How had the large black wolf found her? She shook her head and vowed to never walk out of the apartment again, it would now become her fortress and to hell with her job. *It's not that great anyhow.*

They stared at one another for so long; Trinity even forgot to blink. Her eyes burned with the need for moisture, but she couldn't. What was wrong with her?

She'd lost her will to think rationally tonight on several occasions and that infuriated her. She made a Herculean effort to blink and back away from the window.

An anguished howl rent the air outside. The cry so lonely and pitiful, Trinity herself felt close to tears. When she looked outside again the wolf was gone, with not a trace that it had ever been there.

Eternal Conquest

Clara Verone

RuneStone Publishing

This book is a work of fiction. Names, characters, places and incidents are products of the author's imagination or are used fictitiously. Any resemblance to actual events, locales or persons, living or dead, is entirely coincidental.

RUNESTONE PUBLISHING, LLC

P.O. Box 946
Dover, New Hampshire 03820

Paperback ISBN 1-59648-004-1
E-book ISBN 1-59648-005-X

First RuneStone Publishing printing October 2004

Cover illustration by Regina Brytowski

Printed in the United States of America

Visit RuneStone Publishing online at
http://www.runestonepublishing.com

Dedication

First and foremost I'd like to thank my husband, without whom my dream of writing could never have been realized. Thank you Matt, I love you always.

Second to the constant inspiration of my puppy, you're a miracle son.

Third to my Darn-It gals, Leanne K., Brandi B., Jackie T., Mindy F., AJ Searle, Erin R., Raquell B., and Sharon you girls are the best and I love you all. To Linda W. the goddess of Greek mythology, a font of information and to Carol B. you kicked my butt when you had to and helped me tweak my story into what it is.

To my sister, my mother, and my father for showing me true love really exists.

Trixie and Joyce, you guys were always my biggest fans, reading my stuff and encouraging me to give it a try. Thanks!

A who's who of Greek mythology:

Athena- Zeus's favored daughter. The Goddess of Virgins, peace and war.

Aphrodite- Goddess of Love.

Ares- God of war and Aphrodite's lover.

Hera- If there was a queen of Olympus she'd be it. Married to Zeus. She's Goddess of marriage and married woman and will punish adultery severely.

Zeus- Supreme ruler of Mt. Olympus and the pantheon of gods living there.

Hepheastus- (he-Fee-stus) God of the forge. Son of Hera and Zeus and husband of Aphrodite.

Naiads- (Ny-ids) Protectors of streams, rivers, oceans and ponds. They are water nymphs.

Hades- God of the Underworld and Zeus's brother.

Persephone- (Per-se-phone-e) The Goddess of spring. Hades's wife. Forced into marriage when Hades abducted her from Mt. Olympus. She sealed her fate by eating 3 pomegranate seeds and is now forced to live 6 months each year in the Underworld with Hades.

Gods and Goddesses- Powerful beings who reign Mt. Olympus. Used to be worshipped worldwide during the glories of Greece and Rome.

Demi-god and Demi-goddess- No where near as powerful as the gods, these immortal halflings still wield power in their own right.

The Three Fates- Three sisters who foretell the future. Seers for the Gods.

Harpy- Mythical creature. Half-man and half-bird. Normally these creatures are repulsive, with the head of a woman and body of a vulture. However, they have been known to birth a rare male and he acquires the beauty the females of the species do not possess.

Mt. Olympus- The home of the Gods.

Werewolf- Also known as lycanthropes. Normally thought to be bitten by diseased wolfs, these werewolves are Athena's own personal creations.

Nymph- Protectors of land and water. If you look close you are bound to find one by a stream or ancient oak.

Titan- The original rulers of Mt. Olympus, they were overthrown by Zeus and his followers.

Chapter 1

Athena tapped her fingers against the golden throne and stared out at the beauty Olympus had to offer. Her eyes saw nothing. Her mind burned with the memory of her defeat at Aphrodite‘s hand long ago.

A prince of Troy, Paris, had been chosen to pick from the three goddesses standing before him, Athena, Hera and Aphrodite. His choice would determine who was the most beautiful. They'd each offered him a gift, if he chose them. Athena narrowed her eyes as an earthquake of rage rolled through her.

Hera's bribe had been the gift of power. Aphrodite's, the gift of the world's most beautiful wife, and Athena had offered him glory in battle. Surely, any Greek male in their right mind should have picked her, if only for the gift.

But Aphrodite, with her gorgeous blond mane and mesmerizing blue eyes, had been as tempting as ever and the pathetically weak Paris had drooled and fawned over her like a love-starved child. Athena pounded her fist on the throne.

Aphrodite had kept her word all right, giving him Helen, an

already married woman. Ensuring the bloody battle of Troy would go down in history.

Since then, Aphrodite had been a sworn enemy and Athena did anything in her power to put an end to Aphrodite's petulant scheming. Today offered her the opportunity to do so once again.

She whipped her head around and called to her servant girl, Lilith. "Go, and seek out Nikolas. Bring him to me immediately."

"Yes, Goddess." The frail looking servant ran off, the white skirt of her toga whipping behind her.

Damn Aphrodite and her meddling ways. So she thinks to get away with this, does she? Athena smiled. She'd see Aprhodite fail, no matter the cost.

***

Nikolas Theophilus sat within the shade of a large poplar tree and watched the pack of wolf cubs nip and paw playfully, pouncing at one another from within the large, green blades of grass. A slow grin of contentment spread across his face. The day was beautiful and the cubs were restless, the exercise would do them good. The warm rays of sunshine hit his face and the gurgling of a distant brook was a soothing melody.

His ears picked up the unmistakable sound of running feet and he turned his head, shocked to see Athena's personal servant running full tilt his way.

"Nikolas, come quick," Lilith panted, bending over to catch her breath. "The goddess has requested your presence."

His brows knit together. What could Athena possibly want now? He stood, dusted off his pants and walked to the pack. "Go back home. Playtime is over."

The cubs whined and pleaded but Nikolas was resolute. His favorite, a young female, came up and rubbed against his leg, as if begging not to be sent home. Nikolas growled low in his throat. She yelped and ran straight toward home, tail tucked between her legs.

He turned and followed Lilith, wondering at the oddity of Athena's call.

Arriving at Athena's palace, he found his way inside the familiar confines until he stood before her throne. He made a quick bow and looked up.

Athena was a vision of perfection. Her porcelain skin was framed by large spiraled mahogany curls. Round gray eyes peered at him intently, ruby red lips that at the moment were pursed in a thin line of disgust. Nikolas knew that look and it rocked him to his core. What had Aphrodite done now? Whatever it was, it couldn't possibly be good. And likely he'd be the one to pay for her insolence.

"Come closer, my pet."

Nikolas ground his teeth. He hated that name but did as he was told.

"You will heed my instructions without fail, do you understand me?"

"Yes."

"Then listen and listen well. Aphrodite has released a scourge upon the land. An immortal vampire by the name of Alexander. And he's after Trinity."

Nikolas's heart raced, blood roared in his ears. "How can that be? No one knows about her, she was supposed to be safe." Overwhelming fear to reach Trinity in time and keep her from harm ripped through his soul.

"No one knew about her, until now. Seems our little vixen of lust has kept herself busy meddling into other's affairs, I guess she couldn't resist." Athena's mouth turned down and her eyes flashed fire.

"But why? Why release Alexander after all this time? And why tell him about Trinity?"

"Ares pissed her off again by sleeping with someone other than herself. She wants revenge, and this time she wants to release Ares's own creation-gone-wrong. She thinks that with Trinity by Alexander's side, the duo would be a force to be reckoned with." She shrugged her ivory shoulders. "Truth is, she's probably right, and I don't think that bitch has a clue. Aphrodite's not hurting Ares in this, he's a god after all, but her actions will affect others. Like the entire human race."

Nikolas knew Athena well. She wouldn't concern herself over the demise of the human race, after all, she was an immortal, what did she care? He clenched his jaw, hating how the gods could be so manipulative.

"So this doesn't have anything to do with your hatred of Aprhodite in the least?"

She smirked. "Do not think to be impudent with me. I offer you the opportunity to save your pathetic lover's life."

Heat settled in his gut and it took everything he had not to snap. "How can I stop this?" he asked through clenched teeth.

"I'm so glad you asked." Athena lifted a brow and smiled, though it never reached her eyes.

"With this. My father made it for me." She handed him a small silver pendent and chain.

Nikolas stared in disbelief. "This tiny vial is supposed to stop a monster?" He glanced up at her.

"This tiny vial," she stressed, "is a powerful weapon. One which will instantly incapacitate the victim. A very powerful weapon indeed."

He worked the chain through it and dropped it around his neck. If Zeus and Athena had faith in the vial then so would he. After all, Athena was the goddess of war and peace.

"You will have ample resources at your disposal. Also, Gabriel, Damien and Agape accompanying you." She clapped her hands and all three materialized, looking shaken and a bit confused. "Do not fail me in this, Nikolas. Find her, for she is the key to Alexander's undoing."

Nikolas squeezed his eyes shut and nodded once. Trinity would come to no harm. He would see the Underworld freeze over first.

"So be it. Be gone." She reached out her hand and Nikolas fell through the black void. He would find Trinity, of that he had no doubt.

***

A lone streetlight flickered on and off, casting the dark night in shades of yellow and gray. Overhead the stars shone bright. The hustle and bustle of Nashville rang in his ears. Athena had dropped him off in an alleyway. He looked around for a phone. First things first, he needed to call Trinity and tell her to stay home tonight.

"Spread out," he said to his crew of three. "I will find Trinity. You all keep a look out for Semere activity."

Gabriel spread his large iridescent wings and shot off into the night. Damien bared his long fangs and disappeared in a streak of fog. Agape, the only female of the group, changed to her wolf form and trotted off.

Nikolas was left alone to seek out the unwilling participant of Alexander's nefarious plan.

Alexander, he was sure, would be wanton with bloodlust after his thousand-year incarceration. If that maniac was after Trinity, Nikolas could only imagine the danger lurking around her every corner. He cursed at his stupidity. He'd kept a constant vigil over her for years, praying no one would find her out. However, as the years passed peacefully, he'd grown lax, thinking the threat to her life had finally disappeared.

He ran like a blur in the night. People gasped as they felt the chill of his passing but he didn't care. His only concern was Trinity.

At the end of the fourth block, he found what he was looking for; a phone booth sat on a street corner. Sudden relief washed over him. Maybe luck was on his side.

Entering, he flipped through the phone book until he found her number and dialed it quickly. On the fourth ring, the machine picked up.

Nikolas growled low in his throat, he hated these infernal contraptions. Where was she? Why wasn't she home at this late hour? At the beep he left his message.

"Cat eyes. It's me. I know I haven't spoken with you in a long time but, whatever you do, don't leave the house tonight. There are things we need to talk about. Very important things." Reluctantly he hung up and laid his head against the cool glass.

"Oh God, Trin," he mumbled to himself. "What have you

gotten yourself into this time?"

***

Trinity O'Reily stepped out of her car, wondering why she seldom saw the sunshine anymore. Stars twinkled like silver knives in the heavens. Walking to her apartment, she glanced at the hedges of holly shadowing her doorway and froze. Her heart hammered in her chest. Had something moved?

She couldn't shake the sickening feeling that something or someone was watching her every move.

She walked forward with slow, measured steps. Another movement caught her eye. A bead of sweat trickled between her breasts. Her eyes strained to see through the oppressive black veil of night.

"Who's there?" Her voice quivered.

Trinity slowly backed up and prepared to head for the relative safety of her car. A small cloud floated away from the moon and a loud yowl caused her to scream and jump in fright.

Samuel, her neighbor's tabby, tore through the hedges. Trinity closed her eyes, placed her hand on her chest and attempted to slow her breathing. She shook her head and gave a weak smile. The darkness had a way of disguising innocent looking objects into things of pure malice. *Stupid mind tricks.*

Trinity slipped into her apartment and breathed a huge sigh of relief. Her heart, refusing to calm, continued to pound with the force of a jackhammer.

***

Hidden from view, a man crept around the back of her home. He'd nearly caught her. *Damn the stupid cat.* But it was okay, he was patient. He'd waited a thousand years, after all. This would be nothing to him. And the prize would be well worth the delay. Her beauty astounded him. Red flames curled down her back, deep blue eyes sparkled in the night. She'd be a prize to savor in more than one way. A sound broke him from his fantasizing. Stealthy feet approached. With a last look at her home, Alexander fled into the night.

***

Trinity laughed weakly at her stupidity and made her way to the answering machine on the telephone stand. Being a reporter was a busy job, and she was on call more often than not.

The red light blinked. A big number two appeared on her machine. Trinity pressed the button and shuffled through her mail. Gas bill, car insurance…*same old crap.* She threw it down on the table. Someday she wanted to be one of those lucky people and receive a check instead of bills. That would be nice. She smiled to herself.

"Hi, Trin, it's your mother. You there?" A long pause. Her mother was always so predictable. "Well, sweetie, guess you're not there. I just wanted to tell you I love you, and happy twenty-sixth birthday."

Trinity, giggled. Her mother was so cute. You would think the woman responsible for giving you life would remember how old you were! It was always like this with her. She would either tack a year on, or subtract one. However, she meant well, so it was all water under the bridge. Trinity was just happy to hear her voice.

"Okay bye, sweetie. By the way your present is in the mail." Now that did crack Trinity up, she always said that. It wasn't until she went home for a visit that she would actually get her present. Her mother's attic was full of Christmas and birthday gifts from years back.

She'd once bought her a computer, but by the time Trinity had received it, it was already three years obsolete.

She frowned. It hadn't always been that way. Her mother used to be a June Cleaver type. The downward spiral began when her husband, Trinity's father, had passed away. From that moment on, she'd slowly started to slip. At least she still remembered the important things, and that's all that mattered.

The next message took her breath away.

"Cat eyes. It's me..."

She would remember that voice for the rest of her life. Trinity could practically picture him shoving his fingers through his hair as he spoke to the machine. He'd never liked them. She smiled at the bittersweet memory.

How in the world had he found her? Her heart was gripped by pain.

"I know I haven't spoken to you in a long time…" She couldn't take this. Quickly she deleted the message, he didn't even have the decency to remember her birthday. She'd obviously meant little to him, if he could forget. Not that she'd given him much chance to wish her a happy day, but that was beside the point.

She squeezed her eyes shut against the overwhelming pain thinking of him conjured up. Nikolas Anthony Theophilus was a god. There was no other word for it. A Greek god to be more specific. Fine, well formed features. Smooth, olive complexion. Black hair that shone nearly blue in the sun, and startling sea-green eyes.

She'd lost her virginity to him while she was in college, a big mistake since he'd turned around and broken her heart. He hadn't been in school at the time, and that had been part of the appeal for her.

Nikolas had his own job and means to support himself. She'd felt flattered that such an attractive man would even show her the time of day.

She felt as if her heart was being pulled in two different directions. Indecision warred within her. On the one hand, she loved to hear his sultry voice. But on the other, the memories it brought up conjured a pain she thought she'd buried forever.

Nevertheless, she couldn't really hate him. Nikolas was the only person in the world who knew her. Really knew her. He knew the secret she kept hidden in her heart, and for that she'd always think fondly of him. If not with a touch of pain as well. It's not that she didn't trust her girlfriends, but she was sure they'd try to get her committed.

With Nikolas, it'd been different. He'd never once made her feel like she was insane. On the contrary, he seemed to accept it with absolute ease. There were so many facets to him that she'd longed to get to know, but never would.

Trinity blinked back hot tears and walked toward her large bay window, seeking solace in the refuge of the night. A stray sheet of paper danced on the asphalt and tree limbs swayed through the darkening night. The long brown branches looked like wooden claws, ready to swipe her up and force her into their sappy maws. She shivered and let the heavy golden drapes fall back into place.

She walked around the room lit only by the faint light of the moon and struck a match, then touched flame to wick lighting the candles scattered throughout. The soft yellow illumination soothed her and she sank into her plush black recliner.

Trinity gave a disgusted sigh and turned her head to stare at the corrugated bark of a mock palm tree resting in the corner of her home. So tacky, she thought.

But no matter how much she resisted thinking about Nikolas, her thoughts invariably turned to him once again.

Her mind swirled, threatening to choke her with memories. She would be lying to herself if she said she didn't enjoy hearing from him. Her head fell heavily on the armrest and she inhaled the tangy leather scent of it.

She hated to admit it, even to herself, but her body still responded to the purely masculine strength of his voice. Curls of heat spread through her gut. Thinking of him was like an old wound that ached on a rainy day. *No more.*

Quickly she stood and marched off to the shower. A whole year and a half and she still wondered why. It wasn't as if she still loved him, she was way over that. But the one question that haunted her was, *why?* What exactly had she done? She swore silently and her heart crumbled. *Great birthday this is turning out to be.* With jerky movements, she turned on the water, stripped off her clothing, and stood under the warm spray.

Trinity tilted her head to face the deluge, loving the feel of the water rolling over her skin. The heat was like a velvet glove, surrounding her in its warmth. She couldn't continue with the charade, it was time to move on.

"Okay girl, snap out of it. Today's your birthday." She took deep cleansing breaths through her nose and shoved them forcefully out her mouth. She worked her fingers through her soapy lion's mane, allowing the sweet scent of almond and vanilla to soothe her frayed nerves. Moping had never been her forte. Admittedly, she had gotten hurt, but enough was enough.

That was almost two years in the past. She had come a long way since then. A satisfied smile touched her lips with her resolution. Tonight was meant for fun, and nothing would intrude on her newfound peace of mind.

Quickly she rinsed off and wrapped a maroon towel around her dripping body. She loved her bathroom. It was her private haven from outside worries. Trinity stepped out of the shower, grabbed her crimson robe off a hook and swathed herself in it. It felt like soft cashmere against her sensitive skin. Her reflection flickered in and out from the glow of a candle.

She hated florescent lighting with a passion, preferring instead to light her home with hundreds of candles. Fat, tall, short, thin. Didn't matter to her, just as long as they were made out of wax. To say she had a candle fetish was a slight understatement. She smiled at her reflection. "Probably why my friends call me a vampire." Trinity licked her canines. *Nope, still human*. She shrugged nonchalantly.

She swiped a path down the steamed mirror and studied her reflection.

Her pale ivory cheeks were flushed red from the swirling fog of heat around her. The glint of her diamond nose ring caught her eye and she wondered whether Nikolas would approve. *Bah, why should I care? He means nothing to me*. All that really mattered was that she liked it. She smiled and the blue of her eyes stood out in stark relief. Almond shaped eyes had earned her the nickname, Cat eyes from those closest to her. Overall, she was satisfied with her looks, but she really didn't think she was some raving beauty.

Maybe that was why Nikolas had left her. Her brows dipped,

marring the smooth beauty of her face. *Hmm. Best to not go down that road again.*

A sudden pain struck her like a lightning bolt. She gasped and squeezed her eyes shut. Her temple throbbed unmercifully. Shooting daggers of light flared behind her eyes, and her heart palpitated in her chest.

Trinity, groaned. *Not now.*

Chapter 2

She groped blindly for support seconds before she fell face first to the cold floor.

Disjointed images of a brunette flashed though her mind. Some unknown woman laughing in the woods. An outstretched hand grasping her shoulders and pinning her against the trunk of a tree. Then it zipped from there to blood. Lots and lots of crimson blood.

Trinity felt the woman's heartache as if it were her own, and she gasped between clenched teeth. As quickly as it had begun, it ended. Always the same.

She opened her eyes and stared at the black marble tile, not really seeing what was before her. A soft cream colored rug cradled her head. Her heart pounded violently in her throat and she thought she was going to be sick. On trembling hands and knees, she made her way toward the toilet bowl and gagged.

She hated when this happened. Moreover, each vision left her confused and depressed. Trinity had never told anyone about the sweet faced brunette with blue-green eyes. She had haunted her life since childhood.

For years Trinity thought she might be insane. Then she started to hear the voices, and she knew she was. Spirits, ghosts-- call them what you will-- they spoke to her. About their lives, and hers. She eventually learned to filter them out until they were just a buzz in the background of her life, so they couldn't overwhelm and consume her. Then her father had died and everything changed.

His post-death visit to her had been a shock to say the least. He'd appointed himself her guardian and stuck close to her side, rarely giving her time to even breathe. But he wasn't the only one. With her father's coming, she'd been unable to shut out the ghosts any longer. They all came to visit, clamoring for attention. There was no sanctuary from them, from their thoughts or from their pain. Even blocking it the best she could, she still experienced an uncomfortable tingling sensation when they were around.

But this woman was different. It wasn't the matter of a ghost telling her something, but rather a memory she was reliving. If she could figure out what it was, maybe she could fix it and move on with her life instead of always being reminded about this one spirit who could find no peace.

The ghosts never gave her enough information to help them, though. It was always a smattering of details and time periods, all disjointed and nonsensical. It was as if they just needed to tell their story.

Ugh. She sighed and wrinkled her nose. *This is exactly why I don't think about these things. It's all nonsense and I need help.* She threw up her hands, and got to her feet.

Then a soothing balm touched her mind. A Nordic face smiled down at her, flashing brilliant white teeth. One of a few spirits she actually enjoyed being around. He'd never spoken to her, but being in his presence had always brought her peace, and for that reason she found herself intrigued.

Normally apparitions were quick to tell her of their past lives, but this one was a complete enigma. Instinct told her his life had not been easy. She smiled warmly.

"Who are you?" she asked, her voice trembling. Fearing he would vanish, Trinity had never asked him before. But he didn't disappear, instead, he just stared at her.

Pierce...he spoke in her mind. His gaze never wavered from her face as he floated closer.

She gasped, wide-eyed. He'd actually spoken to her. What should she say next?

"What is your story, Pierce?" Her voice was a whisper of sound. Adrenaline surged through her veins. Would he stay, or would he go?

His translucent figure began to shimmer into obscurity. "No, Pierce." She flung out her hand. "Don't go." She nibbled on her lower lip, unsure of where to go with this. Trinity could sense he wanted to talk. To share with her the horrific moment of his death that had resigned him to living his semi-life as a shade.

Pierce's lips drooped in a frown, and he began to solidify once more. "Lonely. I'm lonely."

Those words caused ice to freeze on her soul, his sadness was palpable, and she wanted to cry from it. "I'm always here for you, Pierce, if you need me."

His body swayed from side to side. "I can't find her. No matter how much I look."

"Who's her?" Trinity kept her tone soft and coaxing. This was more than she'd ever expected to hear from him, and her curiosity got the best of her.

"Storm. My joy." His green eyes searched the room, as if seeking the woman he spoke of. Pierce glided closer to her side and reached out his hand. She shivered from the obdurate cold emanating from him. His body began to dissolve.

"Will you come back to see me again?" The few spirits she never tired of were also the ones who never stayed long enough.

"When you need me." Then he vanished.

A ragged sigh ripped through her. She wanted to help, she really did. Because these spirits had not found peace in their deaths, they were perpetually depressed, which in turn left her feeling their acute sense of loss. Trinity exhaled a noisy breath. She hoped Pierce would find his happiness one day.

Shades were able to return to corporal form, but only once they found that which made them most happy. In Pierce's case, Trinity suspected it was a past lover. Once in her life had she seen that happen, it was extremely rare and she doubted Pierce would be so lucky. Dragging her feet, she went to the closet and pulled out a dress. Her mind was a whirlwind of activity and she frowned. How could she help him?

***

Outside and hidden behind a large oak tree, Nikolas watched Trinity slip from her apartment and into her baby blue mustang. She'd refused to heed his warning. His fists clenched at his sides. She was so beautiful and vulnerable. If he had to follow her for the rest of his life, he would. She would never be out of his sight again. And he dared anyone to try and hurt her, he'd kill them first. As her car sped out of the parking lot, he ran after her, careful to keep his distance.

***

Trinity sat in a circular booth listening to the live jazz band playing on stage. Freddy's was a swanky club in downtown Nashville that she and her girlfriends frequented.

Soft blue lights pulsed with the music and she tapped her foot against the floor. The smoky room gave everything a certain dark ambience she found appealing.

"So, how's your birthday been today, miss big two-five?" Mercedes's deep honeyed eyes smiled down at her. Her best friend since grade school, she was a brash Hispanic with a no holds barred personality. Trinity smiled at her and shifted in her seat.

The cool feel of silk rubbed against her thighs. She was glad she'd chosen to wear the sexy black dress today. Two-inch heels finished off her ensemble, already adding to her impressive five-foot-ten inch frame, but she didn't care. After her earlier musings, she'd needed to feel as if she was desirable to the opposite sex, and this dress did just that.

Trinity turned and gave Mercedes a sincere smile. "Work was brutal, but it's always nice when I get to hang out with my friends."

Trish piped up with, "I'm glad I could come tonight." Her voice sounded pained and she slid her sunglasses further up her nose.

Trinity stared at her withdrawn friend. Trish had pulled inside herself these past few months; it had been awful trying to convince her to come to the birthday party. Ever since she'd met and become engaged to Brett, she'd changed radically.

"Trish, why are you wearing sunglasses in here?" Trinity was almost afraid to ask, because the answer had become very clear to her in the past weeks.

"It's nothing."

Mercedes laid her hand on Trish's shoulder and spoke low, "He hit you again, didn't he?"

Trish shrugged off her hand. "I said it's nothing." Her voice was cold steel, silencing any further questions.

"Look, Trish, it's never all right for anyone to hit you, and I hope you know that." Mercedes glanced at Trinity. "Trin and I are here for you, when you're ready to talk about it."

A laugh, too loud and a bit hysterical, forced passed Trish's lips. "I said leave it alone. Everything's fine. I can't believe this. I'm gone." She grabbed her purse and stood, ready to leave.

Mercedes held out her hand. "Look. I'm sorry. I overstepped my boundaries. Please stay. We'll talk about something else, okay?"

Trish frowned but nodded, and carefully took her seat. Her lower lip trembled; she looked ready to flee at any moment.

Trinity hated to turn the other cheek, but if Trish wasn't ready to talk, then it certainly wasn't her place to push the subject. She'd be patient and wait until Trish felt ready to speak about it with her. Mercedes eyes were sad and somber. Trinity sighed and attempted to add levity to her voice, hoping to squelch the choking tension surrounding them.

"What are you guys doing tomorrow?"

Trish nibbled on her lower lip and her blond brows dipped in thought. "Got some clients coming in tomorrow. My artwork is being reviewed for the gallery."

"Good for you, Trish, you're gonna knock 'em dead." Trinity

looked at Mercedes. “And you, M?”

“Nothing that I know of. Why?” She tossed her thick nut-brown braid over her shoulder.

“I’m doing an article on the football team for the paper.” She shrugged. “Just wanted to see if you’d like to tag along.”

“I’m game, Trin.”

Trinity nodded and played with the salt rimming her strawberry margarita.

“Hi, Cat eyes.” A deep voice sounded behind her. All eyes widened in response. Her heart slammed forcefully against her rib cage. What was Nikolas doing here?

Chapter 3

"Hello, Nikolas." Mercedes's voice was as cold as a block of ice.

Trinity swallowed, her stomach churned in apprehension. She turned and stared at him. Nikolas looked a little sad and tired. Lines she'd never seen before rimmed the corners of his eyes, as if he'd been under a considerable amount of stress. That aside, he was still as heart shattering as ever. A day's worth of stubble covered his cheeks, giving him that rugged, manly look she so loved. Despite herself, she was curious to see what he had to say.

She held up her hand and looked at her girlfriends. "It's alright, girls," she said calmly, belying the waves of trepidation inside her. Her temple was beginning to throb. She was going to be sick, how could being in his presence disrupt her equilibrium this bad? Trinity turned back to gaze at Nikolas, her mouth set in a grim line. "Give us some space will ya?"

"Trin," Mercedes, spoke up. "We'll stay if you want us to."

Trinity flashed a tight, swift smile. "I'll be fine." She couldn't understand why he was here and was loathe to let her friends listen in on what he had to say to her.

The girls stood, gave Nikolas a look clearly meant to insult, and walked away.

"So what do you want, Nikolas?" her voice was clipped in anger. "And when did you get to town? Or should I even ask?" She bit down on her lip and turned her face to the side.

He sighed heavily. "Why didn't you ask me how I found you?" He gave a weak laugh.

Trinity rolled her eyes and nervously tapped her foot on the floor. Sounds of soft jazz buzzed in her ears. "Because that's what you do." She waved her hands through the air. "That's your job, isn't it? To find the un-findable." Her brow dipped in thought. Was that even a word? She shrugged. What did she care if he thought her grammar sucked. "Just what is it you do? Why can't you ever share your life with me?" She hated herself the moment it had left her mouth. Why was the pain still so raw and fresh?

"I'm sorry, Cat eyes, I can't tell you that."

His warm, caring voice made her frown. Why couldn't he ever be mean to her? Why was he always so nice? She hated him for that.

"Whatever. What are you doing here, Nikolas?" Trinity stared deep into his eyes. His odd, sea green orbs stared back at her; wise and calm. Nikolas was not what he appeared; she'd always known that. Even the year and a half they'd dated, he'd left her with many unanswered questions. Maybe it was the mystery that had so intrigued her. However, that was then, this was now.

Nikolas walked around her, his black trench coat heavy around his ankles, and took a seat in the chair opposite her. He sighed again and dropped his head on his chest; tendrils of coal black hair covered his face.

He wore it long, one of the many things about him she'd found so interesting. Nikolas wasn't like other men; he was a different breed entirely.

"I need your help with the case I'm on," he said, his words muffled against the dark tan of his shirt.

"Oh no. Uh-uh. I don't know what you're involved in, Nikolas, but I have a reputation to uphold." Trinity shook her head, her eyes wide in her face.

She didn't know what his job was, but the year they'd dated, it wasn't strange to see him come home with his clothes ripped and tattered. Sometimes even brown bloodstains could be found. Trinity had been too afraid to ask questions. She assumed whatever it was it wasn't good. Probably the mafia. That would be just my luck, she thought cynically.

"No way." Her voice dropped down to a whisper and she glanced around. "I'm a reporter, and a darn good one. This is my life and you're not going to come in and ruin things for me." What she didn't admit was that the pain of him leaving once he finished with her caused a fresh gash to open in her soul.

His aquamarine eyes were alive with raw, unchecked pain. "Look, Trin. I'm sorry for the pain I've caused you, but believe me when I say, I'm all wrong for you."

"Oh please, buster, don't flatter yourself." She sneered. "That was a long time ago."

"Just let me explain a little bit, then I'll let you decide on your own time." His flat, unspeaking eyes prolonged the moment.

Finally, she gave in to her curiosity. "Fine, but make it snappy, it's my birthday."

"I know. Happy birthday." He sounded sincere, then pointed to his nose. "Nice nose ring." He smiled.

Warmth spread through her limbs, he noticed. Pleased at his comment she gave a tight-lipped smile. She knew she was acting like a jaded fool; she took a deep breath and smiled tentatively. "Thank you." Her mind whirled with conflicting emotions. She felt nothing for him, so why couldn't they be friends? On the other hand, was that just another lie she told herself?

"Look, before you continue, let me just say I'm sorry. Honestly, I'm still confused about things that happened between us, but that's in the past now and I'd like to leave it there. Truce?"

He clipped his head once, betraying none of his thoughts. "I agree. And I want to add, there are some things you don't know about me, Trinity. Things better left in the dark. I never lied about loving you."

Her nostrils flared and she bit down on the inside of her cheek. *What the piss does that mean?* That had always been her problem with him. His answers always left a million questions buzzing in her mind.

Nikolas inhaled deeply and continued. "Have you heard about the killings?"

A groan ripped from her heart. She didn't want to listen to this. It was so much easier to pretend she was normal when he wasn't in her life. Immediately she realized he meant to ask her to use her channeling in one form or another. She couldn't say why she felt that way, she just did. Trinity leaned her head in closer and spoke quietly. "Yes."

Nikolas looked at her face and debated whether or not to tell her the full truth. Her beautiful blue eyes were narrowed and had a panicked gleam to them. The rapid beating of her pulse in her throat told him no, so instead he opted for the half-truth. Eventually he'd tell her everything. Just not now.

"It's bad. Real bad. Seven bodies hacked up." He spread his large tanned hands wide and added, "Bodies drained of their blood. Men, women and children. The killer is indiscriminate." He noticed that her breathing had quickened, she was not taking this well.

He sighed and wondered what he should do with her. She was no longer safe alone; all he could do now was to bring her with him. But would that put her in more harm? Nikolas had no way of knowing.

"So you've come to track a killer? That's it, that's the whole reason for you being here?"

He winced at the pain in her voice as it seared through his heart like a red-hot poker. How could he tell her that she'd meant so much more to him and still did? He couldn't, so he swallowed his pride and pretend to be unaffected, when the truth of the matter was, Trinity meant the world to him.

"Yes, I've been assigned to this case."

"Who? Who assigned this? Tell me, damn it! Don't leave me in the dark again." Trinity rubbed her temples in a vain attempt to get rid of the building throb behind her eyes.

"Please trust me when I say, I can't tell you that. All I can say is that I need the use of your powers to catch the killer." His sad looking eyes lit with anticipation.

"I told you before, Nikolas, I hate messing with this stuff." She sighed and looked him squarely in his face. "You're the only one who knows my secret. Anybody ever finds out and I'm going to be considered a quack. I've got a good life…" her voice trailed off and she snorted.

Her heart tightened in her chest and she squeezed her eyes shut.

His voice rumbled through her head. "I know, Trin. I'm sorry, but there are people dying, and you're the only one I know who can help me on this case. You're the only one I would trust with my life."

"Just because I saved your life once doesn't mean I've made it my full-time job." Her gaze focused on a black spot on the wall behind his head.

Trinity remembered as if it were yesterday. She and Nikolas had been enjoying a fabulous night out on the town. As they were driving past the open hillside, they spotted a carnival and decided to stop. A fateful decision to be sure. The night had been calm and lovely. Stars twinkled overhead, the moon hung like an ivory sickle and garish neon lights lit up the night sky. Sweet smelling cotton candy and funnel cakes were a heady enticement to her grumbling stomach. Everything had been going fine until he decided to go for a ride on the rickety wooden coaster.

An overwhelming sensation of panic and fear stole over her, urging her to leave. Spirits crowded around her, moaning loudly in anguish, their cold hands reached for her, to turn her around.

As he was about to step on, he turned around and gave her a thumbs-up sign. His brilliant white teeth flashed through the dark olive tone of his handsome face. Her heart thumped with love as she returned his smile. A flash, or image of the future, seared through her brain. Nikolas, his body broken, sprawled on the ground, pieces of wooden coaster littered around him. Twelve lifeless bodies staring with unseeing eyes into the black heavens.

She had screamed and called him to her, begging to leave. Everyone in the park had looked at her as if she was insane, and truthfully, she had felt that way. In typical Nikolas fashion, he'd grabbed her hand and steered her back toward the car. Just as she was beginning to feel like the world's greatest fool, a loud clap of thunder sounded behind them. She turned around and gaped at the scene of destruction.

A portion of the track had become unhinged and fallen twenty feet to crash against the hard, unyielding earth. Everyone had died on the car.

That was the night Nikolas had learned her terrible secret.

"I…I don't think I can do this, Nikolas," her voice cracked.

His face fell and he gave her a half smile. "I understand. I'm going to leave you my card. I'm staying at the local hotel, so if you change your mind…"

Nikolas reached into his coat pocket and slid his card under her margarita shaker. He got up slowly and walked away, then turned back around and stared down at her. "It's a gift, Cat eyes. Think of all the people you could save." Then he was gone.

***

That night she lay in her sleigh bed and thought long and hard about what Nikolas had said to her. Was it worth it? How could she possibly benefit from doing something so painful? Conversing with spirits tore at her. Not her spirit guides, but the others. The one's unwilling to let go of their past. Trinity knew they meant her no harm, but the pain of their deaths stuck to her like poison, infecting her with their agony.

She looked at the strange shadows upon her wall, and wondered if a ghost would show up tonight. She hoped not, she needed some peace and quiet. Trinity pulled back the lavender coverlet and slipped beneath, loving the feel of the satin sheets against her nude body. If only her mind could be so easily assuaged.

Her parakeet trilled a lonely song in the corner. A soft glow emitted from the fish tank, and she stared at the languid movements of her angelfish. Such an exotic and lovely creature, with no path in life. All it lived for, breathed for, was to swim, mate, and eat. She snorted. Maybe they were on to something there. How much more simple would life be if she were just a fish?

"Trinity." Her father's dry voice broke her from her pity party. She squeezed her eyes shut, willing him silently to leave her alone. His translucent specter floated at the end of her bed.

She rolled onto her stomach and wrapped a pillow around her head. "You're not gonna get rid of me, girl. So just look at me now, and get this over with."

Exhausted with constantly trying to keep her visitors at bay, she sighed and sat up. Trinity clutched the satin sheet tightly to her chest. "What, Dad?"

"I've come with some information I think you might like to hear." His firm looking porcelain skin shone white in the moonlight. A blue aura surrounding him pulsed with a life force of its own.

This couldn't be good news. Her forehead wrinkled in consternation. "Okay give it to me."

A broad smile split his face. "That's my girl."

She smiled despite her misgivings. This was, after all, her father, how many people wouldn't die to be in her shoes. No pun intended.

"The word is you've met your soul's destiny."

"What the piss does that mean?" She always hated how vague the spirits tended to be.

"Really, Trinity, I wish you wouldn't speak such vulgarities." He frowned with disapproval.

"So I suppose you'd prefer me to say, what the hell?"

He shrugged. "Sure, why not? Certainly sounds better than piss."

Trinity smirked and shook her head. "Because father, I'm trying to stop cussing. Besides piss works for me."

"If only your mother could hear you." His once twinkling eyes turned sad and introspective. He sighed heavily and turned his face.

Every time her father visited, her heart broke for him. His love for her mother was still very evident. "She can't know about this, Dad. No one can know about this." Her voice was sad. "But I always make sure to tell her how much she meant to you."

His silver-blue eyes drooped with weariness. "I know, baby. I know."

"Anyhow, what were you saying?" It was always wise to break a spirit from getting too depressed, because boy could they mourn.

He gave a tight-lipped smile and continued. "As to your question about your soul's destiny, it's your soul mate. Very few people have them. We're a rare breed, indeed."

Soul mate. Did he actually say that? Why was her life so weird and complicated? "What do you mean by soul mate?" She closed her eyes and chanted through her mind...*please don't let it be what I think he means.*

"You know, two halves of the same whole." His chuckle was like the shriek of wind in autumn. "Believe me, you'll know once you've met him. Your mother and I are soul mates." His eyes lit with excitement and he sighed heavily. "I'll meet my Bess again real soon."

Well she didn't know why she was shocked by anything anymore. If she could talk to spirits, then she supposed anything was possible. On a whim, she decided to ask him a question that had been nagging her for hours. "Is it Nikolas?" Her heart pounded so violently she could almost taste the adrenaline coursing through her.

"That I cannot tell you."

"You've got to tell me something."

"Trin, you already know."

Trinity squeezed her eyes shut. It had to be Nikolas, there had never been another. Was that even possible though? He'd already broken up with her. However, the spirits never lied; it just wasn't in their nature. His obscure statement caused her to believe with her heart. She couldn't decide whether to cry or laugh, so she did neither.

She nibbled on her bottom lip in frustration and stared at her father.

"What's his secret, Dad?"

"I cannot tell you that, either. Only he can."

She blew out a perturbed breath. How aggravating that Nikolas knew all her most intimate secrets, and she'd never learned much about him, other than his name and favorite meal, spaghetti and meatballs. A lot of good that did her now.

"So what's the second part of what you had to tell me?"

"Work on the case."

Her mouth dropped open and a lead weight settled in her gut. "Why? Just give me one good reason. You know what happens to me when I'm around all that horror."

"All I can tell you, baby, is that it will be the catalyst for you to find peace in your life."

She snorted and rolled her eyes. That was questionable indeed, but she wouldn't voice her opinion. "I've tried so hard to establish some sort of normalcy in my life. This will open up doors I would rather see dead bolted and rusted shut."

"Honey, you were never meant to be normal. You've got the gift, now use it."

How could he always make her feel so guilty for not being able to appreciate *the gift*?

"So tell me more about my soul's destiny." If she couldn't beat them, join them. She'd bucked the spirits long enough, now she just had to try to figure out a happy medium. Because they weren't going anywhere, anytime soon.

"You know more than you should. You're smart enough to figure out what to do from here." He blew her a kiss and faded from sight.

Trinity licked her parched lips and her heart leapt to her throat. "Nikolas." His name rolled like warm honey off her tongue. That was an intriguing notion. A slow grin spread across her face.

She reached over and grabbed her purse off the nightstand. Her fingers shook as she pulled his card out. Warm tendrils of desire pooled in her gut. Trinity snuggled deep into her mattress and stared at the white business card lying atop her pillow. Was it possible?

Chapter 4

"So what did you and Nikolas talk about last night, Trin?" Mercedes words were whipped away in the muggy breeze.

Trinity sped the Mustang down the two-lane highway, top down. The sun peaked over the horizon and cast brilliant shades of pink and orange on the landscape. Trees passed in a blur creating the illusion that they were driving through a Salvador Dali painting. Only early morning and already, another steamy day was in progress.

She glanced at Mercedes. Her beautiful nut-brown hair was tied back by a kerchief, and she sported Tommy Hilfiger sunglasses.

"Nothing."

Mercedes lowered the glasses on the bridge of her nose and stared at her. Trinity looked straight ahead, refusing to meet her friend's gaze. "What's it going to take for you to trust me, Trin? I've been your friend for how long? Sometimes I feel like there're parts to you I just don't know."

Trinity blew out a disgusted breath. She well understood what Mercedes meant. She felt much the same way about Nikolas.

She hadn't slept well last night after her talk with her father.

The excitement of the moment had faded quickly back to reality. Nikolas was an enigma she wasn't sure she wanted to be near again. Look how long it had taken her to get over him, which was a joke because she'd never really been over him, had she?

"He wants me to work on a case with him."

Mercedes shook her head vehemently. "Don't you dare do it. Don't let that dog back into your life again, Trin. I had to pick you up off the floor last time, you were a wreck, and so was I."

Trinity frowned. Her heart sank. "Don't call him that." Mercedes scoffed and threw her hands in the air. "Really, M, he's a good guy. Don't hold it against him that things just didn't work out between us. He's never been anything but kind to you."

Mercedes rolled her eyes. "That's not going to stop me from caring about you." Her warm honey eyes pierced Trinity's. "Nikolas hurt you once, and I'll be all over him like white on rice if he hurts you again."

Trinity giggled at her. "White on rice?" She shook her head. "Isn't that kind of grade school?"

A smile cut her caramel colored face. "Yeah, well, with you not cussing, I was just trying to refrain in your presence."

"Aren't you sweet."

Mercedes flicked her hand in the air. "Bah."

Trinity laughed and sped toward the stadium.

***

Her tires crunched over the gravel as she turned into Adelphia Stadium. Blue and red lights swirled in unison. Six patrol cruisers sectioned off areas of the parking lot.

"Ay Dios mio." Mercedes always reverted to Spanish when

nervous. "What do you think happened?"

It was a sinister looking assemblage, and Trinity didn't know what to make of it.

Black uniforms milled around like marching ants, cordoning off the entranceway with yellow crime scene tape.

Trinity grabbed her notepad and pen and shot from the car, her mind consumed by the story in front of her.

"Hey, wait up," Mercedes called out.

She barely registered her friend trailing behind. Trinity's sneakers pounded the pavement. Once her colleagues found out about this, they'd be all over. She needed to get in there while the getting was good, and before the cops got tired of all their pestering and sent them home. This could finally be her big break.

Breathless, she approached the first cop she saw.

"Excuse me, sir. What happened here?" She pointed her pen at the yellow tape.

A handsome looking man turned to her. His coffee skin beaded with perspiration from the muggy climate. His eyes narrowed and crinkled at the corners. "Who are you?"

"I'm a reporter from *The Rapid Express Journal*. I came here to do story on the new team today."

He seemed satisfied with her answer and scratched his head in thought. "Don't really know much myself." He leaned in and spoke behind his hand. "Don't quote me on anything, but the groundskeeper was found dead this morning. His throat had been viciously slit from ear to ear."

Trinity's nostrils flared while she scribbled furiously on her notepad. Her stomach heaved and she wondered if she was going to lose her lunch. Just the thought of gore made her squeamish, but she had a job to do.

"The worst part though," his peppermint breath wafted under her nostrils, "he was ripped completely in half." The officer made a ripping motion with his hand. "Like a piece of paper just right down the middle."

Mercedes gasped in the background. *Ugh.* Okay, she was really about to lose her breakfast, lunch and dinner from yesterday. It was obvious this handsome stranger was definitely a rookie. No one with any time on the job would give a reporter any details and she thanked her lucky stars for it.

"Any clues?"

He shook his head. A look of bewilderment crossed his face. "That's the thing. Blood everywhere, but no shoe prints other than the victims. Only one set of tracks can be seen on the grass. I mean nothing. Zilch." He made a cutting motion at his neck. "We'll know more when we get a forensic test done but…" --he looked around-- "you didn't hear this from me. Gossip buzzing around says that this fit's the same MO of the last unsolved seven cases."

She winced at the loud sound of a siren as an ambulance approached. "So other than a complete lack of evidence, there's no other connection to the last seven homicides?"

He shrugged and offered an apologetic grin.

The ambulance pulled up, two men jumped down and ran inside the stadium. Trinity was frozen in place and watched with rapt attention. The men returned moments later with a black body bag on a stretcher. Her mouth turned down in a frown. For all her bravado about wanting to chase down the next big story, seeing the dead body brought her back home. Someone died. A brother, uncle, maybe even a husband. The need to figure out this story suddenly became a burning compulsion.

She clipped her head at the friendly officer, grabbed Mercedes gently by the elbow, and walked back toward her car. The article on the football team wasn't so important, anyhow.

"My God, Trin. That was awful." Mercedes lower lip trembled and Trinity patted her shoulder affectionately.

"I know, M. I know." She gazed at the retreating ambulance and vowed to call Nikolas as soon as she got home.

***

Nikolas sat up in bed. The shrill cry of the phone's ring echoed off the high-ceilinged room. He scrubbed a hand over his face and stared at his blinking bedside clock. Ten in the morning. Whoever said the early bird catches the worm was insane. He for one could never be called an early riser.

"Yeah," his voice croaked like a bullfrog and he massaged his throat.

"Niky."

Only one woman called him that; his heart slammed in his chest. "Cat eyes, what's wrong?" He threw off his blanket and placed his feet on the thick Persian carpet.

"Umm. I thought a lot about what you said the last night and well…" she paused for a moment. Nikolas's gut swirled with emotion. He'd missed that angelic voice. "I'm in."

"What made you change your mind?" He ran his hand over his head. His heart was doing double time in his chest, and a wolfish grin split his face.

"I…I talked to my dad." Nikolas nodded, knowing what she meant. Her father was her spirit guide, and always pointed her in the right direction. A conflict of emotions warred within him. He loved Trinity, of that he had no doubt, but his desire to keep her at a safe distance conflicted with his desire to keep her by his side.

"I also witnessed a homicide today. It kind of struck home." She sounded lethargic and sad.

"Trin, what do you mean that you witnessed it?" Even though his voice was low and calm, he felt like he'd just been sucker punched. There were things about this case he'd failed to tell her about. Very important things.

"Well, let me take that back. I didn't actually witness it, but I saw the body bag. Plus I got the police description, so I just put two and two together."

Nikolas breathed a sigh of relief, releasing the knot of tension that had been festering inside of him. "I need to shower and get dressed. I'll come get you soon. Where are you?"

"I'll be at the park by the fishing pier."

"Good, just wait for me. There are things we need to discuss first." He hung up the phone and made his way to the bathroom.

He shed his boxer briefs and A-shirt and then stepped under the cold spray.

Nikolas gritted his teeth and pounded his fist against the shower tile. He felt it. The fireworks of pain that coursed through his body, warning him his time approached. He had maybe two more good days before he needed to go into hiding. Time was of the essence for him. He could only hope his secret would never be discovered.

***

Trinity leaned heavily against the wooden pier and stared into the lake's green murky depths. A few enthusiasts already settled in, relaxed in their lawn chairs with a can of beer in one hand and their fishing rod in the other.

Two dragonflies zipped in a mating dance along the shallows. Both were a deep metallic blue. Their wings buzzed through the stillness creating a hypnotic effect. A large mouth bass jumped up and snatched one in its maw then landed with a splash back in the water.

Her mouth turned down in a frown. The food chain at its best and worst. *Poor dragonfly, fish food just like that.* Life could be fleeting in the blink of an eye and it was all over.

A deep sensual voice cut her from her thoughts. "Cat eyes."

A flurry of butterflies danced in her stomach. Was she really ready to face him? Too late now, she squared her shoulders. Bravely she turned around and had to catch her jaw before it hit the wooden planks. He was breathtaking.

He wore blue jeans tapered to his slim hips, a white button down shirt with the sleeves partially rolled up. Two shell necklaces were wrapped around his thick neck. His blue black hair was held away from his face. The contrast between his white shirt and tanned skin nearly caused her to choke. Unconsciously, she lifted her hand and took a step forward when suddenly she recalled they were no longer together and dropped it at her side.

She felt stupid and foolish. He was probably having a good chuckle at her expense.

Standing next to the Greek god, she felt sorely under dressed in her pink baby tee and blue jean shorts. She patted her hair, wondering all the while, why she still felt the desire to look presentable for him.

Nikolas rushed to her side, dropped a kiss on her forehead then walked away and stared morosely out at the quiet lake.

She wanted to stomp her foot in frustration and smile with glee all at the same time. How could he always do this to her? She was a lovesick fool.

Trinity got her emotions in order and stood at the opposite end of the pier. "So you said you needed to talk to me?" This was a stupid idea. She was an idiot for ever thinking she meant more to him than just a casual fling.

He closed his eyes and let out a deep breath, then opened them. His sea green eyes continued to stare at the horizon. *Is he going to stand there all day like a chunk of marble?*

The awkward silence stretched between them, taking on a life of its own, filling her with dread. Trinity fought the sickness overwhelming her. With each second that ticked past, her stomach twisted even worse, tightening it's vice grip. If he didn't say something soon she was going to turn around and head back home.

"You said you saw the body bag?" He turned his head. His white teeth flashed as he spoke. "Did you happen to see the body?"

"No."

"Look, Cat eyes, I'm gonna be straight with you here." He took a deep breath and continued, "These aren't your typical run of the mill killings."

Her ears perked up. Mentally she kicked herself for not bringing her notepad along. "What do you know about all of this?"

"A lot more than any cop. That's for sure."

Trinity had talked to her boss earlier and had received the go ahead to do a little snooping into the investigation. Her heart hammered in her chest, this was just the inside scoop she needed. With his mafia connections, he was sure to know something good. Maybe even who the killer was.

His eyes grew hooded and pensive. She could almost read the debate warring in his mind whether or not to tell her. Her stomach already sick, she wanted to scream to relieve the tension infecting her. "You can't not tell me now, Nikolas."

He gave a weak smile. "Yeah. I know you, always the reporter."

She rubbed her clammy palms down her shorts and licked her lips.

"Vampires." His mouth twisted into a sneer.

Trinity's eyes narrowed in response. Her nose curled and her mouth pursed into a thin line. "What the piss are you telling me?" At the moment, she seriously doubted his sanity. *Maybe I am better off without him. He's nuts.*

"Listen to me, Trin, before you criticize."

He looked dead serious and she had to refrain from laughing at his high jinks. He was pulling her leg, although she couldn't remember him being anything other than serious. For a brief moment she wondered at the validity of his statement, and then tossed it from her mind like rubbish. Anger replaced her earlier shock.

"Do you take me for a fool? You're the one who asked me to help you out on this case. Don't yank my chain." She tapped her sandaled foot on the wooden beam and crossed her arms.

"It's not a joke, Trin. And I'm not stupid, so you can wipe that look off your face." He continued before she had a moment to retort. “It’s an ancient race of Vampires, called the Semeres.”

Nikolas heaved a weary sigh and plopped himself down on the wooden park bench. “To make a long story short. The leader, Alexander, is creating a mass race of followers.”

She threw her hands into the air and squeezed her eyes shut, no longer able to keep silent. “Whoa boy. Hold it right there.” She took a deep breath and stared into his eyes. “Just what do you think you’re selling me? Is this some sort of sick joke? If you need help, Nikolas, I’m sure we can find it for you.”

He reached out and tucked a wayward red curl behind her ear. She shivered from the warm contact of his finger against her lobe, hating that her body still responded to his.

“Listen to me, Cat eyes, and if you still don’t believe me then ask your father. Spirits don’t lie. They’ll confirm what I tell you to be true.”

He was right about that. Fine. She would listen to what he had to say, but that didn’t mean she had to believe him. The jury was still pending on that one.

“Anyhow,” his deep voice rumbled sending shooting spikes of desire through her veins.

Darn that man and his tempting ways. The urge to drop a profane word got more tempting by the moment. She chewed on her lower lip and tried to still her frantically beating heart. The soft breeze picked up his heady scent and she inhaled deeply. The man got to her on a very deep and personal level. She couldn’t deny her attraction anymore than she could deny her ability to speak with the dead. It just was.

Chapter 5

"The Semere," he spread his hands, "were a gift shall we say from our favorite goddess Aphrodite," his voice dripped sarcasm.

Aphrodite…this just kept getting stranger and stranger. Next, he was going to say 'beam me up Scotty.' That would tie in nicely with all this bologna he was feeding her. Trinity rubbed the bridge of her nose and exhaled. A promise was a promise, albeit a reluctant one.

"Let me start from the beginning. Long ago, the god Ares created a race of killers. The Semere. Their leader being Alexander. Basically they were his lackeys; they did his bidding and were locked up until such a time Ares felt they were useful again."

Oh, jeez…was it to late to just walk away?

"And that's how things remained for thousands of years. Until the day, the slave thought he was better than the master who'd given him life. A great uprising occurred and when Ares found out, he smote them all in a rage. The only survivor was the most feared of all. Alexander. "

His face animated as he talked and she became wrapped up in what she affectionately termed his tale of mythology. It was interesting and she wondered if he had read it in a book somewhere.

"Ares ultimate vengeance was to lock Alexander up, in a state of limbo. Unable to move, breath, speak…basically in a comatose state. He heard all that was around him, but was useless to affect anything. Ares placed him in a golden sarcophagus and forgot his little problem." Nikolas illustrated by dusting his hands off.

His aquamarine eyes stared boldly into hers. "I assume you know your basic Greek mythology, correct?"

She quirked her lips into a semi-smile and mentally ticked off listings of psych wards in the area.

"It has long been known about the love affair between Aphrodite and Ares. Hell hath no fury like a woman scorned would fit Aphrodite's personality well. All in all, she's a spiteful goddess and Ares screwed up one too many times. Literally."

By this point Trinity was completely numb. She couldn't make heads or tails of what he was telling her.

"So in a fit of rage she released the Semere."

"Why the piss would she do that?" His tale was so riveting she found herself involuntarily getting upset at the bitchy goddess. Nikolas definitely had a knack for telling a good yarn.

"In a few words, for revenge. Ares screwed a nymph and Aphrodite felt slighted. Not like, she isn't cheating on her husband, but I'm sure she sees it otherwise. Who can know the workings of her crazy mind?" He shrugged. "Anyhow she told him she hoped Alexander would succeed with his uprising and kill him."

"But I thought gods can't be killed?" Her lips turned down.

"They can't. She knew that, she was just furious with Ares and wanted to pester him with his nemesis all over again. The problem is while the Semere is a minor annoyance to Ares; he poses a very real threat to humanity."

She nodded her head. Oh yeah, he was an excellent storyteller. Trinity hadn't expected to get a refresher course on her Greek mythology today, but it was a nice break in monotony.

"So where do you come in?"

"I work for the goddess Athena. She's the virgin goddess of wisdom. Most especially dealing in the realm of peace and war. But more notably, she's Aphrodite's archenemy. Anything she can do to foil Aphrodite she will. They despise one another. She sent me and a few of my colleagues out here to deal with the problem."

"So it really has nothing to do with her wanting to save the mere mortals, it's more of her putting a damper on Aphrodite's release of the vampire."

He shook his head and mumbled low in his throat.

"Kind of shallow, isn't it?"

"One thing you need to know about the gods. They are immortals and stopped caring long ago about petty human plights. Why do they care if the Semere decimates the human race? It's of absolutely no concern to them whatsoever."

He said it so matter-of-factly she found herself wanting to curse those gods who thought they ruled the world. Nobody even believed in them any more, except maybe this delicious looking man sitting before her. What a pity. Her mouth turned down. When had he spiraled out of control like this?

"So what's supposed to be done about them?"

Nikolas lifted his arm and withdrew a small vial that hung from around his neck by a thin silver chain. "This. This is the key to destroying the race."

Filigree work laced the silver cap and she longed to reach out and touch it. Inside swirled a hypnotic blend of blue and green fluid. "What is that stuff?" she breathed in awe.

"Athena is a wise and favored daughter of Zeus. She approached him with her request for a weapon against the race of monsters. He gave her this. Cold-fire."

"Cold-fire." Her brows dipped in confusion. Her life seemed to be made up of oxymorons. "What the heck is that supposed to do?" While it looked pretty enough, she seriously doubted its capacity to bring a feared leader to his knees.

"I'm not quite sure."

She rolled her eyes heavenward. *That's just great, this glop of goo is supposed to solve all these problems and yet he doesn't know how. Go figure.*

"All I do know is that we must hit him squarely in the chest. Every single last drop of it. We kill Alexander and they will all perish back into the dust from which they came."

Trinity gave a tight-lipped smile and shuffled to the farthest corner away from him. Even after all his talk of gods and goddesses, she still found his nearness unnerving and exhilarating.

"I know I've given you a lot to digest. Go home. Speak to your father. Once you realize I'm telling the truth then call me." Nikolas walked to her side, clenched his jaw as if he'd wanted to say something and walked away.

She watched him until he was just a black speck in the fading horizon. Deep down, she worried that he just might have told her the truth. "Stranger things have happened, Horatio…" she mumbled to herself and shuffled off toward her car.

***

Trinity paced back and forth in her empty office of *The Rapid Express Journal*. The only light in the building came from her desk lamp. Desks sat empty and wastebaskets full. The crowd had left long ago and she had hoped to drown out Nikolas's words in work. However, it hadn't helped and now seven hours later she felt no closer to the truth.

She didn't normally call a spirit to her in public places, for fear, people would see her talking to herself but she wanted to find out the truth. Needed to, in fact.

"Dad, can you hear me?" her voice was low and she looked around to make sure no janitors came upon her unexpectedly.

Her father's translucent figure solidified and a Cheshire grin split his face. "To what do I owe the honor, Trin?" His steel gray eyes twinkled with mirth.

She gave her father a knowing smile and spoke, "I know, pretty rare, huh?"

"Rarer than finding a T-Rex roaming the streets of Nashville."

She sighed. "I know…I know." She shook her head and quirked her mouth.

"To answer your question, he wasn't lying."

It always shocked her how well the apparitions knew the inner workings of her mind. Either that or she was just extremely transparent.

But his answer left her more confused than ever.

"How can that be? How can my views of the world be so skewed?"

"The gods' popularity faded back during the rule of the Greeks and Romans. With the lack of belief in them they became reclusive, but they've always been around." His eyes searched her face.

Somehow, his answer didn't surprise her. This nonsense just fit into her warped existence anyhow. She nibbled on her lower lip. "But how is Nikolas involved in all this?"

He shook his head and began to dematerialize. "In time, baby…in time."

Trinity stomped her foot in frustration. Well she could try, couldn't she?

She walked over to her desk and picked up the phone, then thought better of it and replaced it. She wasn't sure whether she was ready to face Nikolas again, especially not at night, when the temptation of his nearness caused her to lose her mind and heart. Trinity squeezed her eyes shut for a minute, then grabbed her purse and headed out the door.

***

The inky black of night was cut only by one streetlight sitting at the far corner of the parking lot. Her blue mustang just barely perched within the safety the light heralded. She hated the dark and wondered why she hadn't thought of that earlier. One of her co-workers had offered to walk her out to the car, but Trinity was a workaholic by nature and refused to cut her time short by leaving even ten minutes early.

The rustle of leaves broke her from her thoughts. Her heart accelerated with the rush of adrenaline. The hairs on the back of her neck rose like hackles. A slimy revulsion took hold of her. She turned her head to the side and stared. She could have sworn she'd heard footsteps behind her.

Last time this had happened, it had been nothing but a tabby. She was just giving into her foolish fears again.

Trinity's long legs ate up the distance between herself and the car. Twenty yards separated her from her vehicle.

A wet noise, like a gurgle or something, caused her to freeze. Her mind screamed not to turn around, to just keep heading away from the noise.

Time slowed to a crawl. The wind rustled the grass. The scent of wild onions invaded her senses. Her pulse pounded loudly in her throat and her lungs gasped for oxygen.

A shuffle of feet snapped her back to the present. She ran. They came, faster and faster; heavy footsteps gaining on her. The thing moved with preternatural speed. Her lungs burned with fire and sweat poured freely down her heaving chest.

Two powerful hands clamped her shoulders and swung her around. She screamed and raked her nails down its face. Rancid breath punched her nostrils. Mercurial eyes stared hypnotically into her own.

Her mind rallied, urging her to move but her body disobeyed. She was entranced beneath the gaze of the repulsive and yet handsome creature's face. His hair was blond and spiked. He had piercing's in his chin, his eyebrow and one very large ring in his nose. Sensuous features were distorted by a menacing evil that emanated from within him. The creature wore a spiked dog collar and a metallic silver vampire claw on its pinky.

Her body slumped in his embrace. She no longer fought him, she couldn't. He'd taken away her will to do so. Instead, she stared at the rising welts on his face; glad she'd somehow managed to hurt him.

*Dad...*the rational side of her mind called to her father silently. *If you can hear me, I need help.*

Her heart lurched when the creature bared his long fangs. *My god, Nikolas was telling the truth.* A wicked gleam glinted in his eyes. He smirked. Her eyes widened in response. She was going to die. Her mind became disjointed from the events surrounding her. All she could think was she was too young to die. Trinity couldn't even close her eyes as he slowly lowered his head.

A seeping cold curled itself between her and her captor. Her father's dead fingers wrapped around his wrists and shook him off. The creature wailed in protest and slashed his arm viciously through her father's immaterial substance.

"Run, Trin. Go! I cannot hold him for long."

Fear lent her speed and she turned to flee. The creature ran to catch her. Trinity closed her eyes praying for a miracle.

An eerie howl lit up the night. She paused, mid-flight, and turned around. The creature also turned.

A great black shaggy wolf ran silently toward the vampire.

Her mouth dropped open. *Oh, good god, am I going to be sucked dry by the vampire or torn to shreds by this great beast?*

The two creatures crashed together like goliaths and she literally felt the earth tremble beneath her feet at the raw power.

The black wolf leapt up and slashed the vampire's throat with its long pointed fangs. A sharp yank was all it took to break the windpipe free of its host. The vampire fell with a loud crash against the blacktop. Black springs of blood gushed forth.

Still refusing to die, the monster reached up with its hand and tore open a large gash in the wolf's haunch. A howl of protest rent the air, minutes before the wolf plunged its head into the vampire's chest and ripped it to shreds. Moments later, it came up with the still beating heart and punctured it with its fangs until it resembled nothing more than red dough. Then the wolf spat it out and sat down panting heavily.

Its own blood mingled with the black road. A flame of fire shot through the still vampire and the body incinerated in the inferno, leaving nothing more than ash and dust in its place.

Her heart threatened to jump out of her chest and she swallowed the ball of revulsion trapped in her throat. The wolf continued to stare. Bright green eyes gazed at her, wise and old.

Trinity licked her parched lips. Slowly, painfully, the beast stood to its paws. A bright pink tongue lolled out if its mouth. With one final glance in her direction, it padded off.

Chapter 6

Arriving safely home, Trinity fled her car and ran for her apartment, in no mood to see any shadows jump out at her tonight, not that she'd ever been in the mood for that in the first place.

Inside she marched over to her bay window and peered out, expecting at any moment to see a blood-sucking monster shamble up her sidewalk.

Outside the night was calm. Nothing stirred. No sounds were made. A deserted night met her assessing gaze. The moon, nearly full, overflowed with a generous amount of white-blue light. Her heart felt twice its normal size and about ready to burst through her throat. Shivers wracked Trinity and she wrapped her arms around her chest.

A green glint by the tall oaks in her line of sight caught her attention. A black shadow that crept on four legs. She groaned loudly and allowed the curtain to slip from her fingers back into place. Trinity hugged her bare wall and prayed whatever it was, hadn't seen her.

Beads of sweat tracked down her neck, over her breasts and she squeezed her eyes shut. She couldn't stand the not knowing any longer and gently peeled back a portion of the curtain, making sure all the while to keep herself well hidden. There stood the great black wolf in the exact same spot as before. Its odd green eyes seemed to know exactly where she was, zeroing in on her immediately.

I'm gonna die of a heart attack. I just know it. Her heart beat an uncomfortable mambo in her chest. The shaggy beast mesmerized her. Twice the size of a normal dog, power seemed to ooze from it.

How had the wild animal found her? She shook her head and vowed to never walk out of the apartment again, it would now become her fortress and to hell with her job. *It's not that great anyhow.*

They stared at one another for so long; Trinity even forgot to blink. Her eyes burned with the need for moisture, but she couldn't. What was wrong with her?

She'd lost her will to think rationally tonight on several occasions and that infuriated her. She made a Herculean effort to blink and back away from the window.

An anguished howl rent the air outside. The cry so lonely and pitiful, Trinity herself felt close to tears. When she looked outside again the wolf was gone, with not a trace that it had ever been there.

***

A loud rap on her door caused her to yelp in fright. The culmination of too much stress, she supposed. She needed to get a grip; she was losing her mind. Trinity desperately needed to talk with Nikolas and see what he knew. Why had she doubted him in the first place?

A second knock, louder than the first snapped her out of her trance.

She crept toward the door; one glance in her peephole caused her to nearly swoon with relief. Hastily she threw her door open, a welcoming smile on her face.

Nikolas stood there, his eyes roaming her body hungrily. She shivered despite herself, her body quaking with need.

"Nikolas," Trinity's voice was a breathless whisper in the night.

He closed his eyes and ground his teeth, the tick of a muscle worked in his jaw. When he opened them again, she drowned in their sea-green depths. They glittered with unbearable pain.

"I came…to see how you were doing."

She sensed the roiling tension beneath his calm exterior.

How had Nikolas known she needed to see him? It was almost uncanny. But, for the moment it didn't matter, relief was a soothing balm to her tormented mind and she gave him a tremulous smile.

The thought struck her that he was still standing on her stoop. Heat stole up her neck. Trinity cleared her throat and hastily invited him in. She was really losing her mind tonight; embarrassment and stupidity warred inside her.

"Please, please come in, Nikolas."

He nodded his head once and padded silently into her living room. She closed the door behind him with trembling hands and followed in his wake.

Her eyes traveled the length of his body and she admired the firm movement of his buttocks in his tight blue jeans. A falter in his step grabbed her attention and she frowned. *He hadn't been limping earlier today, had he?*

Trinity rushed ahead of him and quickly threw some pillows on the springy beige carpet. "I'm sorry; I don't really have much in the house. You can sit on the couch or cop a squat on the carpet." She shrugged and gave an apologetic smile.

His reassuring smile caused a flurry of butterflies to swarm through her body. She tingled from head to toe.

"Don't worry about me, Trin, I'll be fine." His white teeth flashed through his dark face. Her eyes widened, he was still as breathtaking as ever. She was seriously about to make a fool of herself and gush like a little girl going to a Beatle's concert.

She made herself busy, attempting to put distance between Nikolas and her wounded heart. She lit the rows of candles atop her fireplace mantle and walked into the kitchen.

"Would you like something to drink?" One arm rested on the refrigerator door and she turned to look at him. Trinity couldn't understand why she was suddenly so nervous. He made her absolutely lose her mind.

A brief grimace of pain flashed over his face as he sat down. And she wondered whether she had seen anything at all, or whether it was a trick of the light.

"A cold beer. Any type, don't care."

She reached inside her refrigerator and grabbed two Coronas. "Trinity, he's just a man," her voice was a mere whisper of sound. "The most adorable, delicious looking man you've ever seen, but he's just a man. Don't embarrass yourself."

She straightened her shoulders and made her way into the living room. Was that a grin she just saw on his face? *Surely, he didn't hear what I said in there.* Nah, she was just being too suspicious. No way could he have heard what she said.

Trinity handed him the beer and sat cross-legged on the floor in front of him. She took a deep swig, hoping for a buzz to help quiet the tumultuous emotions inside her head.

"Well I guess the first question is what are you doing here?" She stared at the liquid perspiration sliding down her glass bottle, anything to keep her from looking in his eyes and getting lost in them.

Nikolas sighed. "I heard about the attack earlier and came over to see if you were okay." His hair fell loose around his shoulders.

Images of him lying naked in her bed with that hair splayed over her body came unbidden to her mind and she coughed into her fist.

Couldn't she have ever affected him at all? How could her emotions for him be so strong and yet he didn't feel anything? Her brows dipped and she chewed on her lower lip.

Nikolas's eyes were riveted to the beauty sitting before him. Those luscious lips of hers had haunted his waking and dreaming hours since they'd broken up. Her soft scent of almonds and vanilla tickled his keen senses and he inhaled deeply.

Her deep blue eyes looked up at him shyly. The fine hairs on the back of his neck rose. He longed to pull her into his arms and forget his past, present and future. The intensifying pain signaled that he needed to make his visit brief. The moon was nearly at its fullest and he needed to go into hiding, before he could wreak havoc.

But he dreaded leaving her. They'd only just come together again after all this time apart, he wanted to enjoy her and bask in her presence. Nikolas knew without a doubt she was not ready for what he had to offer. A relationship with someone like him was impossible, a bitter truth he'd fought for so long.

"How did you hear about that attack? It just happened." She shook her head, her blue eyes round and suspicious.

His heart stuttered a beat; Nikolas forgot how intuitive she had always been. "In my line of work, Trin, I hear things the second they happen." He shrugged and took a swallow of the bitter brew.

"Tell me, Niky, tell me who you work for. Share with me. Show me you still…"

He knew what she couldn't finish saying. That he still cared. He did care, more than she would ever know. His heart gripped in his chest at the pain he heard in her voice. The pain she'd wrapped herself in like a cocoon. Before he thought better of it, he reached out and caressed the side of her face. Trinity's lashes fluttered against her cheeks like butterfly wings. He pulled away with one last caress. His body trembled for the temptress, for his one and only love.

A deep longing for more than just a touch welled inside him until his breath left his lungs. "Ssh. Cat eyes, I'm here now." *I love you.* "You'll never be hurt as long as I'm around, I swear to you." *On my life.*

"I…I was terrified, Nikolas," the words caught in her throat. The memory of the past hour came crashing back and all she wanted was to run into his embrace.

Her hand waving through the air bespoke her agitation. "I'm sorry for ever doubting you." She looked up to see him staring at her intently. His hot gaze devoured her, pools of heat crashed between her thighs.

She pulled her lower lip between her thumb and forefinger and frowned. "This…this vampire," she stumbled over the word, "attacked me from behind." His face twisted with rage and she shivered at its intensity.

"If he'd dared to hurt you…" He clamped his lips shut and uttered not another word. She wondered at his vehemence but didn't comment.

"Then," an empty laugh escaped her. Would he believe the next thing she told him? She could hardly believe it herself. "A…a huge black wolf came to my defense." Her mouth pulled down into a frown. "Or at least that's what it seemed like." Trinity was afraid to look at him, afraid to hear what he would say.

However, when she did look all she noticed was that his aquamarine eyes were sad and contemplative.

Several heartbeats passed before he spoke. "Did it frighten you?"

She cocked her head. What an odd question to ask. Now that she thought on it, she realized it had at first. But, when it failed to attack, the only emotions she'd felt were surprise and curiosity.

"For a split second." Her eyes gazed at nothing. "But then the strangest thing happened. Once it killed the vampire, the wolf just stared at me. Didn't advance, just stared." She laughed at her musings and looked at him. His eyes bored into her seeming to study her intently.

"The wolf was here just now, too." She frowned remembering the stare down she'd just had. "And all it did was look at me. Did you see it?"

An uncomfortable look flashed across his face. Beads of sweat appeared above his brows and she worried that he might not feel well. He clutched at his leg and winced.

"Niky, what's wrong with your leg?"

"Nothing. I'm fine." A stony mask crossed his face as he gingerly made his way to his feet. "I have to go, Trin. I'm going to be out of town tomorrow, but I'll be back the next day. Take care of yourself, please." He lifted a hand and paused in mid-air.

She wanted to scream at him not to go, not to leave her again, but she didn't. Her lashes fluttered shut as his warm hand cupped her cheek. Her body responded to his on a purely physical level and she felt an unyielding ache fill her when he pulled away.

She stood in the living room as he walked off. He opened her door, stared at her for a moment, in which time she read all sorts of emotions on his face. Love, sadness, and pain. Then he left, enveloped by the black void that was night.

Chapter 7

Trinity, paced back and forth in her bedroom the next morning. Her red silk robe flapped behind her like a cape. Now that the fog of Nikolas's arrival had faded, she had a ton of questions buzzing through her mind. Things that just didn't add up.

"Dad," she spoke to the ceiling. She paused and stared around her room, waiting for his appearance. "Dad, if you can hear me I'd really like to talk with you."

She ran her hands through her tangled curls and began to pace once again. Where was he?

A clearing throat had her turning around. She smiled wide expecting to find her father, but found Pierce instead, floating by her fish tank.

"Pierce," her voice squeaked from shock.

He drew closer and gave her a weak smile. "I could go, if you'd like me to," he said shyly.

Trinity walked to his side, close enough to feel his cold aura before she stopped. "No it's not that, I just," she paused and studied him, "Is he all right? I mean last night with that vampire, it didn't hurt him or anything did it?" Honestly, she didn't know what kind of reaction spirits would have being in the presence of evil.

"No, he is fine. He sent me in his place."

She cocked her head and frowned. Why would he do that? Her father was definitely up to something that was for sure.

Trinity threw her hands up in the air and smiled. "Fine; far be it from me to question you guys. I don't get anywhere, anyway."

His hollow laughter rang in her ears. It was the first time she'd ever seen Pierce smile, let alone laugh. He would be fine after all. For so long she'd worried he would be lost to his despair, but apparently, he was made of sterner stuff.

"That is true." His forest green eyes lit with laughter and she mentally compared them to Nikolas's. Nikolas's made her melt and want to rip her clothing off. Pierce's were just nice. She shook her head at her wayward thoughts and returned his smile.

She sat down on her unmade bed and dangled her legs over the side, dragging them against the carpet. Where to start? Now that he was here, she wasn't sure what to ask him and twirled a piece of her hair around her finger.

"Why didn't that wolf attack me last night?" She'd struggled for hours after Nikolas left, wondering at the oddity of it.

Pierce shrugged his translucent shoulders. "That I cannot tell you."

"Oh, you guys are so frustrating sometimes." She blew out a breath. "Fine. But you know something that you're not telling me, don't you?"

"Yes."

"Then, tell me."

"No."

Okay this was going nowhere, change of topic. A red curl fell into her eye and she huffed it away. "Was that thing last night a Semere?"

"Yes."

Now they were getting somewhere. She would go along this vein of thought for a while. "Why did it attack me?"

"Why do they ever?" His eyes twinkled and she wanted to scream from frustration. "Are you mocking me, Pierce?"

"No, but that was a rather nonsensical question. It's a vampire. I suppose to drink your blood."

She grimaced and felt about as big as a thumbtack. *Boy, I'm sure not winning any genius points at the moment.* "All right, Pierce, you got me there." She tipped her head and laughed at her own foolishness.

He smirked. "Perhaps you meant to ask if there was a specific reason the creature waited for you." His eyes danced with mirth.

Trinity was shocked. Had he actually offered her some information? She licked her lips and pounced. "Yes, that's exactly what I meant. What do you know, Pierce?" Fat chance in Hades of her ever owning up to the fact she hadn't meant that at all. Obviously, he was trying to supply her with some sorely needed information.

"Let's just say Alexander has plans for you. You wouldn't have been harmed. At least not right then."

Her eyes widened, and blood rushed in her ears like a roaring tsunami. "What?"

Nikolas, her heart cried out. The words Pierce spoke were chilling and she desperately ached to have Nikolas by her side.

"Be careful, Trin." Pierce's image began to fade; she didn't want him to leave her now. She was all alone and Nikolas was god knew where at the moment.

"Don't leave me, Pierce. I need company."

"I'll stay for as long as you need." His green eyes stared down at her sincerely.

She tipped her head and gave a tight-lipped smile. A ball of tension was beginning to form behind her temple. "What kind of plans does Alexander have for me?" She was afraid to hear what he would say. Either way it couldn't possibly be good.

"To make you his Queen."

Her breath caught in her throat and a peep escaped her numb lips.

"What?" She knew she sounded more and more like a broken record, but right now, she wasn't able to think coherently.

"You have powers he seeks to exploit for his own."

"I have no powers. I mean I can talk with spirits, but that's it."

Pierce's eyes turned sad and he gazed at her fondly. "Why do you think, Trinity, that we come when you call? Or why we do your bidding?"

She shook her head, completely dumbfounded.

He continued. "You have power over us. The undead. With the merest flick of your fingers we would do your will no questions asked."

Why had she remained ignorant of that fact for so long? Her body began to tremble from a mixture of anger and terror. Anger that she was in fact quite abnormal and terror that this lunatic meant to make her his queen. She shuddered with revulsion.

"So what if you can do my bidding. How can you as spirits affect anything physically? I mean I saw my father take a hold of the vampire's hand, but it was a slight push. How could that possibly have any affect?"

"It's a meld of all our essences. At your word, we would become a raging inferno, devouring anything that stood in your path."

"Well take it back, I don't want it." She held out her hands, hoping he'd somehow magically snatch her powers away.

Pierce shook his head. "Can't do that. It's yours and has always been yours."

"What if I no longer want to wield power like this?"

Pierce shrugged and turned up his mouth. "You are the eternal bearer of the gift, Trinity."

She stared at her hands in revulsion. *Absolute power corrupts absolutely,* danced through her mind. Her stomach heaved. She didn't want the responsibility. Life had been so much easier for her when she'd been ignorant, thinking she could talk to the random ghost here and there. However, this…this was a horse of a different color.

"Where is Nikolas? I need to find him."

"He's with his goddess."

Trinity gulped audibly and had to swallow a greasy ball of jealousy that settled in her gut.

"He will be back tomorrow morning," Pierce supplied helpfully.

She suffered an overwhelming sense of the house closing in on her and jumped to her feet. She needed to get out and do some thinking, inhale the fresh summer scent and soak up some rays. "Thank you, Pierce. I have to go."

He bowed and for a fleeting moment, she wanted to run into his arms and give him a squeeze, just as a thank you. His face looked sad and forlorn. "I will come when you call for me."

Trinity nodded and ran to the shower.

***

The sun's weak rays caressed her face. She crossed her legs in a vain attempt to get comfortable on the rickety park bench. She'd sat staring at the calm lake for nearly five hours.

Her heart ached for Nikolas more than she would have cared to admit. His reappearance in her life threw her equilibrium completely off balance. She sighed, broke off another piece of bread, and fed it to the pigeons.

The conversation she'd had with Pierce made her lose her breath when she thought on it too long. She felt stupid for ever doubting Nikolas and wished they could make things right again. Trinity desperately needed to see him, to feel warm and protected with him by her side. Ever since he'd come back into her life nothing seemed normal.

Vampires, stray wolves, her mystical powers. She knew there was a connection there, but at the moment, her mind couldn't begin to fathom it.

The breeze picked up the scent of a rose garden that sat to the right of her. They were a splash of color against the green of the grass, all yellows, whites, blues, and reds.

So beautiful and yet her mind refused to see the beauty before her. This had been a dumb idea, all she wanted to do now was go home and lose herself in her exhaustion.

The disgusting pop of her legs separating from the bench

caused her to grimace. If she'd sat there for another two minutes, she would have been super-glued for sure. She tossed the rest of the loaf into the lake and dusted off her hands.

The sun was beginning its descent toward the horizon and she could just barely make out the full moon in the indigo hues of the sky.

A whole day without him by her side felt like an eternity. How had she ever survived nearly two years without him?

The two-mile trek back to her car was refreshing and helped clear the remaining spider webs from her brain. The moon shimmered with a silvery brilliance, as she reached for her car handle.

The sound of tiny stones pinging against one another caught her attention.

Trinity's breathing quickened. Someone stood behind her. She was sure of it. Vampires shouldn't be out all ready. Her throat constricted. The moon had just barely hung itself in the night sky.

"Don't worry about me. I promise I won't hurt you."

Her heart palpitated in her chest. The deep voice was unfamiliar, yet strangely calming.

Trinity turned and stared at the black clad figure. A tall man, towering over her by at least six inches, stood no more than a foot or two from her. How had he come upon her so quickly?

He smiled and flashed two lethal sets of canines. A small cry escaped her and she fumbled with her keys, dropping them through lax fingers to the blacktop. Blood surged through her veins.

She hadn't seen him move and yet there he stood jangling her car keys in his hand. She hesitated, blinking with bafflement.

The musical tinkle of her keys was her escape and that thing had them. Mentally, she started to call for her spirits and rallied her courage around her like a cloak. But before she had time to fully open herself to the shades, the vampire broke her train of thought.

"Trinity, I'm not here to hurt you." His accent sounded vaguely Italian, causing his words to come out more poetic than menacing.

Her nostrils flared and her brows dipped. How had he known her name?

The haunting sense of evil she'd felt the other night could not be found in him. She relaxed a hair's breath and studied his appearance.

Long blond hair was tied back at his nape. His swirling silver eyes didn't appear threatening in the slightest; on the contrary, they seemed to shine with a congenial light. He was attractive certainly, but his appeal was lost on her. Instead, curiosity burned through her.

"Are you finished gawking?" A smile broke through his moonstone complexion. He walked toward her, his hand stretched out to hand her the keys.

Involuntarily, she stepped closer to her car.

"My name's Damiano. But most people just call me, Damien."

Why was he being so friendly? Weren't the vampires after her? How could this one be so different?

As if he read her mind he continued, "I'm Nikolas's friend." She breathed a sigh of relief and experienced a warm tingle at the mention of Nikolas's name.

Finally, she found her voice. "What are you doing here?"

"Saving you from yourself." He shrugged casually.

Her eyes narrowed at the implied insult. "I don't need your

rescuing."

His calculating look surveyed the patch of forest surrounding them. "Oh no? Well I think four Semere lurking behind those trees would say otherwise."

A shiver of fear stole over her and she attempted to stare through the thickening gloom.

"Come on, get in the car. I'll drive. I'm sure you have tons of questions. Nikolas has talked much about you." His smirk was friendly. A paradox in terms for sure.

Trinity hesitated for the briefest of moments, but figured she was probably safer with just one vampire to contend with instead of four. Quickly, she ran to her passenger side and slid in.

Damien took off in a peal of rubber. His driving could be called nothing short of erratic, and her heart hammered in her chest. She kept pressing the invisible break on her side and her knuckles whitened from the death grip she had on her door.

He chuckled. "Great gadgets, these cars. This baby sure has got power."

She groaned loudly and closed her eyes. Maybe if she couldn't see that he'd nearly killed them three times, she wouldn't worry so much about it.

"Who are you exactly?"

"It's about time you asked me. Nikolas told me how curious you were. I would have expected you to ask much sooner."

She snorted. "I was trying to keep my lunch down. Your driving is terrible."

Damien laughed uproariously. "You are a little spit fire, aren't you? I can certainly see why you've snagged Nik's interest."

Mention of Nikolas's name caused her toes to curl and she nearly forgot where she was. Nearly.

"To answer your question, I work with him. Which I assume you must know, considering my mention of the Semeres didn't rattle your nerves."

"No, not really. I've heard worse in the past two days. Where is he?"

"By he, I assume you mean Nik?"

She shook her head, fighting off the nauseating feeling of vertigo.

"He's in hiding. The whole phase of the moon thing really throws him off balance."

She snapped her eyes opened and looked at him. "What do you mean?"

Damien turned to look at her and she screamed internally for him to pay attention to the road.

"You don't know, do you?"

"Know what?" *Oh god, please stop looking at me.* "You're gonna give me a heart attack if you don't pay attention to the road," her words were terse.

"You're the one," Damien said in shock. He turned back around and appeared to be in deep thought.

"What the piss are you talking about?" She'd had enough, the result of a major headache about to explode in her temple. *First Pierce, now this.* Trinity couldn't believe how quickly her normal life had spiraled out of control.

"Trinity, for your sake forget I ever mentioned anything."

Chapter 8

Surprisingly, they arrived at her home in one piece. Trinity breathed a silent thanks to God and exited the car. Her legs sagged like gelatin and she sincerely doubted she'd make it to her front door.

Damien followed her inside and took a seat in her recliner.

"Makin' yourself pretty comfortable, aren't you?"

Damien gave another friendly smirk and crossed his arms behind his head.

No longer able to stand she fell upon the throw pillows lying in a pile on the living room floor and heaved a sigh of relief.

"I need to know what you meant in the car, Damien." Her voice sounded weak and tired to her own ears.

He shook his head and stared at her. "I've said too much already. This is something you need to resolve with Nikolas."

She figured that's what he would say. As far as Nikolas's secret was concerned, no one seemed to be willing to tell her the truth. His secret was such a large, gaping void in their past relationship and it seemed as if she was the only one in the dark about it. Trinity was exhausted with all the mind games she'd been subjected to and couldn't bear much more tonight.

"What did you mean I'm the one?"

His silver eyes looked worried and he glanced away. "I cannot…"

She held up a hand and shook her head. "Let me guess, you can't tell me." She smirked. Trinity laid her head on her arm and took a deep breath. Tonight there was no soft glow from the candles, but she didn't really care.

"You don't seem like a typical vampire. If you're a Semere, why are you being so nice to me?"

"Oh, please," he scoffed. "You insult me. I'm no more a Semere than you are a bug."

Trinity laughed drowsily. "Has anyone ever told you, you have an awful way with words?"

"Once or twice." He smiled exposing his long fangs.

Her lashes fluttered up and down, sleep was inevitable. Vaguely she recalled Damien vanishing.

She dreamt of the moon, the wolf, and the man she loved.

***

Bright rays of sunlight filtered through the window. Trinity moaned. Her back and neck were kinked and stiff. Slowly she made her way to her hands and looked around. She must have been tired if she'd fallen asleep on the hard floor.

"Oomph." She blew out a tired breath and stood. She crossed the living room into the adjoining kitchen and retrieved the bottle of aspirin from the counter top, popped two in her mouth and took a sip of warm tap water to wash it down.

She dragged the kitchen chair back, its feet squealing in protest against the tile floor and plopped down. Soon she would have to get dressed for work, but dreaded the idea of having to do so. All she wanted was just to relax in front of her television and drown out the voices in her head.

Sketchy memories of last night flashed through her mind. Damien driving like a maniac and their conversation about Nikolas in the car.

The mystery that was Nikolas called to her, teasing the edge of her consciousness. All the answers to her questions would be found if she just dug a little deeper. The clues were in her brain, she just needed to piece them together.

"Okay, let's give this brain a go." She tapped her foot against the floor.

She thought back to the day she and Nikolas talked at the pier.

"He'd never once grouped himself in the mere mortal category." Her face burned as she remembered. "Maybe he's not."

Nervous energy made her stand and pace between her kitchen and living room. She laid a finger on her chin. "Athena is a goddess. Come on, Trin, see the connection." She pushed herself to delve further into the mystery.

"Would a goddess surround herself with mortals and place a human in charge of killing off vampires?" The thought that he might not be human caused her to pause. Did it really matter? She wasn't sure yet.

"Maybe he's a warrior or something?" She paused in her pacing and her heart fluttered. "Maybe he's a vampire himself." After meeting Damien, she was convinced they weren't all bad. "But if he is, where does the moon tie in? It didn't seem to bother Damien." She sighed. "Although I forgot the obvious, Nikolas can walk around during the day."

Frustrated, she resumed walking. Her pace was fast and clipped. Trinity knew she was close. She could taste it.

A loud knock at the door caused her to turn her head. Earlier thoughts fled with the hope that Nikolas stood on the other side. Her face lit into a smile, butterflies tickled her belly and she ran to check.

She peeked out the window and then nearly ripped the door off its hinges.

His long, black hair hung free, a pair of blue jeans tapered to his waist, and a green button down shirt accented the taut muscles of his chest. Trinity's fingers twitched as she imagined herself raking her nails down his gleaming bronzed chest. She licked her lips, attempting to settle her raging hormones before she made a fool out of herself.

"Nikolas." She reached out, enjoying the feel of his callused fingers clasped within her own and walked into her bedroom.

His deep rumble of laughter caused her to bite down on her lip. Tendrils of desire squeezed her heart, making her breathless.

She turned to stare at him and laughed at his raised eyebrow and suggestive look. "Whatever it is your thinking, Nikolas, stop. I need to get ready for work…" she peeked at him from beneath her long fringed lashes. "But, I'm happy to see you."

He pulled her into his arms and wrapped them tight around her waist. She rested her head on his shoulder, inhaling the citrus scent of his aftershave.

Her mind swirled, wondering at his display of affection. With the way his head tilted, she thought he meant to give her a kiss, but instead he pushed her away. "I needed to see you. See if you were safe."

For a minute, she'd thought the old Nikolas was back but the veil of secrecy enshrouded him once more. Heavy-hearted she marched over to her closet and pulled out a pair of black jeans and white tank top.

"I'm fine. Your friend Damien saw to that." Her mouth quirked as she thought about the eccentric vampire.

He smirked and sat down on her bed. "I sent him to see to you. I hope you didn't mind."

"No." *But you would have been better.* She clamped down on her thoughts and strolled into her bathroom calling behind her, "There's stuff we need to talk about, Nikolas. I found out some rather strange things about myself yesterday."

***

The sound of rushing water and the scrape of a toothbrush caused his ears to perk up. Her wintergreen scented toothpaste wafted to his nostrils. Nikolas shifted ever so slightly on the bed, so he could get a good look at her.

Trinity's flaming hair curled long and heavy down to her waist. She was so beautiful, his heart stopped beating for a second and he clutched at his chest. He wanted so badly to tell her, to share his burning secret. But she hadn't handled it well before and he wasn't sure she could handle it now.

Nikolas knew everything. Each reincarnated life of hers. He'd been there for every one of them. She was as a phoenix rising from the ashes. Trinity could never really die and nothing she had to tell him would surprise him in the slightest.

In the last incarnation he'd made the mistake of telling her about himself and she'd run from him in fright. He'd tried to find her and tell her he would never hurt her.

However, when he'd walked out on the cobbled streets, much to his horror he found her hunter green cape drenched in her blood. A carriage had killed her instantly and with her death went every memory they'd ever shared. Only he remembered them all. He knew how to unlock her repressed memories, if only she'd let him. Still badly shaken from her past rejection, Nikolas was unsure how to approach her.

She shifted and his eyes roamed her body. Trinity began to shed her clothing. Nikolas stiffened as her fingers peeled off her jeans, next came her t-shirt, until she stood in nothing but her black, lacy panties and bra. He couldn't tear his gaze away and trembled at the luscious demi-goddess. She was a fine work of art that he ached to run his fingers over. He'd never shared another lover. For two thousand years she'd been all his and the forced separation of this incarnation was driving him mad for her.

His fingers itched to trace her tempting swells and curves. She shook her head and crossed the bathroom to turn on the water.

Steam rolled around the bathroom and he could make out each pearl of sweat that glistened on her body. He licked his lips as she pulled off her bra. Her breasts spilled over, like a tempting white wine and her rosy pink nipples beaded up.

His body burned for hers, only she could drive him insane with ecstasy. Passion inched through his veins. One year of forced abstinence was wreaking mayhem inside him. He trembled when she peeled off the final layer of clothing and stood completely naked. Her belly had the slightest of swells he found most attractive, the red curls at the juncture of her thighs caused a groan of suppressed hunger to rip through him.

Nikolas pulled back and lay down on the bed spread eagle. His penis throbbed painfully. Why had he subjected himself to that torture?

Moments later, Trinity walked out of the bathroom, fully dressed and rubbing a towel over her wet curls. None the wiser about his peep show. Thankfully, she'd given him enough time to get himself in order. Once again, he was the stoic Nikolas. How he wished it could be otherwise.

"Niky, did you know I have powers?" Her cobalt-blue eyes sought his.

"What kind of powers?"

She worried her lower lip and the faint stirrings of arousal coursed through him. He ground his teeth together and looked away.

"Well," she continued. "Pierce told me…"

"Who's Pierce?" He hadn't meant for that to sound so jealous. He cleared his throat; his body trembled beneath her sharp assessing gaze.

"One of my spirits." Trinity's mouth tipped up at the corner. He nearly groaned at his stupidity.

She waved her hand through the air and continued, "He told me I have power over the dead. That I can force them, if I so choose, to do my will, right or wrong on my part." Trinity grabbed her hairbrush and sat down next to him. Her body heat poured off her in waves and Nikolas basked in it. She looked innocent and tempting all at the same time.

She began brushing out her sodden hair. Before he thought better of it he spoke up, "Turn around, I'll do that."

She gave him a coquettish smile and did as he asked. Gently, tenderly, he lifted the brush, shivering at the feel of her silky strands beneath his hands. He cleared his throat again. He was certainly a glutton for punishment. “So why should that surprise you, Trin?”

Her hand reached up and stilled his movements. The touch of her hand against his was fire, pure fire. She turned to look at him. “Why does nothing I ever tell you seem to shock you?”

He shrugged and continued swiping the hairbrush down her long hair. “I’ve seen too much to be shocked any longer. I’ve always sensed a deep power inside you.” Reluctantly, he dropped his hands. She felt so right, so good next to his side.

Trinity stood and walked to her vanity, picked up her blow dryer and turned it on. “Did you also know the plans Alexander has for me?” she raised her voice over the noise of the machine.

Nikolas stiffened and rushed to his feet. She hadn’t needed to scream anything, she could have whispered it and still he would have had the same reaction.

“What do you mean?” The hackles on the back of his neck rose. He would kill anyone with his bare hands if they dared to hurt her.

“Supposedly I’m to become his Queen,” she lifted an eyebrow and smirked. “Should I be frightened, Nikolas?”

Chapter 9

Trinity marveled again at the gorgeous man standing before her.

"You have nothing to fear. I will see no harm come to you." His green eyes glittered with almost animalistic anger.

Her body responded to the heat in his eyes and she reached out. His day's worth of stubble scratched her palm.

Nikolas's lids lowered and he trembled beneath her hand. The urge to pull him in for a kiss rocked her and her legs wobbled unsteadily. When her chest heaved for air, she broke contact and walked to her closet to pull out some shoes. Even a mundane task right now would be a welcome relief from the pain and exhilaration she always felt in his presence.

"I believe you." She glanced up. He stood as still as a wall of granite. "What now, Nikolas?"

"We need to search for Alexander's location." His mouth turned into a sneer. "Bastard's been keeping one step ahead of us." He looked up and she caught her breath at the passion glittering in his eyes.

She frowned. *He used to look at me that way. Now his eyes glitter just thinking about his job. Did I mean so little to him, that the job and I are on equal footing?*

"That's where you come in, Cat eyes. You're the link to help us track down the Semere leader."

Trinity gave a weak smile, her heart a tortured mess. "I figured as much."

She crossed the room and sat on her chaise. "I told you I would help, just tell me how."

Nikolas's legs ate up the distance between them and he crouched to be on eye level with her. She bit down on the inside of her cheek to help refrain from reaching out and sliding her hands through his thick, sable hair. Instead, she glanced down at her jeans and flicked at an imaginary piece of lint.

"Look at me, Trin." His voice, deep and sensual, sent a ripple of awareness through her. "You need to summon those souls who lost their mortal bodies to his relentless hunger. Do you think you can do that?" Two inches separated them. She was so close she smelled the cinnamon gum he was so fond of chewing. She had to fight her own personal battle of restraint.

She nodded; knowing if she spoke her voice would betray her.

He tipped her chin up and stared at her. His hungry gaze roamed her face and she squeezed her eyes shut. "When do you need me to do this, Nikolas?"

"Tonight. For the time being though, I need you to pretend life is normal. No one can know about this, the less attention we get the better. If no one else knows, then Alexander shouldn't figure out what we're up to."

A terrifying possibility washed over her and she snapped her eyes open. "Do vampires have some sort of homing device? I mean…" she sputtered, "I know that probably sounds silly but, he won't be able to track me down just because I'm searching for him will he?"

His eyes clouded and he frowned. "Damn, Trin, I don't know. I didn't even think about that. We're gonna have to ask Damien. I'm not a vampire and I don't know their inner workings."

That answered her one nagging question, if only he would tell her the rest.

"Tonight then," she mumbled to herself.

They stood in unison and walked out of the apartment. She trembled at the thought of facing down another Semere, and if Alexander was as bad as he was cracked up to be… *Ugh! I don't even want to think about that.*

***

That night Trinity sat at her kitchen table waiting for Nikolas's arrival. A stale slice of pizza sat untouched in front of her. She turned up her nose and pushed the plate aside.

Leprechauns were doing the jig in her belly and she groaned. "Could I be any more nervous?"

The thought of seeing Nikolas and attempting to tap into Alexander's whereabouts was going to make her crawl out of her skin.

"Trin."

She jumped in fright and whirled around. "Dad. Good Lord. Are you trying to put me into an early grave?" She clutched at her chest and attempted to slow her frantically beating heart.

He chuckled, his image wavering from the glow of candle light behind him.

"You are not funny." Her eyes narrowed.

His blue aura pulsed in and out with his laughter. “Oh, Trin, if I could cry a happy tear right now I would.”

She smirked; happy at least someone found her discomfort humorous. “What can I do you for, Dad?”

Instantly he turned serious. “I know what you are planning tonight, baby. I came for support.”

Trinity gave him a genuine smile. “Thanks, that means a lot.”

She walked once again to her peephole, greatly relieved to see Nikolas striding forward, with Damien in tow. “Finally.” She smoothed out the wrinkles in her clothes, more from habit than necessity and opened the door.

She greeted Damien warmly, but her eyes found Nikolas immediately.

He walked to her side and stared at Damien, as if laying claim to her.

Damien threw up his hands and laughed. “Hey, man,” he said in his melodic Italian accent. “She’s all yours. Don‘t worry I won‘t go barkin’ up your tree.”

She turned to look up at Nikolas and noticed a tick working in his jaw.

“Shut your trap, Damien, and go take a seat.”

She shook her head and stared for a minute longer at them. *Am I missing something here? Why should Nikolas sound so offended by Damien’s innocent teasing?*

“Trin,” her father whispered in her ear. “It’s time.”

The jolt of reality came crashing down around her. *I’m not ready,* her mind screamed.

As if he sensed her nervousness, Nikolas turned to her and

wrapped her in his arms. "It's gonna be okay, Cat eyes. I'm here, Damien's here, and so is your father."

She pulled back and stared at him. "How did you know my father was here? I'm the only one who can see him." Her brows dipped.

"I sensed him, now come on," he spoke impatiently and pulled her behind him.

Obviously, he doesn't want to talk about it…then again when does he ever want to talk about anything? Nikolas never failed to surprise her. She sighed and shut out those distracting thoughts.

Trinity had arranged the living room differently tonight. She'd pushed back all her furniture and created a large circle with candles. They sat gingerly within the circle and she closed her eyes, taking in several deep, calming breaths.

"Damien." She turned to stare at him. He pulled his long blond hair back. Sometime between yesterday and today, he'd acquired a vicious looking gash in his left cheek.

"Yes?"

"Will Alexander be able to get a track on me?"

His eyes shot to Nikolas. She frowned, that was not a good look and in response her palms began to clam up, she wiped them on her jeans and shifted on the rug.

"Truthfully, I do not know. We've never tried this before. That's why I'm here, in case anything happens…"

A loud groan pulled from her lips. *Oh, Lord.* That was not the answer she'd needed to hear. Her fingers trembled as she lifted them to her brow and massaged. Already the rising throb of pain built behind her eyes.

Warm hands clasped her own. She turned to stare at Nikolas. His gaze was warm and reassuring.

The sickness tugged at her. Calling a ghost, other than her spirit guides, had always made her ill and this time was no exception.

Images, disjointed at first, seared through her brain. A vampire ripping human bodies apart and drinking their blood. Entities moaned and wailed. Rising forth, thousands of spirits begged and pleaded with her. She gagged, but pressed on. Sweat poured in rivulets between her breasts.

Trinity called to them. The ones murdered by Alexander's hand. They all clamored, rushing at her. Her soul felt like it was being ripped to shreds by their cold, dead fingers.

Her father whispered softly in her ear. "Take control of them, Trinity, they do not have power over you."

She trembled and called out, "If you can hear me, come all you who have died by that monster's hand." Fire lanced through her, a portal from the spirit realm opened up in her mind's eye.

They spewed forth like a volcanic eruption. Their banshee wails caused her spine to stiffen. She gritted her teeth and focused on maintaining control.

"Me, ask me," cried one blond-headed child.

"No, me!" yelled a spirit in Viking attire.

"Stop!" her voice boomed through the crowded room. "Enough! You will do as I say and then return from where you came." She barely recognized the authority in her voice as her own.

"I need to know where Alexander is. Have any of you just been killed?"

"I have." A shy female entity came forth.

Trinity turned to stare at her. "Where is he?"

"Florida."

A shriek of insanity split the night. "My Queen, at last I've found you."

Trinity gasped for air, she searched frantically for the intruder. Icy fear gripped her heart and twisted painfully.

"You want me? Come find me demi-goddess." Alexander's maniacal laughter caused goose bumps to trail a path down her arms. She stared in horror at the spectral image of a clawed hand reaching for her through the wall. He swiped her and she screamed in agony. Her head felt ready to explode, Alexander had touched her with his poisonous mind.

Nikolas growled low in his throat and threw himself in front of her quaking body. Her vision blurred and her head swam.

Damien threw a silver knife at the specter. It vanished in a pillar of flame. The ghosts keened in despair and disappeared.

Trinity closed her eyes and felt Nikolas sweep her into his arms. Bile rose in her throat and she moaned. Her body became feverish. He jogged into her bedroom and laid her tenderly on the soft mattress.

His eyes looked pensive. "Trinity, baby, stay with me." He lay beside her and pulled her into his arms. "Come on, baby, come on."

"I love you," she whispered drunkenly, minutes before unconsciousness claimed her.

Chapter 10

Trinity fled through a passage of corridors. Darkness was a veil over her mind. Hands reached for her. Her slippered feet ran and ran, yet she could not escape the labyrinth. She turned to glance behind her and her long hair whipped through the breeze. Her breathing became ragged and labored. Time seemed to slow to a crawl.

"I will possess you, Trinity. Your powers shall be mine." Alexander's words snaked through her heart. "Run if you must, but I've touched you. You know me, you want me."

Her heart pounded at his words. She shook her head, denying the fact that she was, in truth, quite intrigued. What had he done to her?

Her mouth dropped in an O of surprise, at the bend stood Pierce. His image floated inches off the ground. Blue light pulsed around his translucent frame. "This way, Trin. Through here." He lifted his arm to show an exit. She ran ahead, still staring behind and nearly collided with him. His cold fingers pulled her through. A few streetlights buzzed, giving off minimal lighting. She panted against a green dumpster and clutched at her white nightgown.

A blood-curdling scream ripped through the building. She took off again, heedless of where she ran. Boxes littered the dockside. Papers lay scattered and blowing in the breeze. She tripped over a rut in the road and Pierce clamped down on her shoulder.

"Follow me, Trinity." He raced ahead to a large yacht moored at the dock. Ripples of seawater lifted and dropped the boat like a yo-yo. Salty sprays of water slapped her face, the wind rose, howling its fury.

She lifted a tentative foot and stepped aboard. They headed below deck to the relative calm of the cabin.

She collapsed in a heap upon a bed and stared at her new surroundings. Colored lights were strung along the interior. Large potted plants stood as sentinels beneath portholes. Oak and cherry wood scents intermingled.

"Where am I, Pierce?" She lifted her head, sapped of strength from her encounter with Alexander.

"I have shown you this place for a reason, Trinity." His deep green eyes penetrated hers. "You must remember this when you wake. This is where you will find him."

She closed her eyes. "Who? Find who?" her voice came out weak and strained.

"Alexander. Now wake up, Trinity, you have a job to do."

"No...just let me...sleep a little...longer." The sandman claimed her once more.

***

"Damn it!" Nikolas paced and pierced Damien with his eyes. "How could we have not been warned about this? Surely, Athena knew this would happen. Why did she not warn us?" His heart slammed in his chest and he turned to stare at Trinity lying on the bed. Her body thrashed wildly. Fever laid claim to her. Dewdrops of sweat lined her brow and forehead.

He ran to her side and lifted her onto his lap. Tenderly he smoothed her hair back. He growled with frustration.

"If she dies, I swear I will rip Aphrodite's heart out myself." He knew he was becoming feral, but was helpless to stop it. Large incisors ripped through his gums. Soon he would go on a rampage if he could not get his temper under control.

Damien's eyes widened. "Okay now relax, Nik. Just relax." He crept forward, hands out in a submissive posture. His voice was calm and measured. "Trinity, will pull through this."

"How do you know?" Nikolas barked out.

The vampire licked his canines. "I know because I've done something similar once or twice. It's a weapon we vampire's have to incapacitate our victims, though it only lasts for a night." He shrugged. "Unless we kill them first."

"And what exactly is this weapon?"

"Trinity received what is known as a mind swipe. It's a surge of electro-kinetic energy that we blast at our victims. Numbs their mind and body."

Damien stood close to the foot of the bed.

"Is there nothing I can do to snap her out of it?" his voice trembled. Nikolas was furious at himself as well as Alexander. How could he have allowed that creature to touch her? He squeezed his eyes shut.

"Nothing. But trust me, Nik, she'll be fine. She is strong; she'll pull out of this. Maybe even sooner than tomorrow."

"How was she hurt by this?" Nikolas couldn't understand it. Trinity was a demi-goddess. They had powers greater than mere vampires.

"Normally she wouldn't, Nik," Damien's voice was soft. "If I had thrown that mind swipe, it would have made no difference to her. But Alexander was created for the express purpose of causing destruction." Damien's mouth turned down in a frown. "You know the god wars. Ares wanted to become all-powerful, greater even than Zeus. So he gave Alexander more than a generous amount of power. While the Semere leader has no effect on gods, he can still render a demi-god or goddess in this case," he glanced toward Trinity, "helpless."

Nikolas heaved for air. That he hadn't known. He'd thought Trinity would be their ultimate weapon against Alexander. Instead, he'd placed her directly in harms way. He shuddered at his stupidity.

"Don't worry though, Nik, she's stronger than she looks. Trinity's not just some mere demi-god. She will be the one to put an end to Alexander. The Fates have told us so."

Nikolas nodded. He just hoped he hadn't become too involved again. When he was around her, she clouded his good sense and judgment.

Damien turned and narrowed his eyes. "Are her spirit guides here?"

"Yes," his tortured voice cracked. Nikolas looked up and pointed to an empty spot beside Damien. "Her father is standing next to you."

Damien's eyes widened and he stepped aside. "Jeez, that's freaky how you and Trinity can see those things."

Nikolas shrugged.

"Does she know that you can see them?"

"No."

Damien exhaled heavily. "Man, I'm not one to tell you what to do but…"

Nikolas's head snapped up. "Then don't," his words were menacing. He knew Damien had nothing to do with what happened to Trinity, but he was not in the mood for small talk.

Damien cocked his head. "Do what you want, but she's gonna find out you're a wolf soon. I would think the surprise would be worse than the knowing. Don't you?"

Nikolas turned his head aside. His heart crumbled in his chest. "No, I don't."

A frown dipped the vampire's head. "Let's go, Nik. Leave her to her spirits. They'll take care of her. We need to go brief Athena on what happened."

"No." He looked up. "You go. I'm staying with her until she wakes up."

"Fine. Just howl when you need me." Damien smirked.

"Wise ass," he said and chuckled.

In a flash, the vampire was gone and Nikolas looked toward Trinity's father. "You can go, trust me to watch your daughter."

The spirit glided closer, reached out and trailed a hand along Trinity's fevered cheek. "You have always been good to her, Nikolas. Watch her well. She has much to tell when she awakens." A soft smile laced the old man's face, then he too vanished.

Nikolas stripped her quickly and laid her nude body beneath the covers. He stood and peeled back the layers of his clothing, then lay beside her, pulling her into his embrace. Her body relaxed in measures and he inhaled the almond and vanilla scent that was uniquely hers.

If anything happened to her… He squeezed his eyes shut at the racking pain in his chest. Leisurely, he trailed his hand down her arms. Trinity was back in his arms, it felt so good. So right. He closed his eyes and waited for daybreak.

***

Trinity awakened to find Nikolas brooding and staring out her bedroom window. Sunlight filtered through the shutters. Her head pounded fiercely and she rubbed at her temple. Someone must have run her over during the night. What other explanation did she have for how she felt? She touched her scalp, feeling for any large wounds. None.

"Ugh."

Instantly Nikolas was at her side. "Cat eyes, how do you feel?" Lines of concern etched their indelible mark in his face.

"Truthfully?" She grimaced, "Like I've been run over by a Mack truck. What happened last night, Niky? And what are you doing in my home? And," she pulled back the sheet a hair's breath, heat stole up her neck, "why am I naked?"

"I, hmm," he coughed into his fist, "I stripped you because you were sick, I needed to warm you up."

"Sick?"

His eyes assessed her. "You don't remember?"

Trinity closed her eyes, willing her mind to come up with the answers. "I remember a ring of fire." She looked up hoping he could supply her with the rest.

Nikolas nodded. "Yes, we sat inside a ring of candles last night. What else do you remember?" His green eyes sparkled.

"Oh…" She squeezed her eyes shut. "Um, spirits. Lots of them." She paused considering. A gasp escaped her. "Oh my God, Alexander."

Her eyes darted frantically around the room. She searched high and low for the menacing evil she'd felt last night. A curl of heat spread through her at his name and she squelched it immediately. What the piss was wrong with her? Fear that something terrible and out of her hands raced through her. She fought the temptation to panic, praying that Nikolas wouldn't catch on. How could she possibly explain to him these strange feelings, when she didn't understand it herself?

"He's not here, baby." Nikolas breathed a sigh of relief and crushed her into his chest. Her arms crept around his back and she slid her hand under his shirt, loving the feel of his corded muscles beneath her questing fingers. He brought her comfort from the madness that was threatening to consume her.

He pulled back and she frowned.

"Last night your spirits told you Alexander was in Florida." He stared deeply into her eyes. "Do you know where in Florida?"

Trinity's brow dipped. "How did you know he was in Florida? I never told you that, I didn't get the chance, before he, it…" she shuddered.

"Trinity, I can see your spirits and even hear them. But that's beside the point. We need to find Alexander before he runs again."

She was shocked. Why had he never told her he could see the spirits? For so long she'd thought she was the only one.

"Baby." He gave her a gentle nudge. She looked up at him.

"He's hiding in a warehouse, by the dock. Pierce wasn't able to show me much more."

He stood and began pacing, clasping his hands behind his back. "Do you feel well enough to come with me to Florida?" Nikolas turned his head and glanced at her.

Heat spread through her at his look. A raw look of passion smoldered on his features.

She nodded.

Relief washed over his face, to be quickly replaced with stoic calm.

Damn that man and his infuriating ways. For once, could he just pretend to care for me as I do him? She turned her face aside and bit down on her lip. Hot tears threatened.

"Then let's get you packed. We'll catch the earliest flight out of here."

"And Damien. Will he come?" she asked innocently.

His head whipped around. "Why do you care?"

Indignant that he should make her explain she snapped. "What is wrong with you, Nikolas? In one instant you go from the caring friend to the possessive ex-lover."

His aquamarine eyes clouded and he winced.

"I don't know what you want out of me. I asked because he's your partner in crime, right?"

He shrugged. "I'm sorry, Trinity." He turned his head aside and she wanted to die at the pain that had flashed across his face. She hadn't meant to sound so rude; she was just so frustrated at his odd behavior.

"He will be waiting for us tonight at the airport, along with a few of my other colleagues."

She wanted to cry. His cold, indifference to her drove her mad. She needed him and couldn't believe he didn't feel the same way. How could you love someone so much, without them responding in turn? Trinity's heart wilted, a lonely bitterness dwelt in the cave of her soul. Nikolas meant the world to her and she would willingly sacrifice herself for him. Why couldn't he feel that way for her? Was that too much to ask?

Chapter 11

A million bodies packed the airport heading off to unknown destinations. Television monitors showed arrival and departure times. Some people ran, others walked. Children screamed and mothers pulled their hair out.

Food courts were littered throughout and Trinity's stomach grumbled, but she was too upset to eat.

On the plane ride, she'd tried to catch a few hours of sleep, but Alexander had haunted her dreams even then. Why couldn't she shake him? And what did this mean? Her temples felt near to exploding with pain, a major migraine was brewing and her temper was beginning to rear its ugly head.

The harsh glare of fluorescent lighting caused her to squint. Her shoes squeaked loud against the polished white tile. Nikolas had her hand clasped within his own, panic welled in her throat. She had to get away from the packed crowd. Claustrophobia was setting in.

"Niky." She sidled closer to him. She was exhausted from the long day. They'd landed just moments ago in Florida and she was ready to find a hotel room and collapse.

"Yes, Cat eyes?" He turned his head down to stare at her. Her heart did a little thump-thump. Could a finer specimen of male perfection exist? Trinity sincerely doubted it.

"Where do we go from here? I have a vague idea at best where Alexander is located. What do we do now?"

His nostrils flared and he spoke ominously. "We follow the bread crumbs."

Trinity trembled beneath the force of his gaze.

"Hey, Nik, over here." Damien waved his hand in the air. She turned at the sound and almost laughed when she spotted the eccentric vampire. He seemed so boyish; one could barely tell a killer lurked beneath.

She noticed several women turn to stare and admire the tall, blond man wearing a long black trench coat and sunglasses in the dead of night.

Although how he could manage that getup was beyond Trinity. It was deathly hot out. Within minutes of stepping outside, her tank top clung to her and a fine sheen of perspiration covered her body.

She fanned herself and wondered whether she looked like a drowned rat. Trinity flashed Damien a smile.

Absentmindedly, she noticed a very tall and well-formed man standing to his left, dressed in khaki pants and a loose white shirt. His golden blonde hair even shined in the dim lighting. A complete stranger to her, although Nik and Damien seemed to know him well. She studied him closer and nearly gasped when she noticed he was blind. Both eyes were nearly white. He smiled pleasantly and zeroed in on her location.

"Good evening, Trinity." His voice was smooth and rich like

a fine whiskey. Power radiated from him. She was stunned into silence for a moment. A jab from Nikolas made her remember her manners.

"Umm, hello." She felt foolish; she didn't even know his name.

He laughed musically and shoved Damien in a friendly manner. "So no one's told her my name yet?" He grabbed her hand and gave it a chaste kiss. "My names, Gabriel, glad to be of service."

"Gabe, release her hand." Nikolas spoke gently, yet with force.

Gabriel nodded and winked in her direction.

She grinned, not sure what to do next. A tall, voluptuous woman stepped out from behind his back. All Trinity could do was gasp.

The woman was breathtaking. Instantly Trinity's spine stiffened at the familiar look the lady flashed Nikolas. Her temper simmered just below the surface. Out of the corner of her eye, she studied her rival.

She was a tall woman, nearly as tall as Trinity herself, her hair was so blond as to be nearly white and pulled back in a loose ponytail. Instead of making her look unusual it gave her an alluring mystique. Light amber eyes swirled with mystery. Endless legs that seemed to go on for miles. An enviously trim waist. She was dressed in tight flared hip huggers, a black lace tank top and cowboy boots.

Trinity watched her walk forward, her arm out in greeting toward Nikolas. Her gait was sure-footed and stealthy.

"Greetings, Vrykolaka," her voice was ambrosia to the ears.

Vrykolaka? What the piss type of greeting was that? The mystery deepened and she found herself instantly hating the beautiful woman.

In essence, she was everything Trinity was not. Her heart faltered a step and she lowered her eyes to study the pavement. *Probably Nikolas's new mistress.* Hastily she dropped his hand and stepped away unwilling to give Nikolas the pleasure of seeing her wilt before his eyes.

Nikolas's laughter rumbled through the stale, musty gloom of night. His arm snaked out and wrapped itself around Trinity's waist, bringing her once again to his side. She knew she shouldn't but she melted within his embrace.

"Trinity, meet, Agape Stefanos. I have known her since she was a mere cub." Nikolas made a hasty introduction.

Agape turned toward Trinity and smiled warmly. Trinity gritted her teeth and gave a tight-lipped tilt of her mouth.

She noticed the woman had no canines as Damien did. Obviously, she was not a vampire, so what was she? Anger flared inside her. The green seed of jealousy sprouted in her heart.

"Welcome, mate of Nikolas." Agape's voice was low and sensual. Trinity peeked at Nikolas beneath her lashes. He had a wicked smile on his lips and she bristled. So he thought this was funny did he? Well she wouldn't give him the pleasure.

"I am not Nikolas's mate," her tone was stern and clipped with anger. Right now, she was furious with Agape and Nikolas both. And if Damien or Gabriel didn't watch it, they'd be next. She was cranky, looked like a gutter rat next to the beauty standing before her and Nikolas had the nerve to delight in her jealousy.

Agape's smooth features contorted with confusion. "Then you are not the…"

"Enough, Agape." Nikolas cut the woman off. Instantly Agape lowered her eyes.

Trinity took umbrage at his tone. Who did he think he was? She wanted answers and she wanted them now. If she were a child she'd stomp her foot petulantly. "I'm not what, Agape?" She turned and glared at Nikolas daring him to stop her.

He did nothing, so she looked back toward Agape. The woman did not strike her as one to cower and Trinity couldn't understand her sudden reluctance to speak.

"I was mistaken. It was nothing." Agape gave her a tremulous smile.

Trinity spoke through clenched teeth. "That somehow does not surprise me."

Nikolas lifted a brow and hugged her tighter, a mysterious smile on his lips.

Damien stepped forward and clapped Nikolas on his back. "Well now that the women are done squaring off, I've taken the liberty of renting a car for each of us." He winked at Trinity.

That's it. He's on my bad list, too. Was it to late to turn around and forget the whole lot of them? Somehow, she thought so. Reluctantly, she trailed in the group's wake sure they were discussing the case. Her sandals kicked up tiny pebbles in the paved road.

The noise of planes landing and taking off drowned the noises in her head. She squeezed her eyes shut and sighed. Why did she care for Nikolas so much? She always acted like a fool around him. Better, he leave with the lovely Agape and forget her. Her heart wrenched in her chest at the thought. Florida was a lovers' haven. She sighed once again and trotted to catch up with them.

***

"Athena was not pleased when she heard what happened to Trinity." Agape whispered in an aside to Nikolas.

He chewed on his lower lip. "So she did not know Alexander was capable enough to hurt a demi-god?"

Damien cocked his head. His golden blond hair whipped back and forth. "Apparently not. Zeus is, of course, furious with Ares and Aphrodite, but what's he gonna do about that." Damien's eyebrows rose in a disgusted look.

Nikolas sneered. "He's gonna give them a little wrist slap and send them off. Lot of good that will do us." He turned back to see Trinity pacing a few steps behind. His heart twisted in his chest. She looked so lovely and forlorn. He ached to hold her, possess her again.

Gabriel spoke up, "Athena advised me to tell you the mind swipe may have damaged Trinity in more ways then one."

Instantly Nikolas went on high alert. His heart stuttered momentarily in his chest. "What do you mean by that?" His eyes narrowed into dangerous slits.

"She suspects Alexander may have somehow planted a seed of desire in her heart for him."

"What?"

"Athena's not sure mind you, but she wants you to be on the lookout. Study Trinity, make sure nothing strange is going on with her."

"Why would she suspect that then?"

"Because she thinks that would be the easiest way for Alexander to capture her. How much easier could it get than to have a willing victim?"

Murderous rage filled him and he breathed heavily. "I will kill that creature with my bare hands if he dares."

Agape shuffled closer to Nikolas. "Then let's have another séance. We can find Alexander's whereabouts and put an end to this quickly."

"I will not subject Trinity to that again. We will find another way."

She gasped. "Nik, the Fates have told us she would be pivotal. Trinity must be involved."

"I forbid it. Trinity is my soul's destiny. No harm will come to her," he growled low in his throat.

She lowered her eyes. "Forgive me."

"Gods, Nik, must you always assert your authority?" Damien whispered. He looked toward Agape protectively. "She is correct, regardless if you want to admit it or not. And since I am not one of your pack mates, I can respectfully disagree with you." His silver eyes swirled with anger. His face set in challenge.

Nikolas heaved a disgusted sigh. "We have to find another way. Trinity is my life and I can't wait another two hundred years for her rebirth. I will see no harm come to her again."

Damien grimaced, exposing his long fangs. "Do what you must, Nik. Me, I've got vampires to track."

They arrived at the cars. Two Lamborghini's, one red, one black and a silver Hummer sat in a row.

Agape lifted a brow. Her gaze amused. "I see you do not care if we get noticed, Damien? Undercover ring a bell with you?"

Nikolas smirked.

Damien slid his glasses down his nose. "I love fast cars, don't you, Gabriel?"

Gabriel grinned. "I wouldn't know."

Damien laughed with delight. Nikolas was glad to see him back to his former playful self.

Trinity arrived and stood slightly apart and to his left. He ached to draw her to him.

Nikolas barked out orders. "Fine. We split up. Each of us will stay within a five mile radius and check in daily."

Agape, Gabriel and Damien nodded. Their faces set in stern seriousness.

Agape walked toward the red vehicle, got in and sped off in a peal of rubber.

Damien turned toward the silver hummer. "I want power beneath me tonight. You take the other Lamb." He tossed Nikolas the key and walked away-- then turned around. "Heed my warning, Nikolas; don't allow what's right to be clouded by your desires. Your decision will affect the entire human race. I trust you to do what's right." Damien lit the ignition. The Hummer rumbled threateningly, and then he took off.

"Where's your car, Gabriel?" Trinity looked confused. "Are you to come with us?"

He lifted a blond eyebrow. "No, I have my own means of transportation. Although, Nik, if you wouldn't mind…" Gabriel tugged at his shirt. "It's my favorite and I'd hate to see it get torn."

Nikolas grinned and extended his arm out. Quickly, Gabriel pulled off his shirt and flexed his long wings. They shimmered like the colors of the rainbow. In the background, Nikolas heard Trinity gasp.

"Thanks, buddy. See you later." Gabriel handed him the shirt and flew off. The downdraft was powerful and Trinity stumbled back a step.

"Is he an angel?"

Nikolas smirked at her innocent tone. "Not hardly. He's what you would call a harpy. Half-man, half-bird, although I'm sure he wouldn't mind if you called him one. He sorta plays up to the boy scout role."

She nibbled on her lower lip. "Niky, how come Gabriel was able to zero in on me? Isn't he blind? He sure didn't act that way."

"He's sorta like a bat. Gabe can't exactly see, but the way he explains it is that he has some sort of sonar device in his head. Just as good as sight I would imagine." He shrugged.

Trinity turned her head upward and stared in awe, Nikolas wasn't too sure he liked that look.

"Come on, let's get going," his tone indicated his displeasure.

"Right." She suddenly looked washed out from exhaustion. Quickly he ushered her into the car and headed to the nearest hotel.

***

Trinity's head lolled on the seat. Her eyes closed and visions of Agape danced in her mind.

"Nikolas." She turned her head to stare at his profile.

"Yes." He glanced at her and she licked her lips.

"What is Agape to you?" She hated herself for asking, but

could no longer refrain.

"A sister." His mouth set. Trinity sensed he hid something from her but couldn't place her finger on it.

"Literally?"

He turned to stare at her. His aquamarine eyes looked speculative. "Why do you care, Trin?"

She shrugged and casually flipped her hair over her shoulder. "Curious."

"We are not related by blood, but I've known her since she was born. She's never been anything other than a sister to me." He stared straight ahead, refusing to meet her gaze.

Trinity sighed. His answer helped soothe her jagged nerves. Now that the assumed threat of Agape was out of the way, she realized the woman had been quite nice. And she despised herself for acting so immature.

"Is she Damien's…"

"Cat eyes, can we stop talking about Agape? I'd much rather talk about you." His deep baritone caressed her body. Her stomach flopped and moist heat trickled between her thighs.

"Me," she squeaked out. She'd waited so long to hear him say that. Her eyes narrowed and she stared at him speculatively. "What are you getting at, Niky?" She refused to put her heart on the line again. Trinity waited, breathless for his answer.

Nikolas turned into the hotel parking lot and cut the engine. Deathly silence greeted her ears. She nibbled on her lower lip.

"Come on, baby, let's check in." He clipped his head and exited the car.

Sadness and pain welled in throat. She quietly stepped out of the vehicle and followed him inside, silent and heartbroken. Why had she expected Nikolas to answer her for once?

Chapter 12

As they walked up the carpeted hallway to their room, Nikolas glanced at Trinity. She'd fought to have her own room, which hurt him. He'd insisted she needed protection and reluctantly she had acquiesced.

His heart squeezed in his chest. How much longer could he keep away from her? He needed to lose himself in her. To forget the painful past. Was it possible she was ready to hear his secret? Or would she run away from the truth and their love as she'd done the last time he'd told her everything?

Nikolas stopped at their door, key in hand. He opened it and gently ushered her in. He stood just inside the door and observed her reaction.

She gasped and flung her hand to her mouth. The room was aglow with white candles. Plush Persian carpets covered the floor and in the center, stood a large four-poster bed. A gentle gust of wind fluttered the white curtains and washed the room in the exotic perfume of orchids.

A metal and stone patio gazed out over the Flori

She slipped off her shoes and ran to the balcony. Nikolas padded softly behind her, his arms clasped behind his back. He'd called ahead of time and given his order for how the room was to look when they arrived. He just hoped she approved.

Blue sky met the black silhouette of palm trees. Salt from the ocean carried on the warm breeze. Trinity's hair was a beacon in the night, glowing like warm embers from a banked fire. She gripped the railing and Nikolas worried he'd messed up somehow.

Slowly she turned around and his face fell. Her eyes shone with fresh tears.

"I…" She threw out her arm, encompassing her surroundings. "I…love it," she said breathlessly.

Nikolas smiled. He stepped forward, his eyes trailed down her body. She was so beautiful in her green summer dress. His fingers itched to scoop her up. He longed to nip and lick at her most sensitive areas and make her groan with pleasure from beneath him. His penis throbbed painfully.

Trinity's chest heaved and he made out each dewdrop of sweat smattered along the swells of her breast. He ground his teeth together and fought to maintain a modicum of control.

"I'm glad you approve." He cleared his throat and shook his head, his mind swimming with naked images of her. "I'm going to take a shower. Make yourself comfortable." Quickly he walked off, his movements stiff and jerky.

***

Trinity gazed at his retreating backside. There was hope, she felt it and knew it to be so in the depths of her heart. No man would go to the trouble he had for her tonight. Silently she walked around the room and swept her arms out; she twirled in place smiling. The softness of the carpet tickled her toes and she curled them in deeper. She threw her head back and her hair whipped around her like a cloak. She giggled and dropped down on the bed.

She massaged the scarlet coverlet. The sound of rushing water echoed from the bathroom. Before she could think better of it, she peeled off her dress and let it fall to the floor. She crossed the room and lifted her fist to rap on the bathroom door, then decided against it. She wanted the element of surprise on her side. Quietly, she let herself in and was instantly engulfed by warm steam. The bathroom was also lit with candles. How she loved him. The shower curtain was all that separated her from his loving embrace. Could she do it? Should she? Her heart pounded fiercely in her throat. She took one step, two, three and before she knew it, she was within arm's reach of heaven.

With trembling fingers, she pushed back the shower curtain. Nikolas stood under the hot jets. His nude body tanned and sculpted to perfection. Black hair clung to his shoulders and arms. Sad green eyes stared at her for a heartbeat. Of their own accord, her eyes traveled down to witness his jutting organ, eight inches of velvet steel.

Trinity's mouth parted. It was too late for her to turn around. The next move was his.

His body trembled visibly. Nikolas sucked in a deep breath; his tortured eyes stared at her. He lifted his arm and pulled her inside the claw foot tub.

Her body quaked at his light touch. Heat centered in her groin and she moaned from the beautiful torture. His roughened fingers traced the length of her arm. Goosebumps of fire trailed a path wherever he touched. No words were spoken, they weren't needed.

Water dripped down the strong arms that encircled her so tenderly. Her throat raw and parched she licked her lips. She needed this…him.

Roughly, he pulled her into his chest and growled deep in his throat. His velvet shaft pressed heavily against her stomach. Butterflies dove Kamikaze style in her gut.

"Cat eyes." His voice was husky. "If you don't push me away now, I will not be able to refrain myself." He squeezed his eyes closed, as if in torture.

She lifted her hand and placed them on his smooth tanned checks, forcing him to look at her. "I've never wanted anything more in my life."

He swooped and captured her lips. She mewled with pleasure and wrapped her arms around his neck drawing him closer. He nibbled on her lower lip, she parted her mouth slightly and their hot breath intermingled. Nikolas thrust his tongue inside the warm heat of her mouth, tasting and devouring her. Her head swam with passion.

She rubbed herself wantonly against him, urging him to take her. He twisted and pinned her to the bathroom wall, then placed her hands above her head.

"Don't move," his words came out strained between breaths.

She closed her eyes and inhaled his body wash.

He nuzzled her neck and then scraped his teeth along her neckline, sending tremors through her body. He lavished attention on her with his mouth and tongue; he drew wet circles in the hollow of her throat. Trinity shivered. Her breathing became shallow, more ragged.

Nikolas's hands slowly moved down, skimming either side of her rib cage. Adding pressure then withdrawing. His head dipped lower and she opened her eyes. His warm mouth encircled one of her nipples and she moaned. Her hands came down to rest against his head.

He looked up. "No, Trin, don't touch me. Not yet. I have to taste you, feel you first." He lifted her hand, then lowered his head. She thrashed violently when he nuzzled her breast. Water poured down her in rivulets and he lapped up the stream. Then his tongue flicked her nipple once again, both hardened painfully.

"Nikolas…" the cry escaped her. While he would be merely filling a moment of physical desire, she would be allowing him to tear apart her soul.

He lowered himself to his knees and hugged her tightly. His face flat against her belly. She burned from head to toe. His masterful hands squeezed her inner thighs.

Blood pounded in her brain, leapt to her heart, and made her knees tremble.

Gently he cupped her center.

"Oh God, Niky." She pushed herself down on his palm, loving the feel of him against her springy curls. His finger separated her moist folds. He flicked her engorged nub and she threw herself forward wrapping her arms around his neck. "Save me, Nikolas. I'm dying…"

His answer was to lower his head and blow gently. She squeezed her eyes shut. Her world began to fragment before her eyes.

"Niky…Niky…I need you now."

His laughter vibrated through her body and she clenched her pelvic muscle in response. Then his tongue encircled her and she sucked in a deep breath.

Comets and falling stars exploded in her mind. Fireworks danced along her veins.

Quickly he shot to his feet and lifted her up placing her center mere inches from his stiff penis. She wrapped her legs around him. Her lashes fluttered open, drugged and heavy. His aqua eyes dripped with suppressed passion.

"I love you, Trinity." Then he shoved himself inside her.

Her arms wrapped around the strong contours of his back. His muscles clenched beneath her hands.

Nikolas pushed her against the wall. Up and down, up and down. Whimpers escaped her. He filled her so completely.

"I love you, Nikolas." She panted heavily. He pushed himself to the hilt and pounded into her.

He grunted against her wet hair. "Come with me, baby."

She surrendered to the thrumming orgasm threatening to spill over. Heat spiked through her core. "Oh God…oh God." He bit down sharply on her shoulder; she spiraled out of her body.

Sweet death.

She screamed his name and with one final thrust of his hips, he too called out.

Blissful relief laid claim to her languid body. He slipped down with her slowly, still keeping a firm grip on her waist. They lay entwined beneath the now cooling spray. Her body was half ice, half fire.

He laid his head against her forehead and panted heavily. "Thank you, Trinity."

She stiffened. *Thank you. That's all he has to say to me is thank you.* Her heart splintered into a million tiny pieces.

As if he could sense the sudden mood change, he looked at her intently. His hands cradled her chin. "I love you, Trinity. There has never been and will never be another for me, but you."

The cold around her heart shattered and she smiled. She could die now and be happy.

Reverently he lifted her from the cold ceramic tub and walked their dripping bodies over to the king sized bed. He laid her down, his green eyes smoldering as he looked at her. And he proved his love to her for the rest of the night.

Chapter 13

The ringing of the phone broke through Nikolas's fog of sleep. He squinted against the harsh sunlight filtering through their room. A supple leg was intertwined through his own. He smiled and reached for the phone.

"Yeah," he croaked.

Trinity sidled closer to him in her sleep. He draped his arm around her shoulders and cupped one breast in his hand, softly kneading it.

"Nik," Agape's smooth voice spoke through the receiver. "We did some scouting last night…"

He frowned. "Why didn't you guys call me? I should have been there."

Her musical laughter tinkled through the phone. "Because we knew you'd be otherwise occupied."

Nikolas smirked. *True.* "And?"

"Mmhmm. I see you have no other response, obviously we were correct." She laughed once again. "Semere activity is very high down here. We learned more about Alexander's whereabouts before we dispatched two of his cronies."

His heart hammered in his chest. "Yes."

She remained silent for a while. "It's not good, Nik. He's barricaded himself in a tunnel system of abandoned warehouses. It's going to be next to impossible to find him."

"Give us an hour to get ready. We'll meet you downtown at the beach. Damien below ground?"

"Yes. He interred himself over an hour ago."

"Fine. See you then." He hung up the phone.

Trinity moaned and his mouth tipped into a smile. She looked flushed and lovely this morning. He leaned over and delivered a soft kiss against her brow. She smiled and opened her eyes. "Hi you," she said with a shy note to her voice.

Nikolas felt himself stir and wondered whether he'd ever get enough of her. "Hi yourself, gorgeous."

Her arms wrapped around his neck and she pushed herself into him. He groaned, hating that he had to push her away. *Tonight*. He grinned. Tonight he would have her again and again.

"I'm sorry, baby. We gotta meet Agape. Come on, let's go shower." He wiggled his eyebrows.

She nibbled on her lip and shook her head. Lightning quick she ran from the bed. Her nude body bounced enticingly in all the right places and her laughter trailed like the tinkle of bells behind her. He stiffened immediately; she was going to be the death of him. Nikolas growled low in his throat and chased after her.

***

An hour later, they headed toward the beach. Nikolas snarled when several sets of eyes studied her, nearly breaking their necks in the process. A fist had slammed into his chest when he'd seen Trinity walk out of the bathroom in her white bikini. He didn't want anyone but himself to see her like that.

Trinity on the other hand seemed completely oblivious. She hooded her eyes with her hand and stared down the beach. Her blue wrap waved in the breeze, her bright red hair shone like fire. His heart clenched in his chest and he glared at any man stupid enough to stare at her.

Trinity giggled. "Baby, cut that out. Let's look for Agape."

He smirked. "Can you blame me, Trin? I'm just protective of what's mine."

"I'm not yours. If I choose to be with you that's one thing. But nobody owns me, but me." She pointed at her chest and stared at him. Her bright blue eyes sparkled with mirth.

"Whatever you say, Cat eyes." He glared one final time at her entourage and tugged her forward. *Damn, the beach was a stupid idea.*

"Nik…Trinity, over here." Agape waved her hand in the air. She sat beneath a huge blue and white beach umbrella. She'd twisted her pale blond hair into a braid; she wore a blue tank top and shorts.

"Agape," Trinity said. "You're not dressed to swim."

Agape sighed. "I do not wish to be seen as meat before this pack of human, heathen men." She sniffed disdainfully.

"Human, heathen men? What do you mean by that?" Trinity looked confused and pursed her lips.

Nikolas could see the wheels turning in her head and he narrowed his eyes at Agape.

"Just that they are a bunch of vultures."

Quickly Nikolas changed the subject. "Where's Gabe?"

Agape waved her hand through the air. "Oh somewhere, you know how he is. Searching high and low for our sworn enemies." She laughed.

Nikolas shook his head. "Well tell me what you learned last night."

She turned serious and studied the sand. "Please sit, you make me uncomfortable towering above me."

Trinity and Nikolas sat cross-legged beneath the umbrella. A large picnic blanket saved their rears from scorching on the hot summer sand.

Agape leaned in close. "Damien followed three Semere to a warehouse downtown. They were drunk on human blood and unaware of us." Her fingers played through the white sand. "We dispatched two and ordered the third to give us the location of Alexander. He was obstinate and refused. Damien sliced off a hand before he would even respond."

Trinity shuddered. "Ugh." She frowned.

Nikolas draped his arm around her shoulder. It was time she knew more of his life. He'd feel her out, see if she was ready for the full truth.

"The Semere was mad. Laughing one moment then crying the next. Fool." Agape's mouth turned down. Her amber eyes swirled with remorse. "I hate killing them; they must have been normal people once with normal lives." A shudder rippled through her. "Anyhow, he gave us one other promising lead. He mentioned keys and a house. We asked him what he meant by that, but he lunged for me. I had no choice." She turned her head aside.

Trinity patted her hand affectionately. Nikolas stared on in shock.

"I've been in their presence, Agape, they may have been human once, but they are nothing but monsters now. Don't feel bad for doing what you had to do." Her face shone with sincerity.

He couldn't believe it, had she actually offered Agape solace? Maybe he'd misjudged this new Trinity.

"Thank you, Demi-Goddess." Agape bowed her head. Nikolas's heart twisted with fear and he glanced at Trinity.

"Stop calling me that," she giggled. "Believe me, I'm no demi-goddess. I'm just little ol' Trinity O'Reily from Nashville, Tennessee."

Agape turned to stare wide-eyed at Nikolas. He clenched his teeth and gave the merest shake of his head.

"Forgive me, then. It was just an expression."

Trinity stood, dusted herself off and smiled. "I'm going for a swim. It's deathly hot out and those blue waves beckon." She unwound her wrap and made her way to the shoreline. Nikolas couldn't tear his gaze away. Her body swayed, one hip rose then fell. His mind buzzed with screeching sea gulls and squealing children. The ocean water pounded the beach, the roar deafening in his ears.

"Nik…" Agape shook him roughly by the shoulders.

He cocked his head and looked at her. "What?"

"I've called your name twice. Did you not hear me?"

Nikolas turned his head to stare once more at the sizzling beauty.

Agape sighed. "Have you not told her anything?"

He whipped his head around. "No, I haven't." His mouth set

in a grim line.

"She has a right to know. After all, her fate is in your hands." She lifted a brow.

"Agape, I have neither the time nor the patience to speak with you about this. This is a decision I will come to when I feel she is ready."

"More like when you're ready." She crossed her arms. "Stop acting the lovesick fool. You have a job to do…"

He bared his fangs, feral heat curled through him. Agape trembled. "Remember your place. I will tell her when it is time," he stressed.

She bowed her head, her body quaking with anger. But Nikolas knew she would not oppose him, he was the alpha and regardless if she agreed or not she would obey.

"Vrykolaka, I take my leave." Agape stood and padded off.

Nikolas let out a pent up breath. He hadn't meant to be hurtful. Trinity was consuming him once again. How could he protect the woman he loved and also do his duty to his goddess? Shame ripped through him. He would right things with Agape later. She was, after all, correct, he was allowing his love to blind him to what must be done. He stood and walked toward Trinity.

She floated peacefully within the protective netting of the ocean water. She'd closed her eyes and he imagined caressing every inch of her, which was nearly his undoing. He groaned out loud.

The water was crowded and he ached to take her someplace private. Then he had a thought.

"Trinity."

Her blue eyes opened and she smiled lazily. His body burned for her. Nikolas entered the water, reaching her side within minutes.

"Come with me."

She straddled him with her legs and stared into his face. His body lit up in flame. Heat shot through his groin and he stiffened with need.

"Where is Agape?" Her eyes roamed the beach.

"She has gone." He walked with his hands beneath her soft bottom, kneading her with expert fingers. She purred and dropped a kiss on his neck. The hairs on his arm rose in response. He made his way out of the water, keeping his arms around her petite waist.

"Where are you taking me, Niky?" Her silky hair rubbed against his naked chest, he picked up the pace. His feet kicking up mounds of sand in his wake.

She laughed a delicious sound to his newly awakened passions. "It's a surprise, Cat eyes."

Within moments, they topped a dune and left the summer crowd behind. Sharp rocks jutted out of the ocean looking like castle spires. The ocean tide whipped heavily against them. Bits of green lichen clung like tentacles to the gray slabs of stone.

She'd never known Florida to have coves. She gazed on in awe. Where in the world where they?

He entered an alcove that held waist deep ocean water. Rocks surrounded them, hiding them from prying eyes. The tide was calm and soothing. A soft lapping against their skin.

Trinity gasped. "You've been here before." It wasn't a question, more a statement of fact.

"Once or twice. Do you like it?" His voice was low and

sensual.

Her mouth twisted. "How did you know this was here? And where exactly is here? Florida isn't known for its nooks and crannies."

Nikolas roared with laughter. "Do I detect a hint of jealousy?" She raised an eyebrow in response. "To answer your question, this is not the first time I've been to Florida. I stumbled upon this place quite by accident and it has been my private haven since then. As for your nook," he lifted a brow, "magic, I guess." His smile was secretive.

Magic. Well anything was possible. What was this compared to everything else she'd learned? Then a thought struck her and she stiffened.

Trinity inhaled to speak, but Nikolas cut her off. "No, I haven't brought anyone here but you." She rolled her eyes and smiled. "Now, I ask you again. Do you like it?"

Trinity giggled. "It's beautiful." She closed her eyes and laid her head against his chest. He melted beneath her. Gently he tipped her head back and lay claim to her once again.

***

Their bodies sated, they lay nude and intertwined on the beach. The warm rays of sun kissed her bare skin. Nikolas's hair draped around her breast and she trailed her fingers through it, enjoying the feel of him against her body.

Trinity felt at once pleased and worried. She couldn't complain about his lovemaking, it was everything she'd remembered and more. She frowned and nibbled on her lower lip. Her heart was content and screamed at her to leave the mystery that was Nikolas alone. But that wasn't how she wanted to live her life.

Trust was vital to any relationship and she desperately wondered why he'd been less than honest with her. On top of that, lay Agape's peculiar way of addressing her. Why did everyone insist on calling her a demi-goddess, she shuddered. Even Alexander had called her that. Was there something she did not know?

She needed to speak with her father and figure it all out. And find out the meaning of *Vrykolaka*. That was a piece to the frustrating puzzle. She just knew it.

The rocking sound of the ocean lulled her into a deep sleep.

***

Alexander walked up to her; his suntanned skin glistened like gold. Water trickled down his smooth, hard abs. A welcoming smile played on his sensuous lips, he held out his arm to her.

Trinity shivered from the intensity of his gaze. Goosebumps rose on her skin. She hated him and yet desired him all at once. Would he touch her?

He came closer until she felt his hot breath fanning her cool skin. Her lashes fluttered shut. What was happening to her? Panic and bile rose in her throat, she needed to get away. But her passion for him wouldn't allow it. It was revolting and exciting all at once.

"So you desire me already, my queen?" His voice was hollow and devoid of any warmth. He licked his lips, exposing his long, sharp fangs. His lavender eyes swirled with madness. He lifted a finger and trailed it along her jaw line.

Trinity knew she was lost to him. His gaze mesmerized her like nothing else could. "I will never desire you," she spat.

He threw back his head, his long black hair whipped behind him. "You do already, you tasty vixen. You tease me with your rejection. But I know it to be untrue; I can read it in your heart. You and I have a connection, Trinity."

She shook her head. "No, never."

"Oh, but we do." Then he lunged for her. His fangs ripped into her throat.

She screamed. Sand clung to every inch of her body from the sweat she'd formed.

Nikolas sat up quickly. "Baby, what's wrong?"

Her heart hammered in her chest and her mouth tasted of cotton. It couldn't be true, it just couldn't. She lifted a hand and felt a tiny prick of pain in her neck. *No, way*…she shook her head. A bug must have bit her, that's what it was, a bug. Trinity turned to stare at him, noting the wide look to his eyes, no sense in worrying him needlessly. It was after all only a dream. "Nothing, Niky. Just a little nightmare. It was nothing." She only hoped that was true.

***

Alexander wailed with laughter. His ivory chamber resonated the sound; it was like music to his ears. He steepled his fingers together. His plan was working brilliantly. Trinity was dough to be molded and he had her right where he wanted her.

He licked his canines savoring the droplet of blood he'd managed to extract from her, rolling it on his tongue like an expensive wine. She tasted wonderful. A rare delicacy.

So she thought it to be a dream, did she? Oh how he enjoyed the chase. Maybe if she pleased him, he'd make her his queen. Then again, he had no problem using her powers until she ran dry and killing her. Either solution caused him to smile. He'd just have to wait and see.

***

Nikolas and Trinity wiled away the remainder of the day, swimming, making love and stopping at a food shack for a burger and fries. Her earlier fears were all but forgotten. Quickly the sun had begun to set and it was time to get ready for the evening. The first step in seeking out the ever-elusive Semere leader.

***

They roamed the noisy streets of downtown. Bright neon lights blinked and buzzed, proclaiming one bar or dance club as the best in town. Tourists packed the streets. The moon hung, half full and eclipsed by the harsh lights of the rowdy city.

"It's past mid-night. Don't people ever sleep?" Trinity sighed with exasperation. Nikolas laughed and searched the streets. He held tightly to her hand, parting the maddening crowd like the Red Sea with his glare. Her feet were sore and tender. They were supposed to meet Damien at the corner of Fifth and York. But with the way people milled about, a thirty-minute walk would likely take two hours at best.

A sensation of intense sickness swept through her. Nikolas must have felt it as well. He paused, his nostrils flared as if smelling the balmy night breeze.

He turned his head to the side and swore. "Trinity, we've found our bread trail."

Chapter 14

They ran down a side alley. The putrid stench of rotted fruits and vegetables assailed Trinity's nostrils and she gagged.

Nikolas stopped next to an opened back door. Loud techno-music blared through the night. Wooden crates littered the alleyway and he sat her down on one.

"Baby, I have to go…"

Trinity shook her head. "No, Niky. Let me come with you." Her heart pounded in her throat. She couldn't be left alone, not in a strange city, with rogue vampires running amok.

"No, Trin. I will not see you come to harm. I will come back to get you once I am done. I swear it." His aquamarine eyes pleaded silently for her to obey.

She swallowed the lump in her throat. He grasped her wrists tight and held on.

"Promise me, Trinity, my life means nothing if you don't take care of yourself. Promise me."

She nodded, unable to speak. He ran off, a black spec in the night.

The chilling sound of rusted hinges squealed in protest. Rats squeaked and scampered off. Trinity rubbed her arms, tears of frustration threatened to spill over.

"Father." She trembled.

"Yes, baby," a voice spoke behind her. She swiveled on her crate and breathed a sigh of relief. Her father's spectral image floated at her side.

"Where is he?"

"He sniffed out a Semere, actually quite a few. He's gone to take care of them."

The thought that her loving Nikolas was a killer made her quake in response. However, it made perfect sense. He did have a certain ruthlessness she found appealing and exhilarating.

"I need to help him. Where is he?"

"Trinity, I can assure you the boy can take care of himself." He smiled.

Her mouth turned down, she needed to find him. Surely, she would come to no harm in his presence. He was probably done with the Semere by now anyway.

"I can see steam coming out of your ears, Trinity. Don't do it."

"Do what, Dad?"

"Trinity, trust Nikolas to take care of himself. He will come back for you, just be patient."

She shot to her sandaled feet and paced. Her heart raced each minute that ticked past. Where was he? Maybe he'd been hurt.

She cocked her head. The memory of the afternoon flooded her and she remembered wanting to speak with her father. Trinity pierced him with her assessing gaze.

"Dad, I need to ask you a question. You must be honest with me."

He sighed. "It is time for you to know the truth."

Her mouth dropped open. She'd forgotten how well the spirits tended to anticipate her questions.

"You are not what you think, Trinity." His silver blue eyes were sad.

She licked her suddenly parched lips and urged him to continue.

"There is a reason why everyone calls you a demi-goddess."

Her heart hammered in her chest. The beat built in intensity and her head swam. She landed with a soft plop back on the crate.

"I am one," her voice sounded weak and breathless to her ears.

He nodded.

"Why did you not tell me this before?"

"You weren't ready."

"And now…"

"And now you are." He spread his hands wide.

The news was disturbing but not really surprising. She'd always felt strangely out of place and different from all the other girls.

"What abilities do I have?" She imagined the worst and best.

"Basically everything you already know. You can command the dead to do your bidding and speak to them."

She didn't know why that depressed her. The thought of having omniscient power had been a heady prospect for a brief moment. But then she realized she was better off without it.

"If I'm a demi-goddess that means…"

"You cannot die."

Her lashes fluttered. A frown dipped her brows. "But if that is so, how can I vividly remember my childhood and awkward teenage years."

"Because yours is a different immortality, Trinity. Your body dies eventually but your soul continues on, rebirthing itself every two-hundred years."

Her eyes widened in shock. She tripped over her tongue. "How can I not remember any of that?"

"You live under a curse."

"What…what did I do?"

"Zeus admired you beauty and sought repeatedly to make you his newest concubine. When Hera learned of this she cursed you. Since she could not kill you, she did the next best thing. So now, you can die, but will always be reborn. Same body, same person. Just no memories of your past lives." He shrugged.

"Who is Hera?"

"In a word, a bitch." He sighed. "I'm sorry, baby, I know this can't be easy. She's Zeus's wife and very unwilling to share him with anyone, even if it's not the woman's fault. She's spiteful, vindictive and unfortunately she turned her wrath on you."

"Can't I change this?" Panic surged in her throat. She didn't want to forget, she wanted to live and remember everything. *Nikolas*, her eyes squeezed shut. He would die someday. Perhaps not remembering was a boon after all.

"Yes, there is. Nikolas holds the key to your release."

"Niky…Nikolas," she sputtered stupidly. "How can he? Is

he…" her question died in her throat.

A low-slung white wolf raced like a bullet past her. She gasped in shock. *A wolf!* Another wolf, in Florida? How was that possible? The reporter in her could not leave the mystery alone. She took off at a run, following the white blur.

"Trinity, come back." Her father yelled in the background. But she didn't, she couldn't.

The wolf took her on twists and turns. First left then right and left again. She was so lost she feared she'd made a stupid mistake.

The large wolf stopped beneath a lone light post and sniffed the air, it's glowing eyes found her. She stepped back into the shadows of the wall. It growled low in its throat and snapped its jaws, then took off at a trot.

A trot for a wolf was a mad dash for Trinity and her lungs burned. She gasped for air, her body perspiring heavily.

The white wolf entered an abandoned building. The urge to know drove Trinity forward.

The night was eerily quiet. Cicadas chirped; the wind rustled through her hair. Heavy footsteps shuffled behind her. Her breathing became ragged and strained. She deserved to die for her own stupidity.

Trinity turned to see a steely-eyed, brown haired Semere hot on her trail. She screamed and took off at a run. Her hands sought the entryway of the abandoned building and she entered. Everything was so dark she could barely make out hazy outlines. She tripped and fell over a row of empty boxes.

Adrenaline surged through her veins. She had to get out. Get away.

The footsteps were closer. *Oh god!* She panted heavily. She was trapped. Her sight failed her and she turned to meet her death. Her body thrummed with energy. Trinity beckoned her spirits to heed her call.

A loud howl rent the air. A memorable howl, fear snaked down her spine. The Semere turned its head and exited the building. Trinity nearly collapsed. She needed to escape. But escape could only be found through the open doorway, the vampire had just exited.

Gingerly she made her way to the door. As she stepped outside, she spotted a trio of wolves surrounding the lone Semere.

One white, one red and she gasped. The great black she'd seen back home. How could that be? Her eyes darted frantically between them.

A loud whoosh caused her to glance up. A Semere dropped down inches from her. Its exposed fangs gleamed red in the moonlight. Once again, she found herself entrapped by the vampire's gaze. Her heart pounded furiously.

The great black snarled and leapt on the vampire's back. Untamed and deadly, the beast ripped into the howling Semere. The vampire fought to extricate itself from the wolf's death grip on its neck.

Sweat poured down her forehead. Trinity hugged the wall and crept backwards. The red and white wolves fought off three other Semere that had shown up. The black quickly dispatched its prey and glared at her.

She landed with a thud into the arms of another vampire. Trinity screamed and stomped on its foot. Maiden be damned. She meant to live.

"Merda," the vampire roared behind her. She turned to find

herself in Damien's arms. Trinity sagged with relief. "Damn it all, woman, that's the last time I save you," he snapped.

She didn't care; she was finally safe. "Where's Nikolas?" Her voice was hoarse.

"He's fine." His eyes narrowed seconds before he threw her behind him. Faster than light, he flicked out a silver-tipped blade and threw it into another Semere. It landed in its chest with a sickening thud. A column of fire, incinerated the vampire quickly, a hollow scream followed in its wake.

Then two more Semere replaced it. All three wolves were battling again. Trinity panicked and turned her head. The heavy thump-thump of wings flying through the air greeted her ears. The back draft was intense and she stumbled.

Gabriel swooped low and she could only wonder what a blind man was capable of in such a situation.

Damien stood back, and placed his arm against her chest. "Stay back."

She panicked. What was he doing? "Aren't you gonna help him, Damien?" She crept forward, not knowing what she would do, but feeling that something needed to be done.

"Trinity, I said stay back!"

Trinity watched silent and helpless, expecting to see Gabriel devoured by the vampire's mighty hands.

The ones who'd earlier been fighting the wolves also joined their compatriots. A circle of Semere began to close around Gabriel, hissing their displeasure.

Gabriel wrapped his wings about himself and closed his eyes.

Then a beam of pure, white light shot from his forehead. The vampires roared and writhed beneath the light, until they could no longer move, they screamed and raged. They'd become living statues. Flame erupted from within the five Semere and their eerie howls raised the hairs on the back of her neck.

Trinity rubbed her eyes. She couldn't believe the power Gabriel wielded and felt foolish for thinking his handicap was a hindrance. She should have known better.

She breathed a sigh of relief. They were gone. All the Semere had been killed.

The white and red wolf transformed before her eyes. The red, a strange man with long red hair and piercing black eyes. She shivered and glanced in awe at the white.

"Agape," she squeaked. A werewolf? Agape and the other man were completely nude.

Red walked up to the black wolf. "Come we must speak to the goddess."

A brilliant blue flash of lightning surrounded the three.

Her mouth dropped open. Had she just seen Nikolas? Did the black turn into Nikolas?

Her eyes watered at the blinding light and she covered her eyes. When she dropped her hand, all three wolves were gone.

Chapter 15

Nikolas threw his fists into the air. “Alvis, you bastard. Why did you force me to transform in front of Trinity?”

Alvis, a Norse werewolf, growled. They met in the center of an ivory dais, their fists raised.

“Do not think to order me about, Nikolas. I am not of your clan.” Alvis’s face shone red, the same color of his hair.

“Enough!” A female voice instantly broke them apart.

Nikolas shoved a fist through his hair and bowed before Athena. “Forgive me, Goddess,” his voice was clipped with anger. He clamped his jaw tightly, agitation at the situation poured off him in waves.

The beautiful brunette thrummed her fingertips on her golden armrest. Her gray eyes flashed with annoyance. “I’ve summoned you for a reason, Nikolas.”

His heart beat loudly in his chest. Nikolas squeezed his eyes shut. He didn’t want to hear what she would say, so he turned to stare at the rolling green valleys of Athena’s home. The sun shone warm. Butterflies lazed about, twittering from flower to flower. Blue sky and white fluffy clouds met his assessing gaze.

"Face me, Nik."

He straightened his back and faced the goddess head on.

"You have always been a great and respected leader. Do not fail me by disobeying my order."

Nikolas gritted his teeth. He couldn't. "How can I do that to her? She doesn't know…"

"It is not your job to question me." Her chestnut brows dipped, marring the timeless beauty of her face. "You will involve Trinity in this case. She will be the one to bring about the destruction of Alexander." Athena flicked her wrist and stared down at him disdainfully.

"You have disappointed me, Nikolas, but I'm a caring Goddess. I will send you back to the moment after you disappeared so Trinity will know no lapse in time."

Nikolas stood stock-still. How could she ask him to do this? He was breathless with rage. Trinity was an innocent. She didn't need to be involved in this.

"Have a care, Nikolas." Athena's full red lips thinned. "Settle your problems with Trinity soon. Otherwise I will tell her myself and force her to do what's right."

His head snapped up and he bared his fangs. "Right! You tell me what's right. Right is the fact that you've simply involved yourself in this case to thwart Aphrodite." He trembled with rage. Agape slid next to him and laid a calming hand on his shoulder. He shrugged her off.

Athena clapped her hands, thunder rumbled in his ears.

"Bitch…" his word trailed off into the black nothingness that surrounded him like a cocoon.

***

Trinity widened her eyes and looked toward Damien and Gabriel. "Where is he? Was that wolf Nikolas?"

Damien looked uncomfortable and scratched his head. Gabriel coughed into the back of his hand.

The rustle of a stray sheet of paper caught her attention. Trinity turned to look and spotted Nikolas. His long, black coat blew in the breeze. He looked morose and sadness welled in her throat. Without thinking, she ran into his arms.

"Oh god, Niky, I'm sorry," her voice cracked in misery. His strong arms surrounded her and he laid a punishing kiss on her lips. She sobbed from joy.

"Trinity, what were you doing here? Why didn't you wait for me like you promised?" He laid his forehead against hers and traced her jaw with his finger. She shivered and melted into him. He smelled of sea salt and leather. Trinity inhaled deeply.

"I…I saw a wolf." She frowned in thought. "I followed it…Agape." She turned wide eyes to stare at him, wondering whether she should ask him to verify her suspicion. Was she ready to know? Really know, who he was? Her ears buzzed in the quiet that stretched between them.

His aqua eyes swirled with misery. "Yes, she is a werewolf. What do you think…?"

She laid her finger against his lips and kissed him passionately. Not yet. She wasn't ready yet.

"Take me to our room, Nikolas." Her body quaked with need.

He heaved a large sigh, picked her up and walked back to their hotel. Her arms wrapped around his neck and she listened to the steady thump of his heart. She knew what he was. Trinity just needed time to come to terms with it. Regardless, she still loved him.

***

Nikolas kicked open the bedroom door. His breathing was heavy. Fear gripped him. What if she'd seen? What if she didn't want him anymore? His heart twisted in his chest and he crossed the room, laying her down on the bed. She sighed. Her neon blue eyes seemed to pierce through his soul.

He trembled. Nikolas couldn't stand her rejection. He needed her like he needed air. The past two hundred years without her had left him desperate and empty. He meant to hang onto Trinity with his life. He clutched her to his chest, his fingers digging into her back. Her sweet almond and vanilla scent clung to her.

"Nikolas," she gasped. Reluctantly he drew her back; his heart froze over.

"Kiss me." The words spilled out of his mouth before he could take them back.

She placed her knees beneath her and laid her hands gently on his chest. Nikolas closed his eyes.

Her soft lips were a whisper against his mouth. He didn't move, just allowed her to have her way with him.

Fingers worked on the buttons of his shirt. She yanked and tugged, finally exposing his chest to the chill air of the room. He breathed raggedly.

She threw his shirt to the floor and worked her hands over his scalp. All the while, her mouth pushed down harder and harder on his tingling lips. Trinity pulled the leather thong out of his hair.

Long legs straddled his hips and she pushed him down on the bed. Her flaming curls rubbed enticingly against his chest. A moan of desire ripped from his lips.

Her rosy mouth parted and she bit down. Nikolas became entranced by the rise and fall of her chest. Slowly her hands traveled down the sides of her ribcage until they reached the edge of her pink shirt. His breathing quickened, blood rushed to his already engorged erection.

She shed her top quickly. A black lacy bra pushed up her pale ivory breasts. With a deft turn of her wrist, the bra landed in a puddle next to them. Trinity flipped her hair behind her back, baring herself completely.

His hands trembled as he touched her warm, taut skin. She closed her eyes and sighed. Nikolas slid his hand along the swell of her breast, cupping one then the next. He flicked a swollen nipple and she cried out. Her skin was flushed and radiant.

Trinity stood. A moan escaped his lips when she placed her hands on the waistband of his jeans. Quickly he shed them and watched with excitement as she slid her shorts down. Then she crawled back on him like a stalking panther. Nikolas pulled her on top of him, their nude bodies slick with heat.

She nipped at his nipple, before completely encircling it with her wet mouth. He ground his teeth and hissed, bucking beneath her. Trinity walked herself slowly backwards on his chest, her moist haven mere inches from his erection.

"I love you, Nikolas." She impaled herself on him and threw

back her head, looking like some wild fey creature. Her coarse hair rubbed against him, the friction causing him to gasp. Trinity was wet, slick, and tight; it felt so good.

He placed his hands on her hips and surged beneath her. Their tempo increased in speed and need. They groaned like two rutting animals.

Nikolas squeezed his eyes shut against the pleasure and pain. Her tiny hands pushed against his chest. He captured her wrists and forced her to look at him.

Her blue eyes swirled with molten passion. Her face contorted moments before she breathed his name. His hot seed spilled inside her in a fiery explosion. Nikolas arched and called out.

Trinity collapsed on top of him. His arms hugged her tightly to his chest, their bodies still connected.

"I've never loved another," she whispered. Her words carried like the call of trumpets to his ears. Nikolas smiled and succumbed to deep sleep.

***

Early next morning Trinity sat outside on the balcony. The sun was beginning to make its ascent. She took a sip of herbal tea and watched nature's painting unfold.

She was miserable because she knew the truth and she was afraid to approach him about it. How did this change things? If last night was any indication, not by much. However, Nikolas had fought so long and hard to keep the secret from her. Was there a reason why? She just couldn't fathom it.

A cold chill turned her head. Pierce's green eyes drooped wearily.

"What's wrong?" He glided to within arms reach. "I felt you in here." He pointed to his heart.

She gave him a half smile and sighed. "Nik."

He shook his head. "You've finally figured it out. Why does it bother you?"

She shrugged and stared ahead. "It's strange, is all…"

"How so?"

Trinity faced him. He seemed to be genuinely interested, so she unloaded. "It's just the shock of realizing you don't know anything. Life has always been one way and then Niky shows back up and everything's haywire."

"Trinity, that doesn't change how much he loves you. How much he's always loved you."

"What does Vrykolaka mean?"

"It's Greek for werewolf."

She nodded solemnly. The final piece of the puzzle, it all fit.

His face looked sad and bitter. "You've got your chance, don't waste it."

She knew he was right. So what if Nikolas was a werewolf, she was a friggin' demi-god for crying out loud. Nothing changed. Her feelings for him were still just as strong as before.

"But that's not all is it?"

Her head whipped around. Should she tell him? Trinity decided to chance it. Not being able to confide in anyone was slowly driving her mad. "No, it's not."

He nodded his head slowly. "How bad is it?"

She suppressed a sob. "Pierce, Alexander gives me no rest.

Whenever I close my eyes, he's there. Even the most mundane tasks make me think of him. He's a drug for me." She winced at the wild tone of her voice. "And I can't stand it. I love Nikolas. So why this desire for…for evil?"

"All I can say, Trinity, is to dig deep inside yourself and remain strong. Don't let him near your heart."

"What? He couldn't possibly get near my heart, that's always belonged to Nikolas. Nothing's changed."

He smiled sadly. "Just please heed my warning."

She frowned and worried her bottom lip. Pierce was beginning to frighten her. They were only dreams, weren't they?

Cold seeped into her limbs. She would fight him. Alexander would never possess her, even in her dreams. Starting now, Trinity wouldn't allow him to ruin her day. She pushed all thoughts of Alexander from her mind and quickly changed the subject.

"What happened to you, Pierce?" Her voice was soft and soothing.

He sighed, his translucent shape shifted away from her. "I was a sheriff, killed by a reckless gang and my fiancée committed suicide."

She gasped at the depth of his emotion.

"I've looked for her, it seems like forever."

"You haven't found her?"

"No." He began to fade. "Don't do what I did. Hold on real tight to Nikolas and never let go."

She sat staring at nothing with her tea, cold and forgotten in her lap and Pierce's words ringing in her ears.

Chapter 16

Trinity swiveled in the chair and stared at Nikolas's sleeping form. A smile lit her face. One very muscular leg draped over the blanket and his hair covered his face.

She'd give him time to tell her. Maybe he feared her rejection. After all, it wasn't everyday you walked up to a person and said you were a werewolf. However, with the way her life was now, nothing could honestly surprise her anymore.

She turned back around and allowed her leg to dangle over the balcony. The weather was still tolerable, but rapidly turning muggy with the rising of the sun.

Streets came alive with honking horns and people shouting greetings to one another. Another glorious day in balmy Florida was underway. Other thoughts intruded on her peace of mind.

Alexander. The name alone caused tremors to run through her body. Her relationship with Nikolas would have to take a backseat until that maniac was taken care of. She mulled silently. Where did she fit in this picture? Why was Alexander suddenly so interested in possessing her?

She'd taken the time, after Nikolas's revelation a few days ago about Gods and Goddesses, to do a quick study. What she learned didn't bode well for her.

They were selfish creatures concerned with their own personal gain in the competitive hierarchy of Olympus.

She wrinkled her nose. If anyone had asked her a few short months ago whether mythical creatures existed, she would have laughed and called them silly. She shook her head, not only did they exist but she was dating one. Ironic, to say the least.

Something smelled fishy to her and it didn't come from the ocean. The fact that Athena wanted to thwart Aphrodite made sense. That fit perfectly with the profile. But what Trinity couldn't understand and sought desperately was why a goddess didn't choose to take care of the pest herself.

She placed her cup on the table next to her and stood. A Goddess or God could easily dispatch a minor annoyance, so why go through all the drama of sending people much less capable?

Trinity twirled a curl around her finger.

Arms trapped her within a strong embrace. Shocked she turned around and smiled. Nikolas had come up on her unawares. *Silent...like a wolf.* More and more she found she couldn't deny the truth.

"How long you been up?" Nikolas's voice was deep and sexy from just waking. He nuzzled her neck.

She laughed. "A few hours. I needed time to clear the spider webs from my brain."

His eyes became hooded and she sensed him withdraw from her once again. She wouldn't allow that anymore. Her arms crept around his neck. “Niky, Niky, where are you going?” She smiled, her eyes searching his.

“I’m right here, Cat eyes.” He looked tired.

“Don’t withdraw from me anymore, baby. It’s okay. Whatever it is your hiding from me, it’s okay.” She just hoped he’d catch the hint.

Nikolas seemed to be deep in thought and she pulled him in for a kiss.

An amused glint danced in his expressive green eyes. “What was that for?”

She shrugged. “Just because. So what’s the plan for today?”

He narrowed his eyes at her as if in silent wonder, then he shook his head. “The Semere are swarming this city.”

He began to pace back and forth relentlessly.

“We feel…”

“Who’s we?”

“Agape, Damien, Gabriel and myself.” He scrubbed a hand down his face. “Anyhow, we feel this is just a diversion. We don’t think Alexander’s here at all.”

Trinity was taken aback. Her vision had been very clear that Alexander was in Florida. “What makes you feel that way?”

He gripped the railing and stared down. “A feeling. I suspect, Trin, he’s been alerted to our presence.” His tired eyes looked at her.

“How?”

“You.”

She gasped and placed a hand on her beating chest. “Me,” she peeped.

Nikolas rushed to her side and drew her into him. She trembled violently; cold fear gripped her.

"When you sought him out. Athena suspects some sort of transference may have taken place."

"What are you telling me?" Her eyes rounded and her breathing quickened.

"This is all just hypothetical, Trinity. But when we questioned a few Semere last night..." he gritted his teeth and continued, "They mentioned you."

She was breathless.

"I would never let him hurt you." He laid his chin atop her head. "Never, Trin, I vow it."

She clutched at his naked back, fighting for control. "What did they say, concerning me?"

"They...they called you their Queen."

Memories of Alexander calling her just that flooded her mind. Her skin crawled at the possibility. *No, it can't be. It's just an odd coincidence.* "My God, Nik. How do I stop this?"

"Well, baby, if he's half as powerful as I think he is. I'm not sure. I asked Damien for some clues, he's checking on that, but for right now," he shrugged, "I just don't know."

"Nikolas, he's in Florida." Of that, she was sure. Her conviction was strong. The spirits couldn't lie to her. Alexander was here, somewhere in the vast unknown.

"How can you be sure, Cat eyes?"

She shook her head. "I just am. I feel it with every fiber of my being. He wants to lead you astray, but he's here."

Nikolas blew out a frustrated breath. "We'll search some

more tonight. In the meantime, I have something I need to show you."

Curious, she cocked her head.

"I've put this off for far too long. There are things about yourself, Trinity, you need to know." He tugged on her hand and walked back into their bedroom.

She squeezed her eyes shut. How many secrets could she handle before she cracked under the pressure?

***

He wrapped her in his arms and laid his head against her head. "Take a deep breath and relax. It might even help you if you close your eyes."

She studied him. "Where are you taking me?"

"Some place very special. Now; you ready?" He leaned down to peer at her. His green eyes looked worried. That more than anything helped her to relax. Nikolas wouldn't allow anything to happen to her.

Placing a quick kiss on his cheek, she squeezed her eyes shut.

Nikolas muttered under his breath.

A terrible sensation of vertigo rocked her. She swayed from side to side and gripped his shirt tighter. Eventually the dizziness stopped and she cracked open an eye.

"Where are we?" she gasped.

"Mt. Olympus, Trinity. Your home."

They walked hand in hand, along the sprawling meadowlands of Olympus. Nikolas's heart threatened to erupt from his chest. He could only wonder what she was thinking now.

He led her to a bubbling brook and brought her down to sit

with him on a dead tree branch. Deer bounded away, bumblebees flew drunkenly through the still air. Rabbits nibbled on sweet grass, all in all, a very cozy scene.

She was silent and Nikolas worried he'd rushed her. He'd never in the past shown her, her home in Olympus. Never fully trusting she could handle it.

"This is my home?" she breathed.

She turned to stare at him. A golden circlet lay on the crown of her head, her red hair hung in waves down her back. A pleated periwinkle gown clung to her body. The moment they'd stepped through the portal separating earth from Olympus she'd transformed to her regalia of old. Almost as if Olympus itself rejoiced in her return.

He sucked in his breath at the vision of beauty. She reached out her hand-a golden snake band wrapped around her upper arm glinted in the sunlight-and plucked a juicy pomegranate from a cornucopia that had appeared, as if by magic, by her side.

"This is your home." He extracted the fruit from her hand and deftly sliced it in half. The juicy, sweet aroma wafted up.

She kicked her feet in the water and sucked on the seeds. "What exactly do I rule?" Her brows dipped.

"You don't rule anything, Trin, more a sharing of powers."

"With who?"

"Hades. You're a very minor deity."

She snorted and stared at him.

Nikolas smirked. "Not to me, but you aren't exactly well known."

"Fine by me." She shrugged. "I've always preferred my privacy anyhow." She nibbled on her lower lip. "How exactly was I born?"

"Your birth was from a union between Hades and a nymph. Hence, your demi-goddess status. You share many of your father's abilities with the dead. Talking with them and such. But while he can command them all, you're only able to deal with the shades. The not fully dead, if you will."

Her mouth rounded in an O. Nikolas's curiosity got the best of him. "Why is it, Trin, that you don't seem shocked? You're taking this pretty well."

She blushed. "I forgot to tell you I had a similar talk with my father…" She looked at him sharply. "What exactly would he be to me anyhow? He certainly feels like my father, but all this has sort of thrown my perspective on things out of whack."

"Trin, you have one real father. But seeing as how you don't know him, consider Bruce your real dad."

"You're right. Well, Bruce…I mean Dad," she paused. "This is all very confusing. Anyhow, Dad told me who I really was last night. My shock faded already." She smiled.

A beautiful head popped out of the water and Trinity gasped. "What is that?" she pointed.

"Melaina."

At her strange look, he explained further. "A Potameides."

Trinity still stared.

"A sea nymph. Mermaid."

"Oh wow!" A look of enchantment touched her features.

The green haired, golden-eyed lady swam forward. She lifted her upper torso out of the water, exposing her full rounded breasts. A huge smile of greeting was on Melaina's lips.

"I couldn't believe it when I heard." Her voice sounded musical. "Trinity, it is really you?"

Trinity frowned. "Do I know you?"

Melaina's response was to flick water at her. "Of course you do. Why, we practically grew up together." She turned her swirling golden eyes toward Nikolas. "Nik, you look as handsome as ever. It's good to see both of you."

Trinity turned her head sharply and stared at him, curiosity written all over her face.

"And you, Melaina. How goes your search for a mate?" Nikolas smiled warmly.

"Eternally frustrating, as ever. I'm convinced I shall never find one." Her soft laugh sounded like a dulcimer playing in the wind.

"Are you here for good?"

Nikolas shook his head. "No, unfortunately. I was just showing Trinity her birth home."

"Oh my." Melaina brought a dainty hand to her mouth. "I forgot about the curse." She swiveled at the hips and stared at Trinity. "Do you remember anything?"

Trinity looked from him to the mermaid. "No, just what others tell me."

"Oh." A sad look touched the Potameides' face. "Then I suppose you truly don't remember me?"

"No, but I'll never forget you again." She smiled warmly.

The mermaid glided forward, barely disturbing the water. She leaned in, gave Trinity a large hug and chaste kiss on the cheek. "I cannot wait to have you home, Trin. I've missed our talks." She smiled and dove under water. Her rainbow colored tail flipped up one last time, as if waving a good-bye.

Nikolas turned to stare at her. She wore a look of awe. “So much I’ve missed out on.” Trinity looked at him. Her blue eyes shone. She crumpled. “And for what? That I made a Goddess jealous. Did I have any part in Zeus’s seduction of me?”

Nikolas shook his head. “No, baby. But that’s the way of the Gods. They don’t need a reason for what they do, they do it without impunity.”

She picked up a pebble and skipped it across the calm water.

He squinted up at the sun, noting it’s descent in the sky, when a lumbering, shuffling sound greeted his ears. Nikolas stiffened; he knew the gait of the creature walking behind him. He turned to make sure.

A spotted cow broke through the clearing. Its black, beady eyes centered on Trinity.

Nikolas grabbed her hand and shot to his feet.

“Nik?” she said, “what’s wrong? It‘s just a cow.”

He clenched his jaw and shielded her from the cow’s gaze. Hopefully it hadn’t spotted her.

“It’s not just a cow. It’s Hera’s sacred animal. The cow was sent to spy on us. I don’t know if this was random or if Hera has been tipped off to us being here. But, it’s better if we leave now.”

She gulped and nodded.

“Don’t worry, baby, it’s all right. It’s all right.” He only hoped so.

Chapter 17

Trinity dressed in her tight, black leather pants and halter-top. The sun was just beginning to set. Nikolas exited the bathroom, a towel to his damp hair. He smelled fresh and clean. A warm smile from him caused her toes to curl. His appreciative glance was all she could have hoped for and more.

"You sure Hera didn't see me?" She still tasted the fear she'd felt hours ago after nearly being spotted by the cow.

"Absolutely." He laid a kiss on her head. "If she had we would have known by now. It's all right, Trin." Nikolas gave her a heart-stopping smile and she melted.

His assurances went a long way toward calming her down.

Quickly he tied back his hair, slipped on a pair of sunglasses and a black trench coat. She lifted an amused brow. "Going for that dark, mysterious look?"

She giggled and touched the hem of her pants. "We are going to be so hot in leather."

He shrugged a wolfish grin on his face. Her heart thumped loudly in her chest. He was gorgeous.

"It suits me. Besides you can't fight in anything but leather, haven't you seen the movies?" Nikolas grabbed her hand and headed outside. "Let's go find the clan."

***

"It's about damned time," Damien teased. "I was beginning to wonder, whether you two had forgotten your little task." He sat crouched in the shadow of a bakery. The smell of warm bread mocked Trinity, reminding her she'd forgotten to eat.

Like a great cat unfurling itself from a long sleep, Damien stood. He was graceful and predatory all at once. He'd tied his long blond hair back at the nap of his neck. Damien's face was cast in shadows, his lethal fangs exposed.

He flicked his head. "See those five Semere?" he whispered.

Trinity and Nikolas turned in the direction he pointed.

"Agape and I have been trailing them. She's coming at them from the other direction. Gabriel's winging overhead, ready at a moments notice to strike." He glanced at each of them, as if to make sure he had their total attention. "Apparently," his Italian accent became more noticeable with his excitement, "they are five of Alexander's personal entourage."

Trinity shivered.

"What are they doing here?" Nikolas's voice dripped with disgust.

Damien turned on his heels and lowered his sunglasses. His strange silver eyes pierced her. "One can only imagine."

Nikolas threw himself in front of her and growled low in his throat. "You forget yourself, Damien." His body was stiff and rigid.

An amused chuckle escaped Damien. He threw up his hands.

"Nik, just a little touchy aren't we?"

Trinity furrowed her brows. Damien had never been anything but courteous to her. Why did Nikolas always have to act the hero for the damsel in distress? She was no damsel and she certainly wasn't in distress. This male preening ended now. She yanked on his arm. "Back off, Nik. He didn't mean anything by it."

He looked at her and he leaned down. "Trinity, I'll never stop being protective of you. No matter how many times you tell me to stop."

Her stomach went aflutter. "You macho male, I'll deal with you later." She chuckled and threw Damien an amused glance.

A sliver of white in the moonlight drew her attention. Agape crouched on her paws. She turned her regal head and looked at them. That was the signal for them to move out.

Trinity's mouth became dry. She swallowed. Nikolas's hand found hers and he dragged her forward creeping within the safety of the long shadows. Innocuous sounds boomed in her ears. The rustle of grass. Surf pounding the now vacant beach. Her heart threatened to jump out.

"Baby." Nikolas turned to her, a finger against her lips. His warm breath caressed her ear. "Stay here. Damien scouted this place earlier. You'll be safe. I'll come back for you."

She wanted to scream from frustration. Once again, she'd be left to her own devises. He pulled her in for a quick kiss then vanished- a creature of the night welcomed by his mother's dark embrace.

***

Nikolas ran to catch up with Agape. He shifted to wolf form minutes after leaving Trinity's side, delighting in the raw power of his body. Electric ripples shot through him. A slight tingle and the transformation was complete. His breathing was smooth and even. To his left stood Agape. His mouth curled up, his tail held high. Time to fight.

Quietly they padded along the vacant alleyways. His nose low to the ground, the revolting stench of his prey slapped him in the face. Warm human blood mixed with the rot of death. Nikolas picked up the pace and exposed his long fangs.

Agape came in close to his side and rubbed her head into his shoulder. A greeting between clansmen.

He froze and lifted his head. They were to his left, hiding in a decrepit building. So they knew he was after them, much more observant than regular Semeres. He grinned, delighted to have found worthy prey.

A black blur caught his eye. Damien clipped his head and crouched behind a huge dumpster. Gabriel sat perched on top of a brick building. The trap was set.

Silently he stalked them. Agape circled to his left.

A frantic female cry raised the hackles on his neck. One Semere exploded through the door lightning quick, a silver bladed knife in its hand. Agape sailed in the air, jumping for the jugular, she ripped into it. Hot blood assailed his sensitive nostrils.

Damien was a whir of activity, dancing circles around his opponent. His black coat flapping behind him like bat wings.

Gabriel was playing games with his, a fearsome looking vampire with a puckered scar that ran the length of his eye to his lips. Gabriel feinted, twisted and turned.

My turn now. He howled and ran headlong for a Semere trying to creep up on him. A pink Mohawk sat atop the male's head. Nikolas sensed one closing in on him. He'd get to that one later. He would deal with the pink clown in front of him first.

His claws extended until they were razor sharp talons able to pierce through the thickest leather. The vampire swung at him with a mace. Nikolas cocked his head. They circled one another. Finding the vampire's weak spot, he pounced. A gaping wound tore open in the creature's chest. Black blood oozed. The vampire touched his chest and grinned wickedly.

"So it's like 'at, eh, were-beast?" His thick Irish accent accosted Nikolas's senses.

Pathetic creature. Nikolas jumped and ripped into his prey's shoulder. His violently pounding heart sent adrenaline surging through him.

The vampire whimpered and swung madly with its weapon. The mace whistled through the air, mere inches from his head. He swiveled on his paws, confusing the creature, and jumped on him. His claws dug cruelly into its back. The force of the impact threw the monster to the black pavement.

Nikolas transformed and barked out, "Tell me now, before I kill you, where Alexander is."

"Why should I 'elp you out? Nothin' in it for me." He coughed up phlegm and blood.

Nikolas pushed his knee into the man's spine. "You tell me, and I'll give you a merciful death. You don't," he shrugged. "It's your choice."

"Go rot in 'ell." The vampire swiveled and stared at him with its mad, red eyes. "Ye'd better hope ye kill me, 'cause I got me some plans for that delicious strumpet o' yers." He laughed and licked his bloodied canines.

Nikolas saw red.

A can kicked across the pavement alerted him to the other Semere's presence. He turned, still crouched on the man's back.

A beautiful brunette with honeyed eyes grinned wickedly. There was a vicious buck knife held fast in her hand.

He gasped. His eyes widened. It couldn't be.

She smiled, exposing long white fangs and dove for him. His momentary lapse nearly ruined him. The other Semere pushed up, dumping him to the cold ground. Instantly Nikolas transformed and snapped his jaws.

Curls of steam rose from his mouth. Mercedes? But how? How did this happen?

Mercedes gripped the handle of her weapon and sliced down. The man swung his mace. Nikolas backed up. The hackles on his neck rose in warning. The knife ripped through his shoulder blade. Pain, fierce and hot tore through him. He yelped in protest. The mace mercifully missed him.

He latched on with his fangs to Mercedes ankle, shaking his head from side to side. She cried out and kicked him in the muzzle with her boot. Stars exploded behind his head. His shoulder throbbed. Blood, his own, poured freely from the wound.

Gabriel and Damien flew to his side.

Damien threw a Chinese fighting star into the man's heart. He screamed and exploded in a leap of flame. In the confusion of the moment, Mercedes fled.

His heart leapt to his throat. Trinity. He needed to reach her. Oh God! He screwed up again.

***

Trinity sat bored beneath a park gazebo staring at the unusually deserted streets. Fear was quickly replaced with restless energy. The moon was the only illumination she had. She trusted Nikolas completely. He'd told her she'd be safe, so the strange shadows caused her no fear.

Truth be told, she was close to falling asleep. The incoming tide was rhythmic and hypnotic. Palm trees rustled in the breeze. She yawned and tapped her finger against the wooden banister.

A rustle of footsteps caused her to smile. She twirled around. A black clad figure walked slowly toward her. "Oh thank God, Niky. I was beginning to get bored out here waiting for you."

She waited for a response and frowned. The figure kept advancing. Trinity licked her parched lips. *He wouldn't play a joke on me, would he?* A creeping sense of loathing crawled up her spine. She shivered and her eyes searched for an escape.

Her pounding heart drowned out the panic rolling in her head.

Powerful fear caused her to take flight. She jumped over the wooden railing, landing with a hard thud on the packed earth beneath her. Her breath left her in a rush. She glanced behind her. The figure ran with preternatural speed. Bile rose in her throat, she fled, running full tilt through the maze of streets, turning left, then right. Her lungs burned for oxygen and greedily she sucked in air.

The pounding footsteps never once wavered. She paused, dripping sweat, and leaned against a brick building. Her head turned from side to side as she searched for an escape.

Heavy breathing caused her to yell in surprise. Trinity made to run once again, but the figure clawed her back, ripping into her skin. She winced and fell to her knees, her head dipped down. The creature walked in front of her and genuflected. Its fingers grasped her chin and made her look up.

She gasped. Needles of pain lanced through her. "M." Her voice was a mere whisper.

A glimmer of recognition crossed the honeyed eyes. The beautiful Hispanic took a step back as if her humanity warred with the predator within.

Trinity panted. Light-headed, her vision swam in and out of focus. She couldn't believe it. Her friend was now a vampire. They'd only been at the jazz club a few short weeks ago laughing and having fun, how could this be?

Mercedes walked forward with a long knife clenched in her fist. She couldn't, she wouldn't die like this.

Trinity shot to her feet, the blood rushed from her head and she swayed precariously. Without thought or reason, she grabbed Mercedes by her shirt and pulled her close.

Mercedes mouth dropped open. With a rush of power, Trinity called her spirits to her.

Blue and green lights swirled in her mind's eye. Their wails of desperation screeched in the silent night. A bright silver glow encircled them. The spirits erupted from within her.

A quivering mass of light. She clenched her teeth. Sweat poured down her brows. Trinity fought for control. The light swirled faster and faster, becoming bright red. It pulsed with energy. A towering inferno rose in the air and exploded around them. All the torment of the dead blasted them full force.

Mercedes yelled in pain and squirmed in her arms. Trinity threw her head back, gritting her teeth. Fire shot through her arms, scorching Mercedes. The smell of burnt flesh punched Trinity full force.

They were consuming her. The dead. Somewhere, deep in the back of her mind she yelled for them to stop, to release her. Orange and yellow flames licked at her, begging her to keep holding on. With a mighty shove, she forced Mercedes from her grasp. The vampire's eyes rolled to the back of her head. Exposing the whites of her eyes. Blindly, she fled into the night, wails of despair following in her wake.

Trinity was a tower of flame. A breathing, living flame. She fell to her knees and clapped her hands together. "Cease," her voice boomed in the night.

Instantly the shades separated and flew back as separate entities within her. Her head lolled once before she crashed heavily upon the cold blacktop.

Chapter 18

Fear for Trinity beat a crazy rhythm within Nikolas's chest. He kept his nose close to the pavement, sniffing out her trail. He'd arrived at the gazebo and found his worst fears to be true. She was gone and Mercedes had been responsible for it. The Semere's unique scent was all over the place.

Desperately he ran to find her. A red gleam of hair caught his eye.

His movements stilled, his limbs refusing to move. His heart jumped to his throat, a wretchedness of mind consumed him. He let out an eerie howl and ran to her lifeless body. She lay drenched in a puddle. Her cheeks smudged with dirt. He smelled fire, but couldn't detect any. Trinity's faint intake of breath caused him to tremble with relief.

Nikolas changed to human form. He flexed his arm, testing it for weakness. The gash in his shoulder was healing nicely. Already, pink skin replaced the gaping wound.

Panic ate at him. He needed to get her home. Give her time to heal. Nikolas cradled her in his arms and practically flew on the wings of the night. He was but a blur of light.

He said a quick chant, shielding them in a cloak of invisibility. Seconds seemed like minutes, minutes like hours, before he was finally within their room.

Embracing her like a timeless treasure within the safety of his arms, he crossed the room. She was ashen and barely stirring.

He tore off her clothing. His hands and eyes skimmed her for lacerations of any sort. Frustration welled within him, sick and cloying. Nikolas smelled the blood, her precious blood. But, where?

Gently he turned her over and sucked in a deep breath. Three jagged tears in her back seeped warm fluid. Already the wound was swelling and filling with pus. His fingers tested it for depth by pressing down; she squirmed and yelped.

He squeezed his eyes shut. He hated to cause her more pain, but the wound needed tending. His hand trembled as he reached for his suitcase. Within lay the ointment he sought.

He extracted a cylindrical green bottle and uncapped it. A gift from his Goddess, the black cream was a mixture of tree bark, berries and black soil from Olympus. However, the cream burned like hell because one drop of Athena's blood had been added to it. He'd used the ointment once on Damien. He'd said it felt like death. But it worked instantly and that's what Trinity needed.

His blood raced in his ears. If he didn't do this she'd die from infection. Closing his eyes, he prayed for strength and dipped his fingers in the jar.

"I love you, Trin. Trust me to do what's right." He spread the ointment on her back. Immediately he could see the wound repairing itself. Ligaments and tendons stitched themselves together.

Pus exploded like a bullet from a barrel. Red, raw skin bubbled, stretching, melding together.

Trinity sat up in bed and screamed, clawing at her face, neck and chest, whatever she could reach. Nikolas threw himself upon her, spread eagle, his feet locking against hers and his wrists grasping her tight.

She panted and heaved, bucking like crazy beneath him. Her pain became his own. Sweat poured off her in waves. She trembled.

"Breathe, baby, it's almost over." Her eyes flew to him and she gasped. She fought against him, a wild and caged lioness. Her nails dug into his face, but the nicks would heal. The sting only lasted mere seconds.

Then she collapsed. Her eyes rolled back and she lay still. His heart hammered in his chest and he moved off her. She was flushed from exertion. Hair clung to her face and her mouth lay parted.

He turned her over one final time. The wound was gone, as if it had never been. Smooth ivory skin met his inspection.

Heavy hearted he lifted her up and took her to the bath, laying her reverently inside. Nikolas turned on the hot water and bathed her. He washed her hair making sure to use her almond and vanilla scented shampoo. Tonight he would take care of her and give thanks that she was safe with him once more.

***

Fingers reached for her. Trinity gasped and spun around. A merry twinkle danced in Mercedes eyes. She relaxed and smiled at her friend. Then Mercedes dived for her. Long, pearly fangs exposed. Trinity screamed and landed in a heap, wrapping her arms around her head.

"Stop!" Alexander walked forward and pushed Mercedes aside. The evil knight coming to the rescue.

Trinity panted and clutched at her shirt. Her eyes sought wildly for an escape, but the graceful undulation of his body drew her to him.

He was lean and free of any imperfections. Alexander was the embodiment of beauty. Sensual lips curled into a cruel sneer. Cold lavender eyes stared at her. "Come to me, my queen, together we could rule nations."

Her lashes fluttered shut; she wanted to fight him. But his sultry voice caressed her and caused warmth to spread through her body. Against her will, she opened her eyes and studied him brazenly. The thought that this was so unlike her flitted briefly through her mind to be once again forgotten by his captivating presence.

He strolled forward in no hurry. His golden skin rippled with each step he took. Alexander was insidiously beautiful. Her hands crept to her shirt and she began to undo the buttons. The rational side of her mind screamed for her to stop, but his strange beauty entranced her. It was as if she had no control of herself. And the thought was terrifying.

Alexander chuckled and stood before her, tall and proud. His huge erection throbbed. He extended his arm and trailed his finger down her cheek.

Trinity tried to stop it. She screamed for help, for someone to rescue her from herself. "Father! Pierce! Please, please somebody help me." A silent tear rolled down her cheek, she didn't want this.

Alexander boomed with laughter. "Do you think your pathetic spirits could help you now? They cannot reach us here, Trinity. It's just you and me." His hot breath tickled her lobe and he grasped her chin, hauling her in for a kiss.

She squeezed her eyes shut and thought suddenly of Nikolas. Her heart began to pound furiously in her chest. His protectiveness towards her, his utter devotion and she smiled. Trinity heard Alexander hiss and his hold on her lessened. Excitement welled inside her. Nikolas would be her redemption. She remembered the passion they shared, but most importantly the love.

Alexander stared at her wide-eyed. "What are you doing?"

She concentrated harder. Gritting her teeth, Trinity pictured Nikolas's love as her armor in battle and cloaked herself in it. Sweat began to sting the lids of her eyes, her body trembled with fatigue but still she pressed on. Trinity drowned in Nik's love and finally forced Alexander's hand to release her, which broke whatever telepathic hold he had on her. The Semere leader drew back from her as if burned. She'd beat him this time, but barely and her mind became numb with exhaustion.

Alexander roared. "You may have won this round, Trinity, but I'll win the war!" He slapped her brutally on the cheek.

***

Trinity screamed and sat up in bed clutching the sheet to her breast. Drops of sweat formed above her brow. The room was as quiet and still as death. Pale moonlight shone through the drapes. Tentatively she touched her hot cheek and felt a large welt rising up. She gasped. It couldn't be.

Nikolas jumped up and ran to her side.

"Baby, you okay?" Lines on his forehead indicated his worry over her. A shaky sigh escaped her and she fell into his warm embrace.

"That was terrible, Niky." Her words muffled against his chest.

Nikolas sat on the bed and laid her head in his lap. His hands were gentle as he massaged the building knot of tension in her scalp. She sighed, delighting in the feel of him.

"What happened, Cat eyes?" His voice was soothing.

She nestled her head deeper in his lap. "It… it was Mercedes."

Trinity couldn't tell him about Alexander. Nikolas would go mad, besides it was just a dream. She'd probably slapped herself. Although that wasn't a great theory, it was all she had to go by. Besides, how could a dream be true? The stress was starting to affect her in strange ways and she rolled her eyes. Alexander had absolutely nothing to do with this. If he could affect her somehow, Nikolas would have told her. Relief flooded Trinity and slowly her heartbeat returned to normal.

"I know. I saw Mercedes, but was too late to stop her." Nikolas's voice held an edge of steel to it.

Trinity pushed herself up and stared deeply into his eyes. "She came specifically for me, didn't she, Niky?"

He shrugged, a helpless look on his face. "Gods, Trin, I wish I knew. But it was uncanny how easily she found you." His eyes shone with unspoken pain. "I let you down. You were never meant to be in harm's way."

She reached out her hand and pulled him into her chest. Her fingers ran through his silky hair. He clutched her. "Nikolas, you could not have known. Don't be so hard on yourself. Bad things happen, that's just the way life is."

"I don't deserve you, Trin."

A laugh bubbled from her. He pulled back and stared at her as if she were crazy. "Well I don't deserve you either. So I guess that means we were meant for each other."

He lifted a brow. "That's an odd and very roundabout way of putting it." He shrugged and smiled. "But, I'll go with it."

They laughed.

Then a memory struck her like lightning. Mercedes being the mother hen helping Trinity come back to the world of the living after her break up with Nikolas and her heart wrenched in her chest. Her face fell and she stared out at the sky pregnant with twinkling stars. "Why her? She's been my best friend forever. Why Mercedes?"

Nikolas pushed her back on the bed and held her hand. The dark surrounded them like a veil. "Alexander knows you, Trin. He knows what makes you tick. I'm sure it was as easy as him putting two and two together."

"How can I change it? I don't want to kill her. Is there someway to redeem her?"

Nikolas rolled on his side and trailed a finger down her neck. Her lashes fluttered shut. Warm heat centered in her gut.

"I've never heard of it happening. Course that doesn't mean that it couldn't."

"But, Niky, the only way to rid ourselves of Alexander is through the cold-fire. Didn't you tell me, if he dies then so do his minions."

His finger stilled and she stopped breathing. She willed him silently to continue his caress.

He picked up where he left off and her body hummed with energy. “Yes.”

She squeezed her eyes shut. That wasn’t what she’d wanted to hear at all. “There has to be a way. I saw her tonight, Nikolas. When I called her name, for an instant she recognized me. I know I broke through her fog somehow. She’s still in there.”

He blew out a breath, tickling her lobe. Shivers coursed through her body. “I’ll ask Athena. But please, baby, don’t get your hopes up.”

That was enough for her. The fact that he’d ask and maybe, just maybe there was a way.

He rolled to his back, carrying her with him. His penis throbbed between them. She gasped and smiled. A delicious heat curled her toes.

“I was so frightened for you today.” His admission left her breathless. How she loved him.

His teeth nipped her shoulder. Liquid crashed between her thighs and she purred into his neck. “Make love to me, Niky,” *and help me fight off these demons.*

He growled and did just that.

***

After their shower the next morning, they dressed in the bathroom. Steam still swirled around their ankles. Nikolas glanced at Trinity. She looked gaunt and large black circles under her eyes printed their indelible mark on her porcelain skin. He cringed; he’d felt her tossing and turning the whole night long.

He pulled her into him. “Baby, what’s wrong? I sense a change in you.”

She sighed miserably and looked down at the tile. “I’m just tired, Niky. Bad dreams. I‘ve been having very strange dreams.”

His radar went on high alert. Memories of Gabriel telling him to watch for any changes in Trinity had Nikolas studying her closely. Her blue eyes seemed clouded with fatigue but overall she looked fine.

“What kind of dreams?”

Trinity dismissed his question with a flick of her wrist. “Stress related dreams, I’d imagine. It’s nothing really.”

“How often do you have these?”

“A few times, I think last night was just too much for me to handle.” She shrugged and dropped the subject.

Nikolas narrowed his eyes. Physically Trinity seemed fine, but something nagged at him, telling him to keep a close lookout for any other suspicious signs. He grabbed her by the elbow and dragged her to his side. “You would tell me if something was wrong, wouldn’t you?”

She scoffed. “Of course. Don’t worry about me, I’m a big girl.” She laid her hand on his cheek and smiled. “I’m perfectly fine, just very tired, Niky.”

He grumbled but dropped the subject.

Trinity stepped away from him, swiped a hand down the mirror and stared. Her mouth twisted into a frown. She seemed to be studying her back. He knew exactly what she was thinking.

“Why do I have no marks? And come to think of it, why doesn’t it hurt anymore?” She looked at him with rounded blue eyes.

"I used an ointment. You healed instantly." He cocked his head. "Don't remember?"

"Well, I do remember pain. Terrible pain, but I passed out. I just assumed that was from the wound." She turned to stare at herself again. "Whatever that stuff is it's a miracle worker."

Nikolas walked toward her. His hand traced the smooth ivory of her skin. Satisfaction washed over him when he saw goosebumps rise. She gasped and looked at him, her blue eyes shimmering with passion.

He swooped her into his arms and nuzzled her neck.

Trinity exhaled.

"You, trollop. You've got me bewitched," he growled.

"Me?" she giggled and placed a hand on her chest, fluttering her lashes. "Well, trollop, am I? Hmm." She sniffed disdainfully.

"Want to take a tumble with a man who loves you dearly?" His voice was low and husky.

She nibbled on his ear and his skin singed at her touch. Her tongue licked ever so softly against his neck. He groaned low in his throat, drunk with passion.

"Aren't we to meet Agape and Gabriel downtown today?"

Her words brought him up short, they still had a mission to do and he couldn't afford to become distracted. Not now, when her life hung in the balance.

He nodded his head and sat her down. She clutched his hand and flashed him a brilliant smile.

"This is not over." He swatted at her bottom.

"Oh, Nik, I would have been disappointed if it had been."

Nikolas ground his teeth and led the way out of the bathroom.

His erection pushed into his jeans uncomfortably. He groaned, this was going to be a very long day.

***

"I still don't see the reason for visiting every key shop in Florida," Trinity protested.

"Baby, that's the only lead we have so far." He turned to stare at her and Agape. Agape simply shrugged her shoulders and entered the decrepit building. Gabriel grinned, clipped his head once and headed off in a different direction.

Nikolas sighed and turned his attention once more to Trinity. "Agape said the Semere mentioned a key before he was dispatched." He lifted a hand and shook it violently. "I'm beginning to lose faith myself right now though."

She visibly shuddered. "This place looks like it's gonna fall apart soon." Wooden beams looked ready to unhinge themselves from the slightest gust of wind and paint chipped off in the corners exposing pieces of rotted wood. "I tell you it's only held together by the termite colony infesting it." He chuckled, grabbed her hand and entered.

The soft tinkle of bells must have alerted the proprietor. He turned his head and smiled. The short, balding man walked up to them. He took out a red handkerchief from his back pocket and wiped his brow.

"What can I do ya for?"

"Nothing, just browsing." Nikolas looked at Agape. She shook her head, a sullen look on her face.

Trinity sighed. "I could make this search much easier, Niky, if you would let me," she whispered.

He clipped his head at Agape and turned around. “I really didn’t want to have to depend on you for answers, Trinity, I don’t want you to overdo it. But I can see that we have no choice, this search is becoming fruitless.”

“Thank God! I don’t think I could have walked into another twenty key shops just to turn around and walk back out. What exactly was your method?” Her blue eyes twinkled with mirth.

Nikolas frowned. “I don’t know. But damn, Trin, this is getting frustrating. What the hell does key and home mean?” He blew out a breath.

Trinity patted his hand. The gentle touch was soothing to his frayed nerves. He pulled her in close and inhaled.

“One way or another we’ll figure this out, Niky.”

He smoothed the hair back from her face. “Trinity, you’ve gone through so much these past few days, are you sure you can do this?”

Her brows drew together. “Actually, I’m terrified.” She gave him a weak smile. His heart flopped in his chest. “But I’ve got to do this, there’s no other choice.”

He called to Agape.

“Yes, Vrykolaka.” She turned her liquid amber eyes in his direction.

“I want everyone to meet in my room tonight at midnight.”

She nodded her head and made her way out of the building.

Nikolas knew Trinity was right, as much as he hated to admit it. He looked toward her and leaned in. His heart clenched in his chest, she was so beautiful. “I promise I’ll stop it tonight if anything goes wrong.” *I’ll die before harm comes to her ever again.* He clenched his teeth in remembrance of the last time. Alexander would not touch her this time.

***

That night as Nikolas and Trinity were setting up a makeshift circle of candles, Damien barged into their room.

Nikolas looked up. "We thought you'd never make it, Damien." Nikolas searched the room and narrowed his eyes. "Where are Agape and Gabe?"

Damien smirked and licked his canines, as if enjoying the moment. "I told you I'd come through for you, didn't I?"

Trinity turned to look at Nikolas, doubt glittering in her eyes.

"What are you talking about?" Nikolas scrubbed a hand down his face. He was in no mood for games tonight. His fear for Trinity was heightening his agitation.

"I know how to keep her safe."

Trinity gasped and flung a hand to her mouth. "How?" she whispered.

His heart hammered excitedly in his chest, relief that perhaps a repeat of the other night didn't need to happen at all, coursed though his veins. He held his breath expectantly.

"The water. Apparently Athena said Alexander's energy field could not pass through the water." He smirked, a triumphant look on his face. "Now, I'll leave you two. I have plans for the night."

"Such as?" Nikolas quirked his brow.

Damien looked at him and Trinity, and then shrugged. "I'm hungry." With one last smirk, he was gone.

Trinity grabbed his hand and swayed into his side. "I don't

think I'll mind the water much. Do you know of a nice place?" her voice was soft and breathless.

Nikolas stiffened and laughed at his wild vixen. "I think I do." He smiled as they left the room. *I think I do, indeed.*

Chapter 19

Nikolas led her by the elbow. "Careful, there's another stone, step lightly."

Trinity wiggled her eyebrows, trying to lower the bandana tied around her eyes. "This better be good, I'm trusting you." He laughed at her comment and she smiled.

The sound of rushing water and the low hum of crickets in the night was a peaceful song. The warm Florida breeze lifted her hair gently. Was he taking her to the same spot as the other day? A smile stole over her face. That would be nice. Thinking back on that day caused a flurry of butterflies to roam through her gut. Making love in the grotto had been very nice and very exciting.

"Are you ready?"

Her stomach clutched. "Yes!"

Nikolas's laughter rumbled around her. "What are you thinking, Cat eyes?"

She bit her lip. "Oh, nothing."

Suddenly her feet became engulfed by the warm tide and she smiled bigger. Nikolas lowered her bandana. "Okay, look."

It took a moment for her vision to clear.

A soft red glow surrounded the alcove. Tiny fluorescent blue fish danced around her, rubbing against her like tiny puppies. She gasped with sheer delight. Clear crystals jutted up from the waist deep water. Red, wet stone surrounded them, helping to keep them safe from prying eyes. Where was she? It was certainly beautiful, but this was not the grotto she'd been to last time.

"Where are we, Niky?"

The corner of his mouth tilted up into an amused grin. "This is one of Melaina's caves. Do you like it?"

Wide-eyed she turned back to stare at her lovely surroundings. "Yes."

Just then, Melaina's beautiful head popped out of the water. The mermaid's swirling eyes shone gold, her lustrous hair hung in soft waves down her back. "Hello, Nik," she nodded, "and Trinity. I'm so glad I could assist you in your quest."

Trinity took a step forward and lifted her hand. "Thank you very much, Mela…Melaina." She stumbled over the tough sounding name and gave an apologetic smile.

Melaina laughed musically. "No worries, Trinity, just call me Melody. It sounds pretty similar to my own anyhow. I've been trying it out. I'm thinking about looking for my man within the earthly realms and an easier sounding name should help, don't you think?"

Trinity laughed at the gabby mermaid. "Yes, I'm sure it will."

In the dim lighting Trinity could just barely make out a faint blush cross the mermaid's face.

Trinity's mouth twisted with confusion. "How did you know we'd need to be in the water tonight?"

"The Goddess gave me notice." Melaina turned toward Nikolas and nodded. "He was told as well."

Trinity shrugged and gave it no more thought.

"Come with me you two." The mermaid swiveled at the waist and swam out a bit further.

Trinity followed in Nikolas's wake and she began to fear she'd drown if Melaina did not stop soon. The water was already chin deep.

The mermaid turned back. "You can have my home for as long as it takes. I've created a path for you, just swim straight ahead and you shall find it." Then she advanced on Nikolas and held out her hands, cupping his face on either side.

Trinity stared wondering at the oddity of it, but when Melaina kissed him soundly on the lips, she took offense. "Now hold it right…"

Melaina laughed and Trinity's spine stiffened. Nikolas had an amused glint in his eye. "Do not worry, Trinity, I was simply giving him the ability to breath underwater. I shall have to do the same for you." As she said this, she swam slowly closer, then laid her hands on Trinity's face and leaned in.

Her lips were soft and Trinity felt a bit uncomfortable but stood still. A mist passed from Melaina's lips into her mouth and an icy blast of air soon followed. Then all was calm once more.

"Now you may go under. My guards shall allow your entrance. Be well and safe. May the Goddess protect you." With a final hug for Trinity, Melaina waved a good-bye and dove underwater.

Nikolas held out his hand to her. "So my jealous wench, are you ready?" His green eyes twinkled with mirth.

She felt foolish and ignorant at the same time. She slapped

him playfully on the arm. "Tell me you wouldn't have done the same if it had been a man?"

He shrugged. "Yeah, come to think of it I probably would."

Mollified, she squeezed his hand and dunked her head underwater. Fearing for an instant nothing would happen. But the most miraculous thing occurred. She could breath and not only that she could see clearly within the dark waters for miles. Melaina's gift had worked after all. Trinity thanked the Gods and followed Nikolas further within the waters.

An octopus swam drunkenly through the ocean, as if in play. It landed by a huge chunk of coral and picked up what looked like a rock. With one of its tentacles, it began to bang it against the coral. The rock opened and clamped on the octopuses tentacle. It shrieked and squirted out a blot of ink.

For the first time since the dreams started, she allowed herself to enjoy all life had to offer. Trinity giggled and was startled to hear her laugh come out clear. "Oh my."

Nikolas turned to her and smiled. "You didn't realize we'd be able to talk underwater?"

"Umm. No, not really. This is amazing." She'd definitely have to come back when they had more time. She wanted to explore these new environs at her leisure.

They entered an intricate maze of tunnels. A soft green glow surrounded them. The water was a warm blanket, soft and soothing. She gripped his hand tighter afraid they'd somehow be separated.

She was so busy looking around she failed to notice Nikolas had stopped until she bumped into him. Trinity turned her gaze forward and gasped.

Two great white sharks swam before a gated entranceway.

"Niky," she whispered. Her heart pounded forcefully in her chest. The beauty around her had her forgetting for a moment that the ocean could still be a deadly place.

"What are we supposed to do?" One shark stared at her. A long gray scar ran the length of him from snout to tail. Long rows of pointed teeth gleamed menacingly. Trinity groaned and began a frantic search for an escape.

"Trin, baby, don't worry. These are Melaina's guard. Come on." He tugged on her hand. Reluctantly and with not much choice, she followed.

"Couldn't she have found dolphins? Isn't that what mermaids usually hang out with?" She shivered the closer she got and squeezed her eyes shut. Her hand accidentally grazed the side of one shark; it felt coarse. Almost like sandpaper. She snatched her hand back.

"That's all a myth, Trinity."

She laughed hysterically. "Myth. Now you're trying to talk to me about myths. If that don't beat all." Her nails dug into his hand and she swam as close to him as possible.

"You can open your eyes now," he spoke into her ear.

She cracked first one lid then the other and breathed a huge sigh of relief. "Ugh! She shivered. "Those things were enormous. Is there an alternate route out of here?"

Nikolas chuckled. "Is this, Trinity, speaking? It can't be that she's afraid of a couple of tamed sharks?"

She rolled her eyes and smirked.

His face turned serious once more. "Come on, baby, it's

time."

She walked forward admiring the shiny marble floor. "Why are we able to walk as if we're on land?"

"Part of Melaina's magic."

"Hmm." She turned her head and studied the mermaid's immaculate home. High mother-of-pearl archways ushered her further inside the palace. What looked like sea kelp waved in the still water. *Kelp waving in still water, how strange?* Her forehead furrowed in thought. Golden light sprang up around her each step she took. The soft tinkle of music played on in the background. Melaina certainly had good taste.

The further they walked the more confused she became. "Niky, where are you taking me? We've passed five or six sitting rooms." She gestured with her free hand.

"Just a little bit more. I thought you might like it." He smiled boyishly.

She lifted an eyebrow and smiled. "Hmm. That sounds wonderfully surprising. How do you know this place so well?"

He shrugged. "Melaina is lonely and hosts many costume balls down here."

"Okay, I feel much better now. Do show."

Nikolas laughed and shook his head. "You're a piece of work, Cat eyes."

"You have no idea."

They walked a bit further and entered a through a closed medieval looking doorway. Inside and directly to the front of them stood a large stone hearth. As impossible as it was for her to believe, a bright orange fire crackled inside, heat actually emanated from it. She turned delighted eyes toward Nikolas. “This is beautiful.”

Billowy green, purple, pink, red and blue silk cloth hung from the rafters. Thick Turkish rugs lined the intimate room. Two large red and gold striped pillows sat before the fireplace.

Nikolas smiled and jerked his head. “Let’s go take a seat.”

Trinity blew out a steadying breath and walked to the nearest pillow and plopped down. Her hands trembled and she hid them beneath her legs, hoping he hadn’t noticed.

His aquamarine eyes bored into hers. “Cat eyes, are you sure you’re up for this? We can find another way.”

His sincerity touched her and she tried to push away her fears. “You know as well as I do this is the only way.”

His hands sought hers, plucking one out from beneath her thigh. She savored the feel of his warm fingers caressing hers. Trinity just prayed she wouldn’t have any close encounters with Alexander, she wasn’t sure she’d be able to handle it. Closing her eyes, she once again allowed the madness to claim her. The burning built behind her eyes. She expected to be gripped with agony by now, but it never happened.

She was excited to know she could tame the wailing spirits better than before. In no time, she had them standing before her with very little discomfort involved in the process.

She opened her eyes and stared at the spectral assemblage. Their blue bodies swayed in the gentle current.

Trinity addressed them. “You all know what it is I seek. Where is he? Where is Alexander?”

A little blond-haired boy, no older than seven or eight stepped forward. Her heart broke for him. He should never have died by that murderer's hand. He was just a child. He bowed his head and knelt before her. "Can I speak, Demi-Goddess?"

"Please do." She smiled warmly at him.

"He's not here."

Shocked, she shook her head. That's not what she'd expected to hear. The spirits had never lied to her, why would they tell her Alexander was in Florida when he was not?

"If he's not here, then where?"

The blue-eyed child looked up at her. "He killed me in his other realm."

Nikolas turned his head toward her. His face reflected his puzzlement. Apparently, he did not know about this new revelation either.

"And where exactly is this other realm?" She spoke softly. Fear twisted through her gut. She was afraid to hear what the child would say next.

"I don't know exactly, miss. I was stolen in the dead of night and taken there."

"So wherever that is…you just don't know?" She suppressed a sigh.

He shook his tiny head. A forlorn look of disappointment crossed his features.

"Thank you, child." She turned her eyes toward the other entities. "Have any of you any other information to offer me?"

They all shook their heads. Knowing she'd get nothing further from them, she willed them back within her. Trinity rubbed the bridge of her nose, exhaustion overtaking her. At least she wasn't feeling the sickness. Maybe all it took was using her powers more and learning how to fully gain control of the spirits. That was a comforting thought.

"What do we do now, Niky?"

He shrugged helplessly. "I'm going to need to speak with Athena about this. Not one of us knew this. To tell you the truth, Trin, I don't even know if he's gone for good or what. This is very strange." His eyes took on a faraway look.

She nodded in total agreement. What now, she wondered.

Chapter 20

"I know what I heard, Athena." Nikolas impatiently repeated himself for the third time. He blew out a frustrated breath and wondered how much longer he'd have to remain.

The gray-eyed goddess brooded upon her throne, her lips pursed into a thin line of distaste. "How can this be? How can your woman's spirit guides not know where Alexander is?" She didn't seem to be speaking to him, so Nikolas wisely kept his mouth shut. He itched to return to Trinity, to wrap his arms around her and forget this night ever happened.

Athena gasped and whipped her head to the side. "Lilith." The slight woman walked forward, head bowed and her arms held out before her. Lilith's platinum blond hair hung as a veil around her face.

"Yes, Goddess."

"Seek out my father. Tell him I must speak to him at once."

Lilith nodded her head and scampered off.

Nikolas was intrigued with the excited sparkle that glittered in the goddess's eyes. Athena had figured out something and hopefully she'd provide him with some sorely needed information.

A breeze ruffled through his hair and placed a soft kiss against his cheek. He inhaled the fruit and flower tinted air, allowing it to ease his taut nerves. The setting sun shone weak hues of orange and yellow upon his surroundings, causing Athena's temple to ripple with a mirage of flames.

He felt her gaze on him and he raised his brow. "What have you learned, Goddess?"

"Nothing."

His brows knit. "Nothing?" Nikolas pointed to Lilith's vacated spot. "Why then send her to seek Zeus?" Anger burned a hole in his gut. "What are you hiding from me, Athena?"

"How dare you question me?" she spoke through clenched teeth. "I know nothing. Return to your demi-goddess." She turned up her nose, as if disgusted with him. "Go back to your happy, boring lives and come back when you have something good to tell me!"

Nikolas shook with fury and clenched his fists. He pounded upon his chest with a closed fist and took his leave. That spiteful bitch knew something and he'd figure out what it was.

***

Trinity sat nude and cross-legged on the bed awaiting Nikolas's return from Olympus. She popped a marshmallow into her mouth and chewed thoughtfully for a moment, then stood and walked toward the grand bay window. She was restless and exhausted all at once. The white curtains fluttered in the breeze and she noticed a man hailing a taxi. He was cocooned in shadow; a tan fedora covered his face. Did that stranger knew the truth of the world? Or was he, like her two months ago, completely oblivious to the facts?

The past few weeks had been hectic and life altering, to say the least. And now this. Was it all over? Had they come to an impasse, unable to finish what they'd started? What did it mean that Alexander was suddenly gone? And could he come back? No answer came readily to her fogged brain.

She stared at the moon. Black clouds obscured the ivory orb hanging in the sky. It was nearly full and Nikolas would be leaving her soon. The corners of her mouth pulled down, a vague sense of unease filled her at the prospect. She was sure it had nothing to do with impending doom but more so a feeling that all was not right.

She grabbed the edge of the curtain and laid her head against the soft cloth. Her hair blew gently behind her.

She had already passed her deadline to be back at work. She hadn't even called or quit, which wasn't like her. She almost felt the burn of a beginning ulcer. She rubbed her stomach and sighed. She hated to look so irresponsible. But no one there would be able to understand what it was she was going through. The thought of losing the job wasn't as heartbreaking as she once felt it would be. Everyday life suddenly seemed so trivial with all that was going on around her.

Two very powerful arms wrapped themselves around her waist. She sighed and snuggled deeper within the safe confines of her lover's arms. This was her home now.

"How did it go, Niky?"

"Well, Athena wasn't too pleased. None of us were. I believe she knows where Alexander's hiding but refused to give me any information. My guess is she wanted to consult her father first. If anyone knows, it will be Zeus. Until then, she told us to continue as before." Trinity felt him shrug behind her. His tone was weary as if the entire experience had been draining for him.

She well understood how he felt.

"Well then, lover, what should we do in the meantime?" her voice dropped an octave and she wiggled her bottom.

His responding rumble of laughter vibrated through her body. She was tired, but not that tired. A large smile spread across her face, she turned toward him and wrapped her arms around his broad neck.

"What have you got in mind, Cat eyes?" his lips quirked and his devastating eyes twinkled with desire.

"Athena did say to go about our regular business..." She paused and left the rest to his imagination. He grabbed her hand and led her toward the bed, never taking his eyes off her.

***

Trinity knew she was dreaming and yet no matter how much she fought it she couldn't wake up. They were not the dreams of before, but rather dreams of the unknown. Blurred images of a time long past flitted through her mind.

Horse drawn chariots. Lovely women in togas. Large, ivory pillars attached to gargantuan structures. One vaguely resembled the Parthenon.

She thrashed and fought her way out of the deep sleep. Sitting up in bed, she tried to make sense of it all. Trinity frowned. Olympus, maybe? Was that what she'd dreamed about? But a nagging suspicion told her no. Her head throbbed and she squeezed her eyes shut, hoping somehow to block the sensation of nails being dragged against her skull. She needed fresh air.

The night was muggy and the satin sheet clung to her uncomfortably. Throwing it aside, she stood, pulled on a robe and walked outside.

The night was black and unyielding, the sun at least three hours away from rising. Sharp whiffs of sea salt caused her to sneeze. She rubbed her nose violently and sat down. Already, the cooler air was calming her keyed up nerves.

She knew he'd be there even before she called. "Hello, Pierce."

"I thought you'd like some company tonight," he replied.

She turned and gave him an appreciative glance. "Yes…yes I would. I hate to wake Nik. He's been working so hard lately. But I can't sleep well." She shrugged and stared out at a sea of nothingness.

"Your dreams?"

She didn't even pretend to be surprised by his uncanny thinking. Trinity merely nodded.

"You'll figure it out soon enough, I'd expect." His voice was soothing and she closed her eyes.

"I'm tired of trying to figure everything out. Why all the secrecy? What am I still missing, Pierce?" She turned to stare at his calm face.

His ancient looking eyes stared back. "Trinity, there's a reason for it, even if you don't believe us. We spirits know everything, but to tell you would mean we screwed with your choice of free will, thus altering the eventual outcome of your life path. You need to be able to figure these things out yourself." He gave her a half-hearted tilt to his lips. "But you will, I promise." Pierce glided closer to her side and lifted a hand.

She watched him, unsure of what he intended. She frowned when he didn't stop. What was he doing?

"Touch me, Trinity. Show me what I need to know."

"Wh…what?" she pushed herself back in the chair.

He paused. Sadness was a palpable aura around him and nearly caused her to gag. "I need to know."

"Know what? Pierce, what are you talking about?"

"Her. Storm. You can tell me, if you just touch my hand." He lifted his arm once again and waited.

"But, I can't. I'd phase right through you."

"You are my mistress. If the sprits will it, we can allow ourselves to be touched by you."

"Why? Just because I rule over you?"

"That and the fact that you believe in us. Now, please, I beg you, tell me."

She debated what to do. As fond as she was of Pierce, touching him was not a thought she relished. But she couldn't let him flounder; she did care.

"Come here quick." She ushered him forward, needing to do this before she changed her mind.

Relief washed over his features. When his fingers clasped her own the thick stain of death, cold and love enveloped her. Her teeth clattered and her soul quaked. The pain was nearly intolerable. She felt her own life force begin to lessen. She closed her eyes and allowed his memories to wash over her.

A beautiful brunette with strange blue, almost indigo eyes popped into her mind. Trinity gasped. Storm was the woman. The woman in the vision she'd dreamed of since childhood. She felt it then, Storm's spirit. Her special life force, uniquely hers. Trinity knew who she was and intimately. The truth shook her.

"Oh my God!" She pulled away quickly and stared in stunned disbelief at Pierce's face. It couldn't be. It was impossible.

"What? Please, Trinity, what did you see?"

She shook her head. Was it wise? Trish. Trish was the unknown Storm. They were one and the same. How had she never known before? What should she do? How was she to handle something like this?

No one other than her inner circle knew about her ability to speak with the dead. She couldn't just phone Trish and tell her, "Hey by the way your long lost lover is a spirit and oh yeah, he wants to meet you." That would certainly make her look like a quack. She groaned and squeezed her eyes shut.

"Pierce, I do know who she is. But she's engaged to another man."

His sparkling eyes turned morose and his face crumpled. In seconds, he looked hundreds of years old. "Tell me. Either way, I just have to know."

"I'm sorry, Pierce, I just can't."

"Right… I understand." Pierce looked out toward the horizon. "I guess some things are just never meant to be figured out. Thanks anyway, I know you would tell me if you could." Then he vanished like evaporating fog and Trinity cried.

"You sure you couldn't tell him, Cat eyes?" Nikolas dropped to his knees before her. She rubbed her eyes.

"I just don't know how she would handle that? It was Trish and I can't tell her. Trish has absolutely no knowledge of the afterlife and most people wouldn't understand it. Besides, she wouldn't be able to see him anyhow. So how could telling him possibly change anything?"

"Do you know that for sure?"

"What?"

"That she won't be able to see him."

The first faint stirrings of hope nestled within her. "No, not really."

He grabbed her hands. "Then just think about it." His warm smile caused her heart to melt. "Come back to bed."

She nodded and stood, staring at Pierce's vacated spot. Trinity nibbled on her lower lip. Maybe she should tell him after all. What could it hurt?

Just as they were settling into bed there was a loud knock at the door. She stared at Nikolas; his brows drew together.

"Who could that be?"

Like a wolf, he made his way to the door. His naked buttocks flexed with each step he took and bronze skin shone in the moonlight.

He looked through the peephole and then threw her a look of warning. Her stomach clenched. That was not a comforting look.

Quickly, he opened the door and stood aside. The harsh lighting of the hallway illuminated their guests clearly.

Trinity drew in a shaky breath. Damien stood holding an unconscious Mercedes in his arms. The repugnant stench of charred flesh settled over the room. Her stomach flopped in her chest, she knew she shouldn't care about Mercedes anymore, but her ex-friend had been such a vital part of her life that her heart betrayed her.

"I found her near to death." Damien spoke directly to Trinity.

"I couldn't leave her like that."

"Come in." Trinity spoke so softly she was afraid he wouldn't hear, but he entered.

Something was different about Damien. Trinity narrowed her eyes and studied the pair. The way he held Mercedes was almost possessive, reverent even. *Nah. Can't be.* She dismissed the niggling thought from her mind and studied what used to be her friend. Mercedes looked a wreck and Trinity had to swallow a lump in her throat. She still loved her, no matter that Mercedes had tried to kill her just yesterday.

All manner of questions raged in her mind. How did Damien know she knew Mercedes? And above all how did he find her? But for now, those questions would have to wait.

Trinity scooted off the bed. "Lay her here, Damien."

With infinite care, he laid the still form down on the bed. Though he wouldn't let go of her hand. Trinity lifted a brow. "Damien, I'm going to need you to back away. I need to see what's wrong with her."

Nikolas walked toward her until he stood at her side. Just as she reached out, he grabbed her hand and forced her to stare at him. "Are you sure?"

Her heart gripped in pain. She couldn't just let Mercedes die, Trinity knew if the situation were reversed Mercedes would have done the same for her.

"Yes. I have no choice."

"Then let's do this together." He massaged her tired neck and pulled her in for a quick kiss.

"Thank you, Niky."

She stared silently at her friend. Mercedes's beautiful, olive skin looked pasty and drained of blood. Her lustrous, nut-brown hair clung to her clammy forehead. Huge purple bruises dotted her cheeks and eyes. Death was knocking down her door.

Trinity's hands trembled as she once again reached for Mercedes's blouse. Taking the shirt off was simply a matter of pushing aside the charred remains.

Pustules seeped green and yellow fluid. Black flesh, where Trinity had grabbed a hold of her, looked ready to flake off. Dried brown blood dotted her entire abdomen. The stench was revolting.

Self-loathing coiled like a snake around Trinity's heart. She was the one responsible for this and hopefully she could correct it. She just prayed she wasn't making a huge mistake.

Chapter 21

Nikolas gazed at Damien's stark profile. He'd never seen his friend this distraught and wondered at the oddity of it.

"Where did you find her, Damien?"

Damien turned and stared at him. "In a dumpster near the wharf. Seems she had the foresight to seek darkness before she passed out."

Trinity spoke up, "Why did you follow her?"

Nikolas heard the unspoken pain in her voice and knew she felt terrible for the predicament Mercedes was in now.

Damien shoved a fist through his long blond hair and huffed. "I meant to finish her off, but…" He lifted a hand and pointed at Mercedes's still form, "I couldn't. Something stopped me. So I brought her back here."

That wasn't the whole story and Nikolas knew it, but he wouldn't force his friend for details. Instead, he turned and stared hard into Trinity's tired face. He had figured out a way to save Mercedes from the Semere fate. But it would be difficult and perhaps even life threatening.

"I can staunch the wounds, Trin." Nikolas walked to his black bag and extracted Athena's ointment.

"Oh shit, man," Damien said. "Do you really gotta use that? Isn't there some other way?"

Nikolas shook his head. "I'm afraid not. She's beginning to fester. If we don't do this now, she'll be dead by the end of the night." He pointed at Damien. "But first you have to do something. Will you help us save her?"

Pain glittered in Damien's eyes and he swallowed forcefully. "Yes."

"You have to have a blood transfusion. Both of you."

By this point Mercedes began to stir and moan pitifully on the bed. Damien crossed to her side and held her hand.

"Be careful though. In order for this to succeed, you will need to take some of her Semere blood into your system. I don't know what sort of effect that will cause for you. But it has to be, in order for her to survive this."

Damien merely nodded. He knew what to do. With infinite care, he lifted Mercedes in his arms.

Nikolas was astounded at his gentleness. Never in all his twenty-five hundred years had he seen Damien act this way.

Damien pushed aside a strand of her brown hair and lifted his pinky finger. He elongated his nail until it looked like a wicked claw. With a quick flick of his wrist, he tore open his shirt and drew a large gash down his chest. Scarlet drops of blood trickled out. He lifted Mercedes head until her mouth was mere inches from his life force and latched her on.

Trinity gasped and covered her mouth with her hand. Nikolas

knew she'd never witnessed a feeding in her life and wondered how she was taking it. He wrapped his arm around her shoulders and drew her to his side. She looked into his eyes and trembled, the bright blue orbs glittering with shock.

Mercedes's arms crawled around Damien's back as she fed harder. Damien sucked in a deep breath and threw his head back. His face contorted into a look of pleasure and pain. Damien groaned. Finally he tore Mercedes away. She continued to whimper but didn't put up a fight.

Damien glanced at them, fear reflected vividly in his silver eyes. He exposed his sharp white canines and dived for Mercedes's neck.

Slowly, the color began to drain from his face. His already pale skin turned an ashen blue and still he drank. Sweat poured freely from Damien. His eyes took on a shrunken appearance, his skin turned mottled. Nikolas knew Damien was taking too much, and feared for his friend. What in the hell was he thinking?

Just as Nikolas decided to put an end to the feeding, Damien pulled back, allowing Mercedes to slip through his lax fingers. His breathing was harsh and ragged. His features looked pinched in the moonlight. Nikolas sensed the internal change in his friend immediately.

"I'm through. Now finish up the rest," Damien ordered gruffly and wiped his hand across his mouth, smearing the blood.

Suddenly his features contorted into a mask of pain and he doubled over. Trinity began to go to Damien, but Nikolas held her back and whispered in her ear, "Don't. He chose to do this. I know Damien; you have to leave him alone right now, Cat eyes."

"He's hurting, Nik. I can't just leave him. I'm sorry." She ran forward and laid her hand on Damien's back.

Nikolas rushed to her side.

"Leave me!" Damien roared; his silver eyes shone red. His face filled with murderous rage seconds before he lunged for her, arms outstretched.

Nikolas grabbed him by the arms, pinned them behind his back and pushed him forcefully into the wall. Several wall hangings were knocked off in the process.

His incisors ripped through his gums. To see Damien with his hands on Trinity in an aggressive stance caused Nikolas to lose his mind.

"Get a grip on yourself!" his voice hardened ruthlessly. His heart pounded in his chest and it took every ounce of mental fortitude Nikolas possessed not to inflect more damage on Damien for touching her.

When he no longer saw red and felt Damien stop struggling against him, Nikolas released him slowly, wary for any sudden movements on the vampire's part.

Damien drew in a ragged breath and shrugged him off. "Fix her, please…" The plea seemed to tear from his heart.

Before anything else could transpire, Nikolas walked toward Mercedes, ointment in hand.

"Stand by my side, Trinity."

He glanced at her and his heart crumbled. She was sobbing uncontrollably with her arms wrapped tightly around herself. When she reached his side, she laid her head against his back. He felt her tiny quivers.

Nikolas sighed and unscrewed the cap. Taking a generous amount of black cream in his hand, he swiped a path down Mercedes's affected areas.

Her fevered eyes shot open and she screamed. Agonizing screams of torment and Nikolas cringed at the sound.

Before he realized what was happening, Damien ran to her side, picked her up and vanished in a blaze of white light.

It was over. Nikolas dropped the cream, lifted Trinity tenderly and began rocking her all the while dropping tiny kisses on her brow. She shivered in his arms.

"I'm sorry, Niky. I'm so sorry."

"Baby, sshh. It's all right. It's all right."

Nikolas laid her on the bed, spooning her into his hard body. He stroked her hair and murmured soothing encouragements. Nearly an hour later she feel asleep in his arms, leaving him to ponder what he'd just witnessed.

***

Streams of bright sunshine stabbed Trinity's closed eyelids. Her sleep had not been restful in the slightest; images of Mercedes had danced in her head. Questions raged like an inferno in her mind. First and foremost, what had caused Damien to attack her?

She'd been foolish to approach him when Nikolas had forbid it, but she'd felt his fears to be unjustified at the time. After all, she'd thought Damien to be her friend. But the Damien of last night was subtly different, no longer the carefree vampire. An evil stain had settled in him. She trembled at the thought and wondered just how drastically he had changed.

She rolled over, heavy-hearted expecting to find the warm body of Nikolas lying next to her. She touched his empty pillow and gazed around the room. Where was he? Quickly, she sat up and wrapped the sheet around her nude body.

He was on the balcony with his legs crossed in front of him. A pair of black silk boxers hid his nudity from the world and the ripple of his washboard abs caused her heart to flutter. His long black hair lay around his shoulders, shining nearly blue in the bright rays of light.

"Did you sleep well, Trin?" His voice was low and contemplative.

She marveled at his wolfish abilities. Everyday that passed cemented for her that no matter what he was, he would always just be Niky to her.

"No, not really. You?"

He shook his head; his tanned fingers rubbed along his jaw line. Trinity crossed the narrow space between them and sat on his lap. He pulled her closer and laid his head on top of hers.

"Niky, I'm confused."

"About what?"

"Last night." She put her hands on his chest and pushed back, staring into his aquamarine eyes. "What happened with Damien?"

"Near as I can tell, her blood affected him. He's now partly Semere."

Her heart broke for Damien and Mercedes both. How had they all come to this? A few short weeks ago, her world had been normal and monotonous, now life as she knew it had been forever altered. For everyone. "So what exactly does that mean? Is he permanently evil now?"

"Only time can tell, Trinity. In all honesty, I have no clue," he growled out. His frustration was tangible. She laid her head against his chest and listened to the steady thump of his heartbeat.

"What was it about Mercedes? He was so different; I've never seen him like that."

He shook his head and ran his fingers through her hair. "Me neither, Trin."

She frowned hoping the answers would miraculously drop into her lap, but this, as so many other things in life, eluded her. Maybe she was not meant to know. The idea did not sit well with her, but what other recourse did she have?

Trinity turned to stare at Nikolas. "Then I suggest we begin our search for the elusive Semere headquarters."

"And where do you propose we start? We've been everywhere and still nothing," he growled out. "I'm sorry," he sighed, "I'm not mad at you, I just…"

She laid a finger against his lips. "Ssh. Don't apologize. I know exactly how you feel. But I know of a place we haven't looked."

Nikolas clamped onto her shoulders and pushed her away, his eyebrows rose in surprise. "And where is that?"

"The Florida Keys." She grinned broadly, pleased with herself.

His eyes twinkled and he laughed. "Cat eyes, I think you may just be right. Why didn't I think of that?"

"Because women think better in clutch situations, it's no fault of yours. It's a gene pool thing." She shrugged and giggled when he glowered at her.

"Pack your bags woman, we're headed to the Keys."

***

Standing on the dock, bag in hand Trinity tapped her sandaled foot against the wooden planks. The mild breeze tugged at her hair, causing curls to fly every which way. She grumped and tried to pull it back but finally gave it up as a lost cause.

"Did you call Agape and Gabe about our change in plans?"

"Mmm." He nodded his head. "They said they'd meet us there tonight."

"And Damien?"

"Couldn't reach him. Though I'm sure he'll be notified soon enough." He didn't seem to want to continue with this topic of discussion, so she dropped it.

At length, a large, white yacht crept over the horizon. Trinity shaded her eyes and studied the boat. It was pristinely white with wooden railings encircling the deck. It seemed somehow familiar, teasing the edge of her consciousness but it was a fleeting thought, soon replaced by her excitement to get out of the hot sun and ever-blowing breeze.

Once it finally docked, she made her way onboard. Seawater sprayed up, slapping her in the face. The zephyr carried the stench of rotten fish and that combined with the yo-yo effect she experienced standing on the deck nearly caused her to retch. As soon as the ship pulled away from land, she knew she was in trouble. They should have driven across the bridge instead.

Nikolas rushed to her side, concern apparent in his stance. "Are you okay, Cat eyes?"

She dry heaved over the railing. "Yeah, absolutely. Never better..." She gagged harder this time and squeezed her eyes shut. "Is it too late for me to jump overboard? Ugh!" She groaned and clutched at her stomach.

A steward walked up to her. He was short, middle-aged and stood chest level with her. His gray mustache twitched as he spoke. "Ma'am, are you all right? You look a little green around the gills. Haven't got yer sea legs yet, eh?" He teased her and winked playfully.

"Room...please." Nausea roiled in her stomach. Bile rose in her throat, she was going to embarrass herself soon. "Bathroom," she croaked again. *Oh God! Not in front of Niky...please, please, please.* The sway of the ship nearly caused her to collapse.

He turned suddenly serious and pointed to a set of staircases. "Below deck, ma'am. Can't miss it. But, I should warn you, going below might actually make the umm," he flicked his hand at her, "seasickness, worse."

"Oh God," she said. "I don't care. It couldn't be worse than this, right?"

Nikolas guided her by the elbow; she pressed a fist to her lips.

"I should never have chartered this yacht for us. I'm sorry, Cat eyes. If I'd known..."

She mumbled something incoherent and somehow found her way down the flight of steps. Then she ran as fast as her unsteady legs would carry her to the restroom.

After gagging a few more times, she walked to the sink and splashed cool, clean water on her face. Could she feel any worse right now? She seriously doubted it.

She pulled open the door to find Nikolas staring at her. He

tugged her toward the bed and laid her down. She felt like such a wimp. Trinity could fight off a vampire and make love to a werewolf, but a little thing like a ship totally put her in a tailspin.

She turned her head to thank him and that was when she noticed the interior of the cabin. Suddenly her vision swam in her mind. The yacht, the lights, the oak and cherry wood smell. Even the potted plants sitting beneath the portholes. This was in the dream Pierce had shown her. At least she now knew they were heading in the right direction. The mystery nearly solved, or so she thought.

Chapter 22

The sun was beginning to set as they stepped through the beachside bungalow Nikolas rented for them. Trinity leaned her head against the door and sighed.

"Well, we're here." He smiled.

Her eyes drooped with fatigue. "You have no idea how happy that makes me."

"That bad, eh?" He trailed a finger across her jaw line. She shivered and he swung her into his arms. "You need a good long soak in the tub."

"What about our meeting later with the group?"

"Don't worry about that, Cat eyes. Let me take care of everything."

She nuzzled her face into his chest. "That does sound wonderful. Maybe I will." Trinity turned her head. "This place is so beautiful." She glanced quickly at the airy furnishings and smiled. "Thank you, Nikolas, for everything."

He kissed the top of her head and walked toward the bathroom. The marble Jacuzzi tub was filled with red and white rose petals. The room dripped with candles.

"Oh, Nik. You're too good to me. I'm sorry I ruined your surprise by getting sick."

He shrugged. Watching her suffer earlier made him call ahead and get the resort to spruce things up to her taste.

He sat her in the tub and helped her undress. Trinity moaned, making him grind his molars in response. His penis began to stir, needing to feel the safety and warmth that only she could offer him, but now was not the time to give into carnal desire. He swallowed as the pale skin of her breasts popped free of the bra, it took every ounce of fortitude he possessed not to ravage her. She grimaced and massaged her brow.

"I've never felt so sick in my life," she said.

That more than anything helped him to regain his composure. She was ill and needed a lovers tender hand. He smiled, reached toward the knob and turned it on, tendrils of steam curled sinuously through the air.

"Now, I want you to just take it easy, okay?"

"Nik." Her eyes narrowed speculatively. "You're not planning on ditching me tonight are you?" She spread her arms. "This is beautiful. I just hope it isn't some sort of diversion."

Nikolas laughed but refused to give her a straight answer. Yes, he would leave her tonight. She needed the rest and if he knew his wild cat, he wouldn't be able to do it without a fight. He was determined not to give her the opportunity. "Just relax. No conspiracy theories here, Trin."

"Hmm." She twisted her lips and began peeling off her clothes.

He hardened at the provocative image Trinity invoked. She was stripped from the waist up and from the waist down wore nothing but a red, lacy thong. All he wanted to do at the moment was rip it off with his teeth. He blew out a breath, walked toward the bathroom counter top and toyed with a golden swan, which held tiny red heart shaped pieces of soap.

"Any word from Damien?" He turned at her voice. Trinity had already immersed herself in the steamy water. Red hair clung to her shoulders in waves.

He shook his head. "No one's heard anything. I'm not sure what to do about him."

"Nikolas…Trinity." A voice floated in from the hall.

Nikolas jerked his head at the sound. "That's Agape. I'm gonna go see what she needs."

"How did she find us so quickly?"

"I gave her the location after I'd made the reservations."

She closed her eyes and laid her head back against the edge of the tub. "I guess I'll get out then."

Nikolas held up his hand to stave off any further talk on her part. "No, don't worry. I'm sure all she's gonna do is brief me on what she's learned. Take your time."

She gave him a tremulous smile. "Thanks, baby. I won't take long, I swear." She slid underwater to wet her hair.

"Take as long as you want," he mumbled beneath his breath and quickly exited the room.

Agape and Gabriel were walking around the living room. He cleared his throat when he entered.

She pointed her finger, taking in her surroundings. "When did you become interested in the aquatic look?" She laughed. "Everything is shells and fish. Nice!" she said sarcastically. Her booted foot played with a woven rag rug lying across the wooden floor.

Nikolas waved aside her banter. "Look, Trin's, taking a bath. We need to get out of here now, before she gets it in her head to come with us tonight."

Gabriel grimaced. "Are you implying that we run off with no good-bye?"

"Um. Yeah."

Gabriel whistled. "That ain't gonna win you any brownie points man."

Nikolas scrubbed a fist down his face. "What should I do? I'm worried about her. She's overtaxing herself. Trinity needs rest whether she's willing to admit it or not."

Agape pulled open a drawer in the oak desk next to her and extracted a pad and pencil. "Here."

"What?" Nikolas's brows knit together.

"It's called a note, Nikolas. At least leave her that. I hate to be involved in this, but coming from a woman, you'd better do it. Otherwise, she's liable to go psycho on you tonight."

"Fine." He walked forward grabbed the notepad and scribbled a quick note. "Come on, we've already wasted too much time." As he closed the door behind them, Nikolas knew he was going to receive a serious tongue lashing later. He shrugged; it just couldn't be helped.

***

Later that night Trinity was still alone in the rented bungalow. She fumed and mumbled to herself, pacing back and forth between the kitchen and sitting room. The room was aglow with candles casting eerie shadows upon the walls. She stopped and stared out the sliding glass door. The deep blue ocean ebbed and flowed, the stars winked and the black sky reflected vividly the black anger in her heart.

"I can't believe Nikolas would do that to me!" She shook the note in her hand violently.

Her father glided to within reach of her. "Trinity, calm down. He made the correct choice."

Her eyes widened and she twirled on him. She would have jabbed him in the chest with her finger if she could have. "Are you taking his side? He shouldn't have left me," she muttered the last under her breath. "And to leave me a note saying to stay inside, my God! That's so lame."

"If the situation were reversed wouldn't you have done the same, Trin? Every time you go hunting with him, you always get into trouble. He was just trying to prevent that."

She clenched her jaw. "I'm not a child and I could help. He shouldn't have left the way he did. I mean I was taking a bath for crying out loud. Couldn't he have at least waited for me to get out before he ran off?"

"Would you have let him go without you?" Her father's gentle reprimand helped her see the sense of his words. Truth was, she wouldn't have and Nikolas knew that as well.

"Ugh, why must you always be right?"

He laughed and his blue aura pulsed with the sound. "Tomorrow, he'll take you out."

She huffed. "Well, that makes no sense does it? So he won't take me out today but tomorrow is a totally different matter."

"He won't have a choice." He smiled. "Because you won't give him one."

Her shoulders drooped and she gave a half-hearted smile. Her anger was mostly because of her inability to do anything constructive and not directed at Nikolas himself. He was just a convenient scapegoat. She'd nearly gotten herself killed not once, but twice and each time he had come to her rescue. The fact that she was beginning to look like a weakling grated on her nerves. Her whole life she'd prided herself on the ability to be a strong, independent woman. She loved Nikolas but hated this new role she was playing.

Thankfully, the nightmares hadn't come back and if it weren't for the burning knot of apprehension in her gut, she'd be able to breathe much easier. None of her spirits could give a location on Alexander and for Trinity that meant one thing. Somehow, someway he was gone for good. Maybe one of the gods decided to take care of the nuisance themselves.

She squeezed her eyes shut for a moment and rubbed the bridge of her nose. Her stomach flopped with anxiety. She was so tired of obsessing about this case. She'd lived, breathed, and ate Alexander for far too long. She needed to get away from the stress even if just to walk outside and allow the cool water to run over her feet. But Nikolas told her not to leave the beach home, not even to step outside. Frustration mounted inside of her, she felt like a cork ready to pop.

She stalked toward the oak kitchen table, plucked an orange from the fruit bowl and walked back into the sitting room. She plopped herself down on the seashell print couch and propped her feet on the wooden coffee table. Her eyes were drawn to a huge stone fireplace, which took up nearly one wall, above the mantle was mounted a monstrous swordfish. The bungalow was Floridian and beautiful.

And, she hated it. At the moment, it represented for her nothing more than a prison.

"Damn it. I can't take this." She attacked the orange, peeling back the skin with frenzied fingers. Sprays of citrus juice flew into her eyes. "Oh, friggin' piss." She swiped her hand across her eyes. "I'm gonna lose it, Dad." Trinity gave the orange up as a lost cause and allowed it to fall through her fingers to the floor.

"I need to get out of here, breathe the fresh night air. I mean what's gonna happen to me if I just stay in the backyard?" She became increasingly excited at the prospect. "If anything comes I could always just run back into the house…or stand and fight." She shrugged and flipped her hair over her shoulder.

Her father shook his head and a strange look crossed his face. "Don't do it, Trin. You cannot fight what you cannot see." His silver-blue eyes pleaded silently for her to listen.

She smiled. "Dad, I swear I won't follow any shadows or wolves for that matter. I'll be a good girl, but you just don't understand how much I need this. Just a little fresh air, that's never killed anyone."

"I don't know."

"Look, if it would make you feel any better then come with me. There's an inviting tree that's calling my name. It's been a long time since I've climbed one." She flexed her arms. Excitement welled inside her like a volcano ready to explode. "It'll be fun and Nik will be none the wiser. Come on." She jerked her head and bit her bottom lip.

"Trinity, I'm dead and I don't know how much more of this I

can handle." He stared at her for a minute, but when she didn't budge, he sighed. "Fine!" He threw up his hands in capitulation.

She winked and practically ran to the door. She opened it and just stood, taking a moment to inhale the sweet and salty fragrance of the night. The warm breeze ruffled her hair and slowly her anxiety began to fade. She stripped off her sandals and sprinted toward the tree. Trinity curled her toes into the sand and reveled in the movement of her body. The nearly ripe moon gave her all the light she needed.

She reached out and palmed the rough corrugated bark of the tree. She'd always loved climbing when she was a little girl. Placing her hands firmly within a niche, she dragged herself upwards.

"Trinity, please I wish you would reconsider." Her father shimmered beside her.

She panted breathlessly. "Lucky you that you can float. I can tell I haven't done this in a while." She continued her upward progress. Why hadn't the tree looked so large when she was standing on land? Her forehead furrowed, she looked down then back up again. Since she was closer to the top, she pushed onward. By the time, she reached a large enough branch to support her weight her arms were trembling.

"Oh Lord, you ain't no Spring chicken, girl." She laughed at her silliness. The wind rustled through the leaves and she soaked it all in, turning her face up she smiled. Her hair twirled around her like a cloak. It was silent and eerily beautiful.

"Do you want to talk?"

"Mmm. No, I just want to sit. But don't leave me, okay."

"I wouldn't dare."

A warm feeling of contentment spread through her. She

refused to think of anything and anytime her mind tried to she'd clamp down on the thought immediately.

She didn't even know how long she'd been sitting there, but the sound of a man clearing his throat caused her to nearly fall off her precarious perch. Her heart threatened to erupt from her chest and she flung a hand to her mouth.

"Oh, pardon me." A kindly, old man smiled up at her. He was reminiscent of Santa Claus, with the huge potbelly and long white beard. "I didn't mean to frighten you. I always take walks on the beach at night. It's such a beautiful evening, isn't it?"

His brown eyes were warm and she nodded. Without reason Trinity trusted the stranger.

Her father laid his hand on her hand. The touch sent shooting spikes of numbing cold through her arm and she shivered. Trinity turned to stare at him, noting his odd demeanor. He was trembling and kept glancing quickly from the stranger to her. When he opened his mouth to speak, he vanished.

Befuddled by his odd behavior Trinity called his name. "Dad, where'd you go?"

"I'm sorry, miss, was there someone with you?" The gentleman's white beard swayed as he spoke.

Trinity immediately realized where she was and shook her head. She'd speak to her father later. She frowned. That was so unlike him.

She blinked to clear the spider webs and glanced back at the strange man. He hadn't moved an inch. "No, I'm fine. Thanks for asking."

"Would you care to accompany an old man? My joints are

feeling a bit stiff and the company of a beautiful gal would be an added incentive to get these old bones home."

She laughed and shimmied down the tree. Reckless enthusiasm raced through her, she knew she shouldn't but he was just a harmless old man. What harm could possibly come to her?

"Sure. Give me a second." Once she was safely on solid ground, she picked up her sandals and placed her hand on his proffered arm.

The breeze picked up in intensity. A storm was brewing over the horizon.

Chapter 23

"What was a pretty girl like you doing up in that tree all alone at this time of night?" His brown eyes bored into hers. A secretive smile played on his lips.

Trinity fidgeted and wondered at his tone. He seemed to almost know she shouldn't have been out. That was absurd. "I needed the fresh air."

"Mmm." He patted her hand that lay on his arm. "I'm, Brian, by the way. And you are?" He tilted his head.

The feeling that something was very wrong began to gnaw at her. It wasn't so much what he was asking but how he asked it. She licked her lips and looked behind her. The bungalow was becoming a black speck in the distance.

The sound of a clearing throat caused her to whip her head around. "I said your name, miss."

"Trin…Trinity."

"Well, Trin…Trinity that's a lovely name." His teeth shone white and the corners of his eyes wrinkled with a smile. "Which do you prefer?"

"Wha…What?"

He boomed his laughter, the sound snaked down her spine and she shivered. "Is that your standard answer for something?"

She was just going to have to leave. The sense of disgust and revulsion was beginning to make her ill. "I'm sorry. I'm not feeling well all of a sudden."

Brian stopped and placed his hands on either side of her face. Trinity squeezed her eyes shut. His touch was like death. Her heart seemed to stop beating, her breathing became ragged and she broke out in a cold sweat. What was happening to her? Panic was threatening her fragile hold on her sanity.

"What is wrong with you, dear?" His tobacco scented breath punched her in the face and she gagged.

She tried to release her head from his grasp but the more she struggled the harder he gripped.

"Open your eyes, Trinity. Look at me." His words were a spoken command. She gasped and squeezed her eyes shut tighter. She knew that voice, the voice of her nightmares. It couldn't be. She clenched her hand until her nails entered her palm.

"I said open!"

She could no longer resist, her eyes slid open like a blooming flower. Bile rose in her throat. Eyes that had once been molten brown were now swirling lavender. He forced her to continue staring at him and the more she did the less she fought him. A revolting rush of desire swept through her.

"Hello, precious. Do you remember me?"

"Oh my God." the whispered words escaped her.

"I'm not a god yet, dear. But feel free to call me that if you'd like." His face twisted into a mask of evil.

She was lost to the powerful timbre of his words. Passion inched its ways through her veins. Images of Alexander entwined with her caused her to pant and heat rose to her cheeks. What was happening to her? Trinity tried to force the thoughts away but the more she fought it the more he threw at her.

"I feel your desire for me. Why try to hide it, my dear? Soon I will fulfill your most secret needs." He leaned in and licked her neck. She shivered and stood as still as a mannequin. A loud snap of sound roared in her ears. He'd broken through her final attempt at resistance. She was now all his.

"That's how I want you, baby. Pliant and willing. Are you pliant and willing?"

"Yes."

He licked his lips. "Then you should have no problems telling me a few things I need to know."

"No."

Brian grinned wickedly. "What is the man's name who follows you around?"

"Nikolas."

"And what is Nikolas?"

"A werewolf."

"Ohh, that's wonderful!" His laughter boomed through the still night. "So he's Athena's pet. Beautiful. I'm making quite a name for myself in Olympus." He seemed pleased with himself. "And tell me, Trinity, what can kill a werewolf?"

"I don't know."

"Mmm. Yes, the whole curse thing has played with your

mind. Well, I think I can fix that." His fangs lengthened and he rubbed her neck lightly. "Is it okay if I taste you, darling? I could take you by force, but I like my ladies willing."

Heat pooled between her legs and Trinity nodded. His fangs tore into her and the pain was soon negated by the pleasure. It was like riding an orgasmic wave and her pulse quickened. Images played through her mind like a movie.

She, herself, dressed as the other Greek goddesses. A golden circlet on the crown of her head. Her legs entwined with those of Nikolas. They lay in a verdant garden of spring flowers and sweet grass.

"Nikolas, you are so powerful." Trinity traced the curve of his nude back. Bronzed skin glistened in the midday sun. "Nothing can harm you."

His aquamarine eyes studied hers. Love and passion flared within. "One thing can." He propped his head on his arm and traced the curve of her jaw. "Can I trust you, Trinity?"

"With your life." Her reflection shimmered and the memory blurred, as if some part of her knew this to be dangerous.

"Silver in my heart."

"I don't think I like knowing your weakness, Niky."

He leaned in close until his lips were mere inches from hers; his warm breath caressed her face. Trinity closed her eyes and swallowed.

"You would never betray me. I trust you."

"Oh, Niky." She reached out and wrapped her arms around his neck.

Black spots danced before her eyes and Brian's menacing laughter brought her back to the present. Instantly her memory was forgotten.

"How very touching. Oh, Niky," he mimicked. "You have given me a great gift, my dear." Brian leaned in and licked her neck, it felt like the sting of a scorpion. Terrible heat spiked through her and then that too disappeared.

She touched her neck and felt smooth skin.

"Don't worry, Trinity. I've left you unscathed." His fingers traced her jaw-line.

***

"Trinity! For God's sake, Cat eyes, answer me." Nikolas's voice cut through the fog in her head.

She whipped her head around and stared. What was she doing out here? Hadn't someone been here? Trinity rubbed her temple. Was she losing her mind? An image of an old man sprang to mind. But there was no one around. She glanced at her feet and noticed only one set of prints. Her own.

"Trinity," Nikolas sighed with relief. He ran to her side and kissed the top of her head. "Cat eyes, where were you? You weren't to leave the house."

"I…I don't know. All I remember is talking with my father and waking up here."

His green eyes studied hers, his brows creased with worry. "I'm taking you home." He swept her into his arms.

Fear snaked through her spine. Trinity looked at her surroundings, black shadows and waving palm leaves met her assessing gaze. What had just happened?

***

Alexander floated as mist out of the old human's body and allowed him to slump to the sand beneath. Blood oozed out of the man's nose and Alexander knew he was dead. The body had been too frail for him to overtake but at least it had accomplished his mission before passing. He shrugged nonchalantly and dusted himself off. What did he care if the old coot died? He was a worthless air breather anyhow.

He was drunk off of Trinity's precious blood. He licked his canines savoring her essence. Now that he'd tasted her, she was his addiction and he couldn't get enough. Soon she'd be all his and he'd drink to his heart's delight.

The sight of the were-beast carrying her caused him to smirk with glee. Joy wrapped as a constrictor around his lifeless heart, he had them both in the palm of his hands. Soon he'd rid himself of the meddling wolf boy and claim his queen for his own.

Alexander closed his eyes, separated his body into tiny floating particles, each no bigger than a grain of sand, and whipped through the air. The land trembled at his passing and huge waves crashed in his wake.

Moments later, he entered his dwelling. A hidden tunnel system in a dockside warehouse. He had to give it to Trinity for figuring out his approximate location.

"Come to me, my children." He held out his arms benevolently. Semeres clamored for his attention, hissing and clawing at one another.

"Quiet!" Instantly the roar dimmed. "Where is Mercedes?"

The throng parted and a beautiful brunette walked forward. Her caramel skin glistened pale in the moonlight. He smiled and waved her over. "Come, my love. Tell me why you failed."

Mercedes bowed her head and trembled violently. "She was more powerful than I'd thought."

Alexander walked to his throne made out of human skulls and sat down. His nudity was admired by the masses. He smiled and ushered her forward. "Closer."

Mercedes shambled forward, each step seemed more hesitant than the last.

"You will not fail me again," he said through clenched teeth. She bobbed her head and swallowed. Something was amiss; Alexander sensed a change in her. He sniffed the air and detected the unmistakable stench of rogue vampire. A Lysandra had exchanged blood with her. Hatred welled in his belly threatening to spew forth as a geyser.

"And what have we here?" He stalked toward her, his steps predatory and menacing. "A change. But why?" He grasped her chin and elongated his nails until they dug into her flesh. Drops of blood ran a path down his arm.

"It was forced upon me."

Alexander licked the blood from his forearm and threw her from him. "Have you turned rogue? Are you untrue to me?"

The slight hesitation on her part was unmistakable. Alexander would kill her when her mission was complete, it would not do to have one of his own turn rogue. "No, my lord."

He feigned belief. "Good. Then it will not be a problem for you to kill the wolf, will it?"

She turned her eyes to him; their honeyed color swirled with an unasked question. He turned his head and sniffed. "You will kill the wolf."

Mercedes nodded and bowed.

He flicked his wrist. "Be gone, then. I have no use for you. I have no use for any of you. Out!" The vampires rushed off and Alexander once more walked toward his throne. A cruel smile broke his features. The fun was just beginning.

Chapter 24

"Trin, you've got to try to remember. What made you walk two miles away from the bungalow?" Nikolas peered into her cloudy blue eyes. She seemed lost and out of sorts and truthfully, he was frightened for her.

He laid her on the sleigh bed and turned her over on her stomach. "Relax. I'll massage you. Think, honey."

He kneaded her stiff muscles and she moaned beneath him.

"I don't know, Niky. I remember needing some fresh air and I ran to the tree in the backyard. But from that moment on everything is sketchy. I don't really have a clue." She groaned and shoved her face into the pillow.

Candlelight danced across her features, casting her in shadow and light. Her flaming curls shone brightly.

He brushed back her hair and trembled at the feel of her, his relief at finding her safe and somewhat whole was immense. He ached to have her beneath him, to bury himself to the hilt inside of her and hear her call his name. Nikolas took a deep breath; he needed to keep focused.

"He's back. Alexander's back and looking for you."

"What?" Trinity sat up quickly. Her curls were a red veil around her face. "How did you find out?"

"Gabe sensed him. I rushed home to tell you as soon as I found out." Nikolas narrowed his eyes and gripped her shoulders. "Are you sure you can't remember anything?"

She swallowed. "Nothing." Her blue eyes were shaded and downcast.

He pulled her into his chest and squeezed. She began to weep gently in his arms. "Gods, Trin…" He couldn't express in words the fear and guilt he felt for leaving her alone. Streams of early sunshine filtered through the windowpanes. She slumped lower, her breathing slowed and Nikolas felt her relax, until eventually he knew she'd fallen asleep.

He laid her down and undressed her. His eyes devoured her. She looked angelic in sleep, her lips slightly parted, her hair a tousled cloak around her. Nikolas ran a path down her cheek, relief filtered through him. If anything had happened to her, the idea didn't bear thought. He undressed and lay next to Trinity, pulling her into his side. Desperation to keep her safe clawed at him and he drowned in it.

Without warning, his breathing turned ragged and fire lanced through him. Nikolas broke out in a cold sweat. The transformation was nearly upon him once more. He ground his teeth and the black void of pain consumed him.

***

Trinity awoke hours later. The room was awash with midday sun. She rubbed her head and groaned. Since when did she sleep this late? Pain behind her eyes was the deciding factor, kicking off her sheets she stood and wobbled for a moment.

Nikolas moaned and shifted, wrapping the bedding around himself. She smiled and walked to the bathroom.

An hour later, refreshed and dressed for the day she paced in the living room. Restless energy consumed her, the need to get out of the house and explore her exotic surroundings beckoned and since it was light out there was nothing to fear, as far as vampires went

"I can't take this." She grabbed her purse and slipped from the bungalow.

***

Walking along the boardwalk Trinity breathed deeply allowing nature to calm her frazzled nerves. A hotdog vendor stood beneath a yellow umbrella reading a magazine.

Food. That's what she would do; she'd buy the makings for a great dinner and surprise Nikolas. Spaghetti and meatballs sounded wonderful. Her mood lightened as a warm rush of pleasure swept through her.

Last night had been awful and confusing, but after a restful sleep, she was ready to once again face the world. She turned at the sound of a child's laughter.

Seagulls flocked around the water's edge. A little black-haired boy in blue swim trunks kept running up to the birds flapping his arms and squawking loudly. What must have been his mother pulled him to her and wagged her finger in his face.

Trinity shook her head and picked up the pace. She needed to get her groceries before Nikolas woke and found her missing.

***

Pain sliced through its soul. A half-man, half-beast reared up

and howled. Its long muzzle dripped scarlet blood. The were-beast ran blindly through the woods. Branches slapped his face; it snarled and ripped the limbs from the trees. Its mind, a red haze of murder, shrouded him. An owl hooted and the beast's lip curled. It stopped running. Fresh meat. Its sharp eyes glanced up at the fully ripe moon, a long melancholy howl issued from its muzzle.

The black sky was bejeweled with thousands of silver lights. Freedom. The beast roared with victory as it once again claimed dominance of its body. Feral heat tore through it. The sound of a snapping twig made it whip its head to the side. The aromatic scent of prey tickled its keen senses. Flaring its nostrils, it followed the trail. Almonds and vanilla. A spark of memory briefly flared in its heart.

Its feet ate up the distance between it and what it sought. Carnal desire curled in its gut. Images of tearing into warm flesh was a heady enticement and lent it speed. It ripped through the clearing and found her lying within a field of green. Her pale moonstone complexion shimmered in the night and her hair gleamed like molten lava. The beast approached cautiously. Its breath rushed out of its lungs, steam wafted from its muzzle.

The beauty opened her eyes, slowly, as if she felt no fear and smiled. "I knew you'd come for me." She held out a hand to him. "My love."

It took a step back. Confusion at her lack of fear niggled through the fog in its brain.

"Come to me, Nikolas."

Trinity. His lover and his life. The beast roared and exploded. Nikolas stepped forward, nude and gleaming with sweat he slumped to the ground, all breath left him on impact.

***

Nikolas jumped out of the bed. *Trinity, Trinity*, chanted as a melody through his mind. Was it possible that when he transformed he wouldn't hurt her? Nikolas couldn't chance it, but the dream gave him hope. Once a month Nikolas became the beast. Not his wolf form, but a blind maniac capable of killing whatever and whoever was in his path without regret or sorrow. And the pain of his upcoming transformation was ripping through him.

White-hot heat singed through his veins, his pulse roared in his ears. His limbs were sensitive, the bones ready to explode and change him into what he could not control. Panic rose in his throat. He needed Trinity; only she could bring him peace from the madness.

He sought blindly for her. Nikolas flared his nostrils and followed her scent. She'd left the house a half-hour, maybe hour ago. Where was she? He growled and ran to the closet tearing clothing in his haste to dress. The door opened. Light footsteps walked across the floor.

Bags were set on the table, the sound a cacophony to him. Nikolas twirled. Almond and vanilla wafted on the air. Relief flooded him. He tore through the house, covering the distance between them in seconds.

His body responded to her on a primal level. Her back was to him, she wore a baby blue day dress and her long hair hung freely around her waist. Trinity hummed, completely unaware of his presence.

Nikolas strode forward and she gasped. She turned and her eyes widened. "Niky, I didn't see you."

"Where were you, Cat eyes?" His gaze roamed her body. Her chest heaved and her breasts pressed tight against her neckline. He watched her nipples harden and desire slammed him forcefully in the gut. Nikolas's erection pushed against his half zipped jeans.

"I wanted to surprise you." A flush crept up her neck and desire reflected in her eyes. Her irises widened, and she took a step toward him.

Nikolas grabbed her and wrapped her legs around his waist. He walked toward the kitchen table never taking his eyes off her. She shivered and nuzzled her nose into his neck, nipping and licking, driving him mad for her.

He threw everything off the table. A glass bowl full of fruit shattered on the floor. Oranges and apples rolled around his feet. Her grocery bags landed with a soft plop beside him. Nikolas kicked back a chair; it slammed to the ground with a resounding thud.

"I need you, Trinity. Tell me you feel it too." His words came out ragged.

"Yes, oh God, yes."

Reverently he sat her down on the wooden surface and with trembling fingers inched her dress up. His heart nearly stopped beating when he encountered the lace garter she wore. He glanced up at her.

She nibbled her lip. "Dessert."

He growled and lowered his head, his lips claiming hers.

She moaned and her hand trailed down his chest. She grasped his erection and massaged slowly.

Her touch was like fire and he burned from it. His tongue danced with hers; she licked and nibbled. Teasing and tasting him. He broke away from her. Her eyes were drunk with passion, half drooped and begging for him to continue.

Nikolas laid her back and skimmed his hand down her taut stomach.

Trinity nearly screamed from the pleasure his touch incited. The friction of fabric against her sensitive skin was unbelievable; she panted and bucked her hips.

His warm breath tickled her inner thighs, his teeth nibbled gently. He inched closer and closer to the center of her. Liquid heat gathered between her legs and her eyes rolled, a groan tore from her lips. Her sounds seemed to spur him on, because he touched her. His fingers rubbed a circular pattern against her. "Oh God, Niky." She thrashed on the hard table.

His hands slid her panties down her legs, the rush of cool air against the moist heat of her body nearly made her orgasm. Nikolas flicked her engorged nub and Trinity clawed at her hair. The intense pleasure was almost more than she could handle.

He tasted her and she cried out his name. Lights flared behind her eyes and she rode the wave of pleasure. Her soul splintered out of her body, but before she had time to gather her wits about her, his stiff erection pushed through. Her body hummed with electricity and her legs shook. She sat up and wrapped her arms around his naked back.

Nikolas gritted his teeth. She was so warm, a safe haven from his madness. Her love encompassed him and he shoved himself deeper.

Her nails dug into his back and the pain became pleasure. A rush of adrenaline coursed through his veins. Her body kept the tempo, moving with him in an organized rhythm, sending him deeper into the black abyss. The climax was swift and severe. Their grunts of pleasure echoed off the room. His seed exploded within her, his life seemed to seep out of him and he fragmented out of his body.

"Nikolas," she screamed and slumped into him. She giggled and laid him against her. She was soft and pliant; Nikolas stared down at her, his hands on either side of her catching most of his weight.

"Encore," she said.

He laughed and kissed her lips. "You'll be the death of me, Trinity."

She sighed. "Never. I'll never be the death of you."

Chapter 25

Trinity carried two plates heaping with spaghetti and meatballs to the sitting room. Nikolas sat on the couch, his legs crossed before him, staring into the crackling fire.

She handed him one and folded her legs beneath her.

Nikolas smiled and sniffed the air. "Mmm. Smells wonderful. Did you add the mushrooms?"

"Of course, you think I'd forget how to make your favorite dish?"

He winked and dug in. Trinity smiled remembering their earlier romp. Her body tingled and her legs still quivered from their lovemaking. She wrinkled her nose and wrapped noodles around her fork. The thought of eating at the table now though made her blush.

"What are you thinking about, Trin?"

"That we just had sex on a kitchen table that is not our own and I can never look at it the same way again." She laughed. "And you? You were awfully quiet while I cooked. What's percolating through that mind of yours?" She was almost afraid to ask. His fork stopped mid-air and he inhaled.

"I've got to leave tomorrow for Olympus."

"What? Why?" She turned to stare at him. Nikolas looked exhausted; his skin was pinched and pallid. He scrubbed a fist down his face and his hand trembled slightly as he did so. He was sick and she could guess why. The moon. Nikolas was ready to turn, but what the change entailed she didn't have a clue.

"I've got something I need to talk with you about later, Trin, but for now can we change the subject," he implored. His green eyes roamed her face as if sketching her to memory.

The look told her more than anything what he was feeling. Fear of her finding out his true identity. Her heart ached for him but she would let him tell her himself, this was his thing to do as he saw fit. "Fine, Niky. But, that's not all, is it? You're keeping something from me."

A sigh escaped him. "No you're right, that's not it."

"Tell me."

"I'm thinking, Trinity, that in order for me to keep you safe I'm gonna have to bring you with me tonight."

She chewed, savoring the crushed tomato and sage sauce. "Is that so bad?"

"Yes."

His answer surprised her and she dropped her fork with a clatter, she sputtered, blistering with indignation. "Why? Because you think, I'll hold you up. Nikolas, I'm tired of being babied. I'm tired of being the one left behind." She narrowed her eyes. "And if you haven't noticed it brings nothing but trouble. Each time you leave me behind something terrible inevitably happens. I'm not a helpless, friggin maiden." Her anger boiled over. "Dammit, Niky, treat me as an equal."

The tension in her gut abated somewhat under the bright glow of his smile. "I love that about you, Trinity. My wild cat. I never have to worry that you'll go fragile, your inner strength is a constant source of amazement for me." He grasped her hand and squeezed.

She blew out a frustrated breath.

"I don't take you because I lose my mind when you're with me. I can't think straight, I can't do my job. You're all I think about, your welfare." He sat his plate down and turned to her. His aquamarine eyes glittered with the passion and truth of his words. "It tears at me to think of the harm that could befall you, you can die…" He grabbed her plate and put it down on the coffee table, then he gripped her shoulders and gave her a gentle shake. "You could die, Trin. This is not some game, this is real and those creatures would gladly sell their shriveled souls to possess you. Furthermore, I have never thought of you as not being an equal to me. Believe me, I know the powers you hold."

Her blood pounded and her face grew hot with humiliation. "I'm…I'm sorry. It's just…" She stood and ambled toward the sliding glass door. She looked at the black vastness of the beach. She lifted her hands and twirled, "I feel so helpless and I can't take it. It's suffocating. Ugh!"

He padded toward her. "Go get dressed, we leave in ten minutes."

"Really?" She squelched the burgeoning excitement.

He nodded. "I swear not to leave you. Now go, before I change my mind."

Trinity didn't need to be told twice. She fled toward the

bedroom and pulled out a pair of jeans and a white spaghetti strap tank top.

***

Nikolas knew the time was now. He held his hands behind his back and stalked back and forth. The secret of who he really was must be told before he left for Olympus. Tonight, he must tell her the truth. His heart was a tortured mess, paranoia threatened to choke him. He hated to admit it but fear that she'd reject him ate away at his barely controlled sanity.

The bright beams of moonlight were like anathema to his soul. Torment was eating at him from the inside. His skin burned as if he'd fallen into a vat of acid, the pain was horrific and he broke out in beads of sweat. Nikolas had to go into hiding no later than tomorrow.

"I'm ready." A bright smile laced her features.

He forced a tight grin and jerked his head. "Then let's go. We are to meet Agape and Gabe at the Blue Lagoon."

"What's that?"

"A dance club." Nikolas buried the pain deep inside. He'd lived with it for over two thousand years. He could ignore it for the time being.

"Why there?"

"A hunch, let's go." He swept a hand down his brow and gritted his teeth. The soft stirring of the beast pounded in his heart.

"Babe, are you all right?" Her forehead furrowed and her eyes were apprehensive

"Fine, Trin, just fine."

She nodded; not looking entirely convinced but followed him

out the door.

***

Fog swirled around their feet. The beating rhythm of dancers stomping and grinding into one another coursed through her body. Trinity was absorbed in the spectrum of flashing lights and the loud blare of techno music. The musk of cigarettes, sweat and perfume overwhelmed her. She clung to Nikolas's back, fearing separation. Her heart pounded violently in her throat. She licked her parched lips and swallowed the nearly debilitating claustrophobia.

A bald man with caramel skin gleaming with pearls of sweat bumped into her nearly causing her to fall in a heap. The contents of his cup sloshed over the side.

"Move out the way, bitch." His words were slurred and the alcohol-tainted breath gave her a clue why.

Nikolas grasped her wrist and twirled on the stranger. His face contorted into a mask of rage and his green eyes seemed to glow in the barely lit room. "Touch her again and I'll rip you in two."

She shivered but clung even tighter to Nikolas's black shirt.

"Hey, man, if yo' bitch was stupid enough to bump into me, then what do I gotta be sorry for?" He laughed and jerked his thumb at a skinny Hispanic standing next to him. "Yo, chico, is that man seriously threatening me?" The pock-faced friend laughed. Then the stranger pulled out a switchblade and held it threateningly before him. "I don't think he knows who he's messing with, vato."

Before Trinity could get her bearings and panic over the knife, Nikolas grasped the stranger's arm and twisted. The snap of bone being broken was loud enough to hear over the deafening roar of music.

The stranger's eyes bulged and he swayed from side to side.

A look of sheer panic crossed his face, almost as if he hadn't quite registered what just happened.

"You do that again and I'll break the other one," Nikolas growled out.

At that moment the stranger's brain must have gotten the pain signal because he screamed and held his misshapen limb protectively to his side. He turned and ran into the sea of people howling as he went.

Trinity blinked twice, her mouth dropped open and shock numbed her brain. She'd never seen Nikolas so brutal, so fierce, so animalistic.

He hung his head and turned toward her, his eyes held a strange glow. Shrouded in weariness, he pulled her to his side. He inhaled deeply and rubbed her back. "I'm sorry, Trin."

Remembering the look of primal fear on the stranger's face, she trembled. Awkwardly, she cleared her throat. "What was that about, Nik?" While, her sympathies didn't lie with the stranger, Nikolas's uncharacteristic lack of self-control disturbed her.

He stiffened in her arms, rivers of sweat coursed down his face and he clenched his jaw.

She grasped his face and forced him to look her in the eye. "Baby, baby, what's wrong?"

"No…thing, Trin," he gasped out.

"Don't tell me nothing." Fear clawed at her heart. "Tell me what's wrong."

A moment later Nikolas looked at her, his eyes clouded with pain. His muscles relaxed and he took a deep breath. "I'm fine. Come on, we have to find Agape and Gabe."

She yanked her hands away and stood firm. "No, you're obviously not feeling well. Please, Niky, let me help you."

"There is no time. We have to find them now!" He grabbed her and led them through the winding maze of people.

She seethed with barely suppressed anger. Again, he'd shrouded himself in secrecy; she'd thought they were past that. Well, she'd be damned if she'd let that happen again. She meant to fight and win. Grim determination coursed through her.

***

A hand shot through the air. "Trinity. Nikolas. We're over here." Agape waved them over. Nikolas headed in that direction and stopped before the duo. Agape's fingers twitched idly. Black circles under her eyes bespoke her own battle with the demon threatening to break loose.

"Have you found her?" He asked Agape. He studied her. She looked worn and tattered, no better off than he. He read the pain clearly in her eyes and he knew she was close to turning. Agape was much weaker than he and controlling the beast tried her strength. They needed to seek the safety Olympus had to offer.

"Yes."

"What? Found who?" Trinity's words were clipped and devoid of warmth.

She was obviously furious with him, but that could not be helped at the moment. Another wave of pain engulfed him, nearly crippling this time. His anger mounted and frustration boiled in him like an infected wound.

A familiar scent rode the stale air and Nikolas's eyes widened.

Agape bowed her head and rubbed her temples, her eyes

squeezed shut. "Yes, he's here too. Unfortunately he refuses to talk with us."

Nikolas glanced up, the second level of the club pulsed with a sea of moving bodies, but that's not what he sought. In the corner, tucked within a shadow, Damien crouched.

"He's still following her, then?"

Gabe nodded and spoke up. "I think it's beyond his control now; they're somehow connected. Their wavelengths merged, the blood transfusion has screwed with him."

Nikolas nodded slowly; he'd feared that to be the case. "Where is she?"

"I'm here." Mercedes materialized beside him.

Trinity jumped and took two steps back. Nikolas laid his hand on her shoulder and leaned in. "Don't worry, Trin. Gabe and Agape have been trailing her for days, she's safe."

She turned to him and her blue eyes shimmered. "No, I feel it." She pointed to her chest. "I can't tell you how, but this is a trap, Nik."

"Trinity, she's told us everything. We know where Alexander's hide out is. She's not holding back anything."

Trinity glanced around; her lip trembled. Nikolas could make out the pounding of her pulse in the side of her neck. She was terrified.

"You must know." Mercedes's words interrupted them.

Trinity glanced at Mercedes, her face clearly reflecting her distrust.

"Know what, M?" Her voice trembled. "How do we know we can even trust you?"

"You don't. But are you willing to take that chance? Alexander's a monster and he must be stopped."

"Why now? Why help us now? I trusted you once, loved you like a sister. Do you think I can forget that you nearly killed me?" Her voice shook; Nikolas heard her grief and pulled her to his side.

Mercedes glanced up and then back at Trinity. "Something inside me has changed. I remember what we once shared and because of that memory I know I have to talk." Mercedes looked around. "But not here. Let's dance." She grabbed Nikolas's hand. "You must follow me."

Trinity pushed Mercedes aside. "What the piss do you think you're doing?"

"Trin, this message is not for you." Mercedes studied her. "For the friendship we once shared, please trust me."

Nikolas grabbed his head. The pounding was intolerable; the swaying bodies a swirling haze of images. He opened his eyes and growled out, "Tell me here."

He bit the inside of his cheek until he drew blood. The metallic taste lingered on his tongue, exciting him, drawing the beast closer to the edge of release.

"Here." Mercedes pushed a knife into Nikolas's hand. "Kill me if I try to deceive you."

The cold steel singed his sensitized skin and Nikolas dropped it with a clatter to the ground. Trinity picked it up and clenched it tightly. She jerked her hand toward the dance floor. "You lead, we follow, M. And rest assured I will use this if you try anything funny."

Mercedes walked ahead of them, her body's undulations like that of a snake, tight and coiled ready to spring into action at a moments notice. She began to sway in time to the beat.

Nikolas stood near Mercedes and then dragged Trinity into his side. He whispered in her ear, “Make this look natural. Dance for me, baby.”

Trinity bit her lip and inched closer to his side. One hand dug beneath his shirt and her warm skin next to his caused him to tremble. She calmed the raging monster within. Her touch, her love comforted him, soothed him as nothing else could.

Her blue eyes sparkled. She turned and leaned into his frame the soft contours of her body rubbing against him. Nikolas held her and swayed in time to the hypnotic beat, she wrapped one leg around him and arched her back, the blade whipped straight out, pointing directly into Mercedes heart.

“Now speak.” Trinity was a lioness defending her man.

Nikolas's heart swelled with pride.

“Alexander is back,” she said in a trembly voice. Her liquid brown eyes searched the room.

“Tell us something we don’t know,” Nikolas growled.

Mercedes lifted her eyes and stared at him, her gaze never wavering. “I’ve been sent to kill you.”

Nikolas laughed.

“With this.” She lifted her hand and uncurled her fingers. In her palm lay a tiny silver orb.

The laughter died on his lips.

“He knows your weakness, Nikolas. He knows.”

Chapter 26

That stupid bitch! Alexander watched Mercedes unfurl her hand. Fire burned a hole in his gut; he clenched and unclenched his fists. He stood upon the roof beams near the back of the club, hidden safely in the shadows. His eyes studied the layout. Three doors led outside. He licked his canines and smirked, they'd exit through one of those doors and he'd be there. Waiting.

Alexander had known when he told Mercedes to kill Nikolas she'd turn. And now he waited to correct the wrong. The group was five strong with one hidden deep in shadows; Alexander curled his lip, the hidden one responsible for turning Mercedes rogue.

A telepathic push roamed through his body and Alexander turned. Angel boy was gazing with sightless eyes toward him. His mouth curved into an unconscious smile, he was ready for the fight and his plan was brilliant. No one would have a clue until it was too late.

His eyes caressed his queen who stood within the arms of the were-beast, her blood a dangerous intoxicant to his senses. The beating of her heart sent waves of erotic pleasure to pulse through his body, his fangs lengthened and ripped through his gums, the pain mingled with the pleasure. Soon she would be his.

***

Trinity stood and twirled on Mercedes. “What the piss are you talking about?”

Nikolas couldn’t tear his gaze from the silver ball held within Mercedes palm. How had Alexander found out? It was a highly guarded secret. The silver wasn’t the crux, while that maimed, it was the specific type of silver Alexander had located that was lethal.

Hephaestus, god of the forge, had somehow given it to him. He was an excellent craftsman, husband of Aphrodite and son of Hera, now all of a sudden the danger went much deeper than Nikolas had at first anticipated. He needed to speak with Athena at once. Aprhodite was not playing a child’s game. She meant to win. And he sensed her game went beyond Ares, she was challenging Athena, of that he was certain.

Nikolas turned to Trinity and fear beat a crazy rhythm in his chest. “I need to go and speak with Athena and you’re coming with me.” He yanked her arm.

“What is that ball, Nikolas?”

He shook his head and ground his molars together. This was not the way he’d intended for her to find out about himself. He called his group over with a flick of his wrist and began walking to the club’s rear exit.

Agape and Gabriel settled on either side of him, Mercedes trailed in their wake. Nikolas sensed her fear and knew she had no hidden agenda, so he gave her no other thought.

Gabriel leaned in, his mouth inches from Nikolas's ear. “He’s here.”

The surprising news stopped him dead in his tracks. Trinity bumped into him and laid a hand against his back. "Are you sure?"

"Not one-hundred percent but his presence is emanating throughout the room."

Nikolas turned, his eyes darted around the dance club. Men laughed and offered to buy women drinks. The women rolled their eyes and scampered off. The deejay stood on a platform high above the room, dancing in time to the beat. Strobe lights flashed and the sickening smell of sweat-soaked bodies mixed with perfume nearly caused him to retch. The roar of human feet pounding on the floor awakened the predator within, transforming them from humans to prey. Nikolas ground his teeth and flicked the sweat from his brow.

But, Alexander was nowhere to be found. The room spun and Nikolas stumbled toward the door.

"Nikolas," Trinity's words trembled, he could smell her fear.

He closed his eyes and clung to her body, inhaling the fresh scent of almonds and vanilla in her hair. He nuzzled her neck and allowed her into his heart cutting off the transformation. But he was losing the battle and needed desperately to speak with Athena, then go into hiding. Trinity must not be harmed by his hands.

He all but ran out of the building, the others close behind. The door cracked against the bricked exterior of the club. A path led directly to the beach. Nikolas inhaled the salt-rimmed breeze. Sea gulls squawked overhead, flying in lazy circles. The stars twinkled like bejeweled daggers; palm trees gnarled and twisted created a backdrop against the sky. The air was heavy with the stench of rum and tequila.

Pain ripped through his bowels and he doubled over, his chest heaving for oxygen. His bones snapped and Nikolas splashed to his knees in a puddle. The transformation was nearly upon him, he'd failed again.

Trinity ran to him.

"Get back!" His concern for her caused his words to come out harsh and cruel.

He turned his head and witnessed Agape in the same predicament. Then all hell broke loose.

***

A heavy fog shrouded them; the stench of evil permeated the air. Trinity crept toward the shadows, her heart heavy with fear and sadness. She glanced at Nikolas. Sweat dotted his brow and his face contorted with pain. Her eyes darted over the group, with the exception of Nik and Agape the rest were on high alert, crouched into fighting stances.

Gabriel peeled off his coat and extended his long, powerful wings. The iridescent colors shimmered and swirled with a life all their own. Mercedes held a wicked buck knife in her grasp. To her left stood the elusive Damien, his bearing fiercely protective toward Mercedes. He crept ever closer to her side until he stood a hairs breadth away, his pearly fangs, long and exposed.

But Trinity had no chance to wonder about his sudden reappearance. A thin, icy tendril of smoke curled around her face. A chill crept up her spine. Fear rendered her immobile, unable to even blink. Her heart beat a crazy rhythm in her chest, the tempo picking up speed. Insidious whispers of sound echoed in her mind, a disembodied voice. 'You need me. You want me. Have you not tired of the chase yet?' An evil laugh bounced off her skull and she fought down the bile.

Her eyes rolled in her head. The voice, the timbre.

Alexander.

Mercedes screamed, breaking the tight tension of the moment. A force blew her off her feet and slammed her against the wall about twenty feet off the ground. Her breath left her in a sudden rush of sound.

Whatever had held Trinity spellbound was now broken and she ran forward.

Mercedes made a choking sound; her eyes bulged in her neck. Trinity gasped. The beautiful caramel skin was losing its blood flow. She was turning a hideous shade of purple and blue.

Damien leapt and grabbed her hand, then he gave a powerful yank. They crashed in a heap upon the blacktop.

The smoke formed a whirlwind, the shriek of the gale deafening and Trinity clamped her hands over her ears. Sand particles slapped her in the face, her eyes stung and warm liquid oozed down the side of her right cheek.

Nikolas and Agape howled in unison, the sound the likes of which she'd never heard before. From out of the tornado stepped Alexander. His pale skin gleamed like milk in the moonlight. His lavender eyes shone with the madness of his fury.

He walked toward Mercedes and pointed his finger. "I knew you were not to be trusted."

Adrenaline pulsed through Trinity until her skin hummed with energy. In the back of her mind, she heard her spirits wailing; their minds shrieked at her, ready for a fight. She fought the nausea and focused her energy. Daggers of light exploded behind her eyes.

With a flick of Alexander's wrist, the silver bullet in

Mercedes's hand flew from her palm to his.

Nikolas growled; his body pulsated. He slumped forward and Trinity stared on with horror. Black fur ripped through his skin. His face contorted, his eyes bulged. Razor, sharp fangs dripping saliva cut through his muzzle. He pounded his fist on the pavement and bent backwards.

Alexander gazed on with a look of sheer delight and whooped with joy. He exploded in a cloud of gray mist and zoomed toward the transforming shape of Agape. He entered her as a tendril of mist and Agape sprang to her feet with a shriek.

Trinity's skin crawled; a loathsome fear gripped her.

Agape's eyes glowed lavender. White fur covered her body. She threw her head back and the loud snap of bones contorted her once human body into that of a were-beast. Still humanoid in form, but hunched over, with powerful legs, each the size of a tree trunk and a face distorted into that of a wolf. The transformation complete she whipped her head around and loped with preternatural speed toward Nikolas.

Damien snapped out of his trance and ran toward Agape. She flung out her hand and gripped his neck, then flung him like a rag doll to the pavement.

Gabriel closed his eyes and powerful light radiated from him. Agape, still controlled by Alexander, held out her hand and reflected it back at him. The impact tossed him fifty yards through the air where he landed with a soft thud.

An evil leer spread across Agape's face and she lifted her hand. Nikolas stood on clawed feet. His eyes shone blood red, his countenance lethal, and his gait predatory. He ran with suprahuman speed toward Agape.

The world slowed down. From within Agape's hand the silver bullet sped in a deadly trajectory toward Nikolas's heart. And somehow, Trinity knew this would deal death's blow.

Something clicked in her brain and spurred her into action. Unafraid of the beast Nikolas had become or the monster she faced in Agape, Trinity dashed forward and stood slightly apart from the two behemoths. Lifting her arms in the air, she channeled her spirits. A mighty eruption spewed from her mind. She closed her eyes and pictured the inferno devouring not only the silver but also the spirit of Alexander.

The flames surrounded her, licking her body. Sweat stung her eyes, a black void threatened to consume her. She gritted her teeth and bore the excruciating pain. Her skin blistered and then seeped warm fluid. The flames ate her; the stench of burned flesh caused her to retch.

Blue fire arched from her fingertips, raw power crackled around her. The greedy flame caught the bullet two inches from Nikolas's heart, melting it instantly; then continued forward into Agape's mutated form. A horrendous wail rose in the night as black mist shot from Agape and into the fading gloom.

Pure beams of blue light surrounded the pair of werewolves and they disappeared in the brilliance.

The flames surrounding Trinity gutted out, falling to the pavement as fireworks of light. She surrendered to the blackness that threatened to engulf her and pitched forward. Her last conscious thought was that it was finally over.

Chapter 27

Gabriel shook his head and sat up. The warm tropical breeze fluttered through his wings. He shot to his feet and sensed around for anyone's presence. Fifteen yards in front of him lay a barely breathing Trinity. He walked toward her keeping his eyes closed and focused on his surroundings. Not a sound, not even a life source other than Trinity's was present. The night was dark and unyielding.

She moaned and he felt her body heat. It was like an oven the way it poured off her, as if she'd walked through the fires of the Underworld. Gabriel scooped her up, spread his wings and flew off into the shrouded veil of night, covering himself in a quick enchantment of invisibility. Nikolas would never forgive him if he let harm befall her. Her body lay limp and lifeless in his arms.

She was bound to have a million questions when she woke. He winged higher into the sky until he was sure he'd be nothing but a speck of movement to spectators below, and then dropped his spell of invisibility. Her breathing returned to normal and he heaved a sigh of relief. Maybe now she could rest. They had a long flight ahead; he just hoped she wouldn't wake for a while yet.

***

"Why fight me, my beauty?" Alexander's eyes glowed like red coals. The ring of red surrounded by the lavender gave him an even more sinister appearance. Trinity cringed and whimpered, she lifted a hand to her mouth and fought down the bile at the sight of her peeling, black skin. Clear fluid seeped into the blood covering her body. She gasped in horror. What had she done to herself? Her hands shook as reality sank in. She was a monster.

She scooted farther within the safe confines the forest heralded. A night owl hooted, a wolf howled a melancholy song of despair and loneliness. Trinity buried her face and allowed the hot tears to fall.

His laughter rained down on her like icicles. Each vibration stabbed her sensitive psyche, the pain was almost intolerable. She groaned.

"Look what you've done to yourself…tsk, tsk, tsk. I shall have to kill you now, you're worthless to me." He smirked and stalked toward her. He stopped inches from her face and twirled. His nude body glistened from the light of the moon. "Your little bit of magic didn't harm me, my dear." He looked her up and down. "A pity I can't say the same for you."

"What do you want from me?" She was tired and could no longer keep up the fight. Alexander's face contorted, he exposed his fangs and hissed. "To possess your. All of you." He grasped her chin and lowered his head. The heat of his breath sizzled along her skin. "To make you mine!"

***

Trinity moaned. The roar of beating wings pounded inside her skull. A blanket of air engulfed her above and below. Powerful arms cradled her like a baby. She snapped open an eye and gazed upward, she was held within the arms of an angel. Gabriel tilted one corner of his mouth; his white teeth gleamed. "Glad to see you awaken."

Awaken? Was it all a dream? She lifted her hand and she sighed with relief. Her skin was flawless, not a blemish or burn in sight. Why then had she felt her body explode in the inferno? She touched her face and released the last of her pent up breath.

But she had to ask, just in case. "Gabriel was I abducted by Alexander and you rescued me?"

"No, Trin, I rescued you right after you got rid of Alexander last night. When he vanished, you collapsed and I didn't know if he'd return. It was the only way to keep you safe."

"Oh, thank God." The fear of Alexander faded into the webbing of the dream.

Her head pounded and she winced. The sun was beginning its crawl over the horizon. Orange and pink hues merged with the blue and indigo of the night sky. Skyscrapers whizzed beneath her. "Where are you taking me? Where am I?" The fog of sleep slipped away and Trinity's heart beat erratically. Adrenaline surged through her body and fear for Nikolas punched her full force.

"Where's Niky? Gabriel, where are you taking me? I need to find Nik," her voice rose an octave, panic threatened to consume her.

"Nik is in Olympus. And I'm well aware that you now know why. I don't think I need to spell it out for you."

She hung her head and massaged her temples. Somehow, she'd hoped last night had all been a bad dream. "Where are you taking me?" her voice weak and strained, barely came through numb lips. Last night came flooding back to her and she wanted to scream. How had things gotten out of control so quickly?

"I'm taking you to my safe haven. It's not safe for you in Florida. The Semere swarm the town like flies, I'm afraid you're in terrible danger."

"And the others, where have they gone?"

He shrugged, the play of wind in her hair was refreshing and the slight chill to the air brought her fully awake.

"Damien vanished soon after. Mercedes ran; her life is now forfeit by her betrayal. Alexander is again nowhere to be found." His flat voice bespoke his disgust with the situation. Gabriel's face remained impassive but she knew he was furious, she could see it in the rigid cording of his muscles, the flaring of his nostrils. Even his white eyes seemed to blaze with barely disguised fury. Trinity shivered in his arms. Now more than ever she missed Nikolas's kind words and felt empty without him.

She ached for his scent. The leather mixed with salt. His blue-black hair that to some may seem sinister but made her melt. Those unfathomable, sea green eyes that swirled with mystery and intrigue. She brought to mind his every feature. From his aristocratic nose to his sensuous full lips, his strong jaw and chiseled cheeks. She yearned to tell him that she'd known the truth all along and that none of it mattered. She loved him and needed his comforting presence now more than ever. To have him snatched away in the dark of night seemed unfair. A stone of doubt settled in her stomach. The leeching feeling that last night was the last time she'd see him niggled the back of her mind.

She licked her lips and her heart revved up once again. Things were not right. Alexander was not truly gone, the spirits inside her whispered incessantly not to let up her guard. Even the wind rushing through her ears whispered of secrets.

Gabriel stopped flying and slowly descended. Trinity gazed at her new surroundings.

Steam wafted up from the damp ground of a rainforest. Huge palm trees encircled them like a cocoon. Macaws and toucans winged overhead. Their brilliant plumage, showed up as a rainbow of color against the azure sky. Directly in front of them, a waterfall crashed into a large cesspool. It had to be at least two hundred feet high. The world around them smelled of rich earth, coconuts, and orchids. A poisonous dart frog, jumped from one leaf to the next, and the haunting ballad of a howler monkey rang in the distance. The sun shone in all its brilliance upon the tropical heaven.

"Where are we?"

He smiled and sat her down. "Pearl Island off the coast of Panama. Do you like it?"

"Yes, it's beautiful."

"It is, isn't it?"

She turned to stare at him. A look of contentment spread across his handsome features. She could no longer bite her tongue. "The way you speak, the passion of your words…how? You can't see it."

He smiled. "But I can." He lifted a blond brow and spread his hand wide. "Close your eyes and I'll show you what I see."

Biting her lip, she closed her eyes and imagined the place as a blind man might.

His velvety smooth voice broke through her concentration. "The tide is rushing in. This land is infused with the scent of the wild. Bananas and their sweet fruitiness, orchids with their exotic perfume."

She cracked open an eye and marveled at his ability to see the world through eyes that had never known color and still he painted a picture she'd never seen before.

His finger pointed above him. "There, a pair of howlers are getting ready to mate. The male is pounding his chest and preening for her. I can smell her interest. But she doesn't want him to know. She's making him chase her."

Trinity smiled. "But how do you know all this?"

"Listen to the world around you. Open up your ears, Earth has a tale to tell if you're willing to listen to Mother Nature. Over there." He jerked his head. "About forty feet from us is a huge waterfall, the roar is deafening and yet it's a life giving source, the trees grow strong and the animals thrive in this place."

"I never thought it was possible to see without really seeing. But I know now you haven't missed much. Your world sounds beautiful. Although I'm not sure I could give up colors."

"Trinity, the world is a canvas. Don't get so used to one sense that you weaken the rest. Smells, sounds, and touch those can be more powerful than sight. Sometimes what we see isn't really what's there at all. But the rest can never fail you."

She cocked her head. "You're right but thank God I'll never have to learn that lesson the hard way. I'm not sure I could manage without my sight."

He lifted his hands. "I don't think this is a debate either of us will win."

"Smart man." She lifted her eyebrow.

"I've just been around enough temperamental women to know when to keep my mouth shut."

She snorted. The playful banter however, didn't help to alleviate her worry over Nikolas or last night.

Gabriel's countenance turned grim as if he knew where her thoughts were headed. "Look, before we get into a lengthy discussion let's get lunch and settle down."

"Settle down. Where?" She gazed at the endless stretch of beach and mountainess outcroppings. She wasn't sure she was ready to rough it. Last night had left her weary in many ways.

"You'll see. Now follow me."

He turned and strode toward the incoming tide. Gabriel tucked his wings behind his back and knelt, looking very much like an angel of mercy praying to the gods above. The sun shone off his hair, surrounding him in a golden aura. "Come on, Trinity."

She shuffled to where he was and knelt beside him. A million questions buzzed through her mind, she kept glancing at him from beneath her lashes but his face remained expressionless. He lowered his hands into the tide. She did the same.

The clear blue-green water caressed her skin. Farther out fish swam, darting around and through a large coral reef. She was about ready to demand what he had in mind when he whooped with joy. She laid a hand over her heart, willing it to calm down. In his hands, he clutched a struggling lobster. Easily the largest she'd ever seen. Its brown body twitched from side to side, its tiny legs scuttling for release.

"How did you catch that monster?"

"With a lot of patience, which I noticed you didn't have much of," he said with a cheerful note.

Trinity turned down a corner of her mouth. But inside she smiled.

"Let's eat."

***

Twenty minutes later she kicked her legs over the stone ledge near the waterfall. She looked down and the sheer drop caused a moment of vertigo. The smell of roasted lobster accosted her senses. Hunger was a ravenous monster inside her.

Gabriel extinguished the flame he'd cooked the lobster over and walked over with a proud smile on his face. She chuckled at the sight. Nikolas was right when he'd called Gabriel a boy scout. Just the thought of him caused a sadness to well inside her.

"Lunch, madam." Gabriel bowed then cracked the lobster in half. Steam rose and the white meat beckoned her. She snatched it greedily from his hand and ripped into a claw, it seemed like forever since she'd eaten the spaghetti the night before. Spaghetti. Nikolas's favorite food. She frowned and berated herself; she was acting like a fool. It wasn't the end of the world after all; she'd see him again. The doubt returned, but she pushed it aside.

Gabriel sat cross-legged before her. "Ask away," he spoke so soft Trinity barely registered he'd spoken at all.

"I'm not even sure where to start. So much has happened." She discarded the empty claw and shrugged. "Why did Nikolas seem frightened of that silver ball?"

"That's a werewolf's weakness. A carefully guarded secret that very few individuals are entrusted with. There was no reason for Alexander to not only know, but also have possession of such a powerful weapon."

Trinity digested that. "Then how did he find out?"

"There are only four non-werewolves that know. Athena, Damien, myself and you." His colorless eyes roamed her face, his gaze boring a hole into her. She trembled. The look was more powerful for the fact that he shouldn't be able to find her so unerringly.

"I've never told a soul. Athena wouldn't dare and Damien has always been trusted." His mouth turned down in a frown.

The lobster suddenly tasted like cardboard to her and she put it aside. She was disturbed by his insinuation. "And why would you assume it's me? I never even knew," her words came out slow and measured. Trinity clenched her fists. She'd never hurt Nikolas. How dare he assume that?

"Let me ask you this. Have you been having strange dreams lately?"

She froze at his words. "What are you saying? Just spit it out, Gabriel."

"Fine. Athena suspected you might have been under some sort of compulsion. The mind swipe Alexander touched you with has somehow connected you two."

"Wh…What?" she sputtered. The food in her stomach rolled.

"I know this is a shock and we could never be sure until now. He stole that memory from you, Trinity."

The thought that she'd nearly caused Nikolas to be fatally

injured caused a hollowness to well inside her. “Liar!” She refused to believe it. Her eyes widened and she stood. “How dare you even say something like that? I would never harm him. I love Nikolas.”

Gabriel hung his head. “Talk to your father, Trinity.” He stood and dusted himself off. “I was not accusing. You can’t be held responsible. It’s our own fault for not catching on sooner.” He dove off the cliff and flew away in a large updraft.

Trinity trembled and drew in sharp breaths. There was absolutely no way she was responsible for that. She gazed at her beautiful surroundings, lost in her misery.

Chapter 28

Nikolas howled and swiped at the trees surrounding him like a bastion. The beast within fought to escape, to run free, to kill. A red haze of fury shrouded his mind, sinking the monster further into a rage. He threw back his head and sent forth a spine chilling call. The woods came alive with the answers from his brethren.

His eyes darted from the silver daggered sky to the shadowed green and black of the woods. The color of the night amplified by the eyes of the beast. Midnight blue sky, hunter green leaves that shone the color of an emerald. Bright red clay mixed with the rustic umber of dirt. Animals scampered off, as if sensing the presence of evil. Nature didn't stir, didn't breathe. Wind ceased to rustle the leaves. Olympus kept him locked inside a maze of madness. He reached out a furry and clawed hand. Nikolas attempted to bend the tree to his will, to provide an opening. But it refused to budge. He ran headfirst into a thicket of thorns, cutting himself. The scent of his blood triggered the killer's instinct.

He pulled clumps of fur off his body, the pain helping to alleviate the madness. Then a balm touched his frenzied mind. His body shifted to that of the man, covered in his own sweat and blood. Dropping to the ground, he heaved for air. His lungs burned with a lack of oxygen. Dirt, stone and sticks clung to his cheek.

Panting he gazed around. It was still the dead of night. The beast's time to rule and yet he'd transformed. He knit his brows. What had just happened? And with that thought came another. Trinity. His heart froze; he swallowed a thick ball of unease. She'd seen him. It was all over. He lowered his head until his forehead touched the damp grass beneath.

A bright gold light suffused his wooden prison of twisted branches. Nikolas raised his head and gazed at Athena gliding toward his side. Her face remained immobile. Her gray eyes flashed with bolts of lightning. Trees and animals bowed before her.

"The time is now, my pet."

Nikolas ground his teeth and stood on shaky legs. He refused to give in to her goading. "Time for what?" he spat out, his heart heavy with his loss.

"I shall release you this once from confinement. You must save her. Trinity is to be abducted by Alexander."

His eyes widened, the animal in him reared its head seeking dominance once more. His vision swam in and out of focus. Nikolas clenched his fists, pictures of maiming Alexander rolled through his mind. "How do you know this?"

"I asked the Fates. Your role in all this must be played out very soon."

Nikolas threw his fists in the air. "How? I'm still stuck within my prison walls. Send me to her."

"In due time. Once I leave, you shall transform back to your baser side. I need you in a blind rage before you can confront Alexander. Then and only then will I send you. Only then, will you survive."

"What?" he roared. "If I return to werewolf, I'll kill not only Alexander but Trinity as well. I cannot do that to her." His heart shattered. In order to save her from one menace, he'd kill her in his other form. He groaned and Nikolas wanted to yell his fury. The Goddess had used him once again.

"I hate to be the bearer of good news, Nikolas, but she's your soul's destiny. Instinctively your animal side will know her as your own, it will not harm her."

The faint stirrings of hope nestled in his chest. Nikolas licked dry lips, but he squelched the hope. It wouldn't be the first time the Gods lied to him. He narrowed his eyes and studied her moonstone complexion. She gave nothing away. "So help me, Athena, if you lie I'll rip you limb from limb." He exposed his fangs.

Her eyes flashed and she flicked her wrist. He sailed through the air, crashing heavily against the rough bark of a pine tree. The air left his lungs in a rush of sound. It was as if a white-hot poker had stabbed him through the back. Needles fell around him, their pungent scent filling his nostrils.

She glided closer, her periwinkle, pleated gown billowing behind her. "Don't forget who is master and who is slave. I could kill you with a snap of my fingers. You'll do as I say. I don't care about you or your pathetic Demi-goddess," she spat out the word. "I only help you in this because it fulfills a greater purpose for me." A cruel sneer twisted her lips. Athena stared him down. Her look could easily kill a mortal. The gaze horrific, images of death and blood flashed through her eyes. Nikolas stared boldly back at her, refusing to give an inch.

After a while, she composed herself and smiled. "That is why I love you so, my pet. You always surprise me. Honestly, thinking you could hurt me."

He growled but refused to comment. "Wait." He suddenly remembered the news he'd meant to give her. "Hephaestus, Aphrodite and Hera are involved in this."

Her spine stiffened. "What?" A crooked grin appeared on her face. "So that's what it is. I wondered how Aphrodite knew so much. Of course, Hera is involved. It makes so much sense now."

"Why Hera?"

She turned and stared at him. "The spiteful bitch cursed Trinity. Her worst fear is for Trinity to break the enchantment. It will make her lose face." Athena smiled and rubbed her palms together. "I suspect she came into this game a bit late. Trinity's appearance in Olympus no doubt was when she decided to stop our crew at whatever cost. She's been the one to give Aphrodite valuable information."

"I thought we'd gone unnoticed."

Athena shook her head. "Hera was watching through her cow's eyes. I'm sure she figured it all out in the end."

"What information could she have given Aphrodite?"

"Well, for one. The secret to finding the correct silver for the killing blow. Aphrodite in turn told Hephaestus where to mine it and the rest is as they say history."

"How did you know about the silver bullet?"

Athena shrugged. "Damien. The rest I figured out on my

own."

"What else has she told Alexander?"

She lifted a delicately shaped brow. "Wonder where Alexander has been to all those times Gabriel tried to get a read on him and he couldn't be found?"

"Where?"

"Hera taught him a little parlor trick. She showed him how to open a rift in the time-space continuum. He was still on Earth, but in a different time. Old Greece." Athena clenched her jaw and flared her nostrils. "To a time when we were still revered and worshipped." She spat on the ground. "Pack of heathens is what mortals are. Betrayers of our old ways." Her gray eyes brewed threateningly.

Nikolas digested the information. Shock rooted him to the spot. He'd always thought time-travel to be a myth. "And that's where you are to send me?"

Athena nodded and smiled blandly. The giant rubies and diamonds of her rings sparkled like a kaleidoscope. "This has suddenly taken on a very interesting turn. I'm sure father would love to hear about this one." She cackled. Her lustrous brown hair bounced around her head. "I'll leave you now. Have fun." She grinned, clapped her hands and dissolved into a ball of light.

The pain returned punching him in the gut. The cruelty of her words rang in his ears. Nikolas clutched the cold-fire amulet still worn around his neck. The necklace warmed at his touch, the greenish-blue pattern swirled faster. It's beckoning a trumpet call to his ear. Then he remembered no more as the beast claimed its rightful throne.

***

Trinity watched as the sun faded beneath the rocking blue waters of the ocean. Gold prisms of light touched the waves, little fingers of sunshine that refused to allow the moon its reign. She rested her head on her crossed knees, her soul an open wound. Gabriel winged overhead, ever vigilant for an attack of any form.

A lone tear rolled down her cheek. The thought that she could have caused Nikolas to be nearly killed was heartbreaking. But, how could she defeat a monster that sought her in her dreams? Alexander was a coward and fire burned in her belly at the thought of him. She needed to speak with her father. In the commotion of the past few days, she'd completely forgotten how things had ended with him.

Trinity caught in a tree, her father vanishing when the stranger had approached. Who she now suspected was Alexander in disguise.

"Dad," she whispered with a lump in her throat. The roar of the cascading waterfall next to her made her fear he might not hear. Just as she was about to call his name again, his blue spectral image appeared. She nearly sobbed with joy. His kind blue-gray eyes regarded her with sympathy.

"Oh, Daddy."

He floated closer and materialized, laying a cold hand upon her head. His frigid touch seeped the life out of her. Her soul quaked in response, but she didn't want him to pull away just yet. She needed to feel his love.

A few seconds later Bruce pulled away and sat cross-legged before her. "I'm so sorry, Trinity."

Her teeth chattered. Her head felt frozen where he'd touched her. Trinity wiped away a tear and huffed. "What happened that night?"

Bruce didn't seem to need reminding of what night she spoke of, he answered immediately. "You are correct, it was Alexander. He caught me unawares, Trin. I feel responsible for what happened to you. Once I realized what was happening I tried to warn you, but he banished me."

A wretchedness of mind like she'd never known before consumed her. "That was the night, wasn't it?" She held her breath; dread welled in her heart. Instinctively she knew what the answer would be.

Bruce nodded a solemn look on his face. "Yes, baby, that was the night Alexander stole that memory from you."

"Oh God!" She gagged and bit her lip to keep from crying out. "So I am responsible for Alexander knowing Nikolas's weakness?"

"No! He did something no one was prepared for. Trinity, your mind holds a thousand secrets that in due time will be revealed to you. You're an immortal, he knew what he sought and he knew how to find it. Simple as that. You were under a compulsion and not yourself." A reassuring smiled crossed his face. "Besides, no one was injured."

"Agape?" She didn't want to ask but had to know if the bolt of fire she'd shot through Agape had maimed her in someway.

Bruce shook his head. "No. Alexander absorbed the full brunt. You can control who gets hurt and who doesn't regardless of who is in your path."

"Ahhh. It's a great relief to know that."

Bruce looked around and sighed. "I shouldn't tell you this,

Trinity. But, you're my daughter and I love you."

She peeked at him from beneath her lashes. When he didn't continue she spoke up. "What, Dad?"

"Do not depend on your sight. The enemy knows and seeks to maim you. Reach out with what Gabriel taught you and then you shall not fail."

A warning voice whispered in her head. "What?"

A loud bang, uncomfortably close caused Trinity to jump in fright. Nature erupted in chaos, winds howled and the air sizzled with power. The final battle was at hand.

Chapter 28

Alexander nearly whooped with delight. He'd found her. After much searching, he'd finally found Trinity. *And, I want what's mine!* Time to settle things once and for all. He faded into a fine gray mist and flashed toward Gabriel. The winged freak flew overhead, sightless eyes shifting restlessly. He leered; wouldn't angel boy be surprised. The thrill of a fight was a drug for Alexander. A high he could not do without for long.

At the last moment, he solidified and crashed into Gabriel's back, knocking the harpy several feet through the air. Alexander shifted back into mist just as he sensed Gabriel's readying attack.

The harpy twirled through the air, a perplexed look on his face. He closed his eyes and Alexander knew Gabriel was attempting to home in on him. He wouldn't give him the chance. The harpy's white ray was lethal, even to him.

Alexander grew weary of being kept away from Trinity, so he decided to get it over with quickly. He wanted, no, needed his queen now. He materialized and flew toward Gabriel. He extended a clawed hand and with a powerful yank, snapped a wing from Gabriel's back.

He licked his lips, enjoying the sight of torn flesh and spurting blood. The harpy screamed in pain, his face twisting into a mask of agony. He fell head over feet toward the ground and eventually landed with a loud thud. The sight of so much blood, only made Alexander hunger for Trinity even more.

He flung the useless wing away and flew off to find his queen.

***

A sense of dread overcame her and Trinity jumped to her feet. She stood upon a high cliff and peered into the twilight sky. The waterfall roared around her.

Who had screamed and why did her skin suddenly crawl at the thought that all was not well? A black speck zoomed toward her. She gasped and ran, tripping over ruts and upraised roots. She knew that speck. Sheer black fright swept through her.

Her lungs burned, her legs ached, but she couldn't stop. She ran through the jungle, pushing aside leaves and brambles that stood in her path. Dead branches scratched her cheeks. The scent of blood would be a beacon for that monster and she knew it. Trinity wiped the flow away the best she could and turned her head to see whether he still followed. Nothing met her eye. No black speck, no Alexander.

She doubled over resting her palms flat against her thighs and took huge gulps of air. Sweat ran down the side of her face. Her heartbeat slowly returned to normal.

"Were you looking for me?" His voice was absolutely emotionless and it chilled her.

She swallowed hard, lifted her chin, and boldly met his gaze. Only the lavender of his eyes showed, the rest of him stood within shadow.

"Where's Gabriel?"

"Dead maybe," he drawled out with distinct mockery and shrugged. "You ask me as if I cared. Let the rats eat him." Alexander spat on the ground, then turned his cold, unfeeling eyes toward her. Their depths swirled with passion and a fury that nearly caused Trinity to retch. She refused to allow Alexander to witness her weakness.

She tossed her hair across her shoulders. "You don't scare me, Alexander." She grew annoyed when she couldn't keep her hands from shaking and shoved them into her pockets.

His insidious laughter grated on her nerves and Trinity clenched her jaw. "You shake like a sapling in the wind. But I love your audacious personality." He took a step forward. When a shaft of moonlight struck him, Trinity gasped.

He paused and lifted a badly scarred brow. "Did I scare you? Look at what your handiwork did to me," he spat out, his nostrils flared and the earlier civility faded to outright rage.

His lips were black and peeling, the skin ready to rot off. Where once had been a nose was now a gaping black hole. Alexander's cheeks were a mixture of skin, tendon and bone. He looked like he'd dipped his head in a vat of acid. The sight was horrific.

"I never knew, my queen, that you wielded such power." He took another step.

She tripped over her feet in an attempt to run and landed with a plop on the wet mud. "Stop right there." She held up her hand, her words carried the authority of one not wanting to being disobeyed.

He shook his head. "I'm afraid not. You see, you have

something I want, something I need. Don't worry, my dear, soon you won't even notice my frightful appearance."

Razor sharp prickles of fear stabbed her heart. "I'll kill you this time."

"How?"

Trinity closed her eyes and began gathering her power.

"Oh, no, no. None of that." His body slammed into hers, breaking her concentration. Alexander's face mere inches from her own. "My lovely queen, I have you now." He laughed hysterically and lowered his head.

Trinity screamed and pounded her fists on his chest, but he wouldn't budge. His rotted lips touched hers. He groaned in his throat as if in ecstasy. Trinity had to hold back the bile that threatened to spew from her mouth. Pieces of his skin dropped onto her face.

Her eyes rolled in her head; she fought for air. He thrust his tongue deep into her mouth. Trinity clamped down with her teeth and ground her incisors together in a sawing motion.

He pulled back, his continence grim and threatening. "Bitch!" He backhanded her. She whimpered and fell with a soft thud to the ground.

Alexander yanked her hair forcing her to look at him. Uttered words escaped his lips, a chanting rhythm.

Trinity's head lolled in his hand. A spinning vortex surrounded her body and pinpricks of light exploded in her brain. She winced and watched as the colors of the world faded to gray. She screamed and placed her hands against her temples. It felt as though worms crawled through her head. Pain, hot and fierce ripped through her skull.

She finally sank into blissful darkness.

***

"Cat eyes," Nikolas's disembodied voice surrounded her like a velvet glove. She sobbed with joy and twirled looking for his figure in the black valley that surrounded her.

He stood ten paces away, his arms outstretched and a welcoming smile on his face. She ran as fast as her feet would carry her into his arms. When he touched her, she purred with joy and nuzzled his neck. He smelled of sea salt and leather. Nikolas's long, black hair flowed down his back. A slight breeze whispered through the trees.

"Oh God, Niky, it was awful." She buried her face in his chest and sniffled.

He caressed her back in an up and down motion. His touch sent bolts of electric fire to race along her veins. She turned her face and gasped at the raw desire burning in his aquamarine eyes.

"I love you, baby." His husky voice caused warmth to spread through her nether regions.

She felt his body stiffen and he pushed her back. His face contorted, sweat beaded his brow and his breathing became ragged and harsh. Fur sprouted from his body. He released an eerie howl, one that shook her to her core. Before her stood the great, black wolf. Gentle green eyes stared at her, a look of utter devotion and love still simmered within.

***

Trinity gasped and flung out her hands. A dream, another dream. But what did it mean? The sound of shuffling feet and whispered words vibrated around her. The cold touch of metal on her wrists snapped her back to the present.

Alexander chasing her. Gabriel screaming. A kiss. She opened her eyes and realized to her horror they were already open. The only thing that met her gaze was an endless expanse of black. Trinity screamed and tried to run, but the bonds held her fast.

Alexander's laughter made her cringe. It was almost a physical blow to her heart.

"I told you, my queen, I always get what I want. And I want you." The caress of his hand on her cheek felt like death itself. Her heart stuttered in her chest. Tendrils of pain washed over her. The pounding in her head slowly increased in tempo.

"Where am I? Where have you taken me?" She listened for the roar of the falls, but nothing more than whispers greeted her ears.

"My realm; where I rule as king and you shall soon rule as my queen."

She sneered. "Nikolas will find me and then he will rip you limb from limb."

"Sometimes you amaze me with your stupidity."

Her spine stiffened at his words. "How dare you? I'll make you regret the day you ever laid a hand on me, Alexander."

His warm breath caressed her face and she squirmed in surprise, she hadn't even known he was so close. Squeezing her eyes shut, she turned.

Was he getting ready to slap her again? The silence was deafening and her lack of sight was terrifying, she was a sitting duck.

"Trinity," he spoke softly, gently, "Nikolas will never find us." He punched her nose. White lights flared behind her sightless eyes. Tears ran down her face and warm fluid from her nose. "And don't you ever think to threaten me again! You're under my power now, Demi-goddess, and you'll do well to remember that!" he screamed, his hot spittle landing on her cheek.

Trinity whimpered and backed into a corner. He'd won after all. She dropped her head in defeat, then anger at her willingness to give in to him scorched her and she felt ashamed.

"No," she whispered to herself. "No, he hasn't won. I'm not gonna let myself be defeated so easily. Alexander fought for me; I'll show him just what he got."

Chapter 29

Nikolas howled and hesitantly padded forward. He sniffed his surroundings, seeking a trap of any sort. The wooden prison, which had earlier been impenetrable, now bowed before him. Fine tendrils of mist curled from his muzzle as warm breath met the chill touch of night air.

"Nikolas," Athena's voice drifted to him on the currents of the breeze. "Go now. Run. I shall get you to Greece, run straight on. May you fight with valor. My blessings shall see you through." Heat spread through his body, seemingly attaching itself to his heart. "Keep it safe Nikolas at all costs; you'll know what to do when the time comes." It was a pleasant sensation and instantly he realized why. It was Trinity's immortal soul. "You have all you need, now go!"

Nikolas lifted his tail and howled his assent then loped toward the distant horizon.

***

Trinity lifted her head. The faint cry of a wolf sounded in the distance. She gazed with sightless eyes at her surroundings, had she been dreaming? Did she want Nikolas to come to her rescue so badly that she heard things that weren't really there?

She set her jaw and took deep calming breaths, now was not the time for daydreams. Instead she remembered yesterday, a day that felt like it had happened a million years ago. Gabriel telling her how to 'see' the world. She remembered the deep blue-green of the ocean, the howlers calling in the distance. The bright red and yellow of a parrot's feather, the vivid green of the lush jungle. The breeze had carried the scent of salt, coconuts and orchids.

As she remembered, other senses came alive. The scamper of tiny feet, running lightly on stone steps. The rustle of several gowns, whispers between friends. Their words bouncing off the walls around them, echoes of sound, telling Trinity she was in a large dome like room.

Fresh baked bread and tangy cheeses greeted her sensitive nostrils. Trinity's heart raced as she realized what she was doing. She was 'seeing' the world as Gabriel had taught her to do. Licking her lips, she widened her other senses and sought for one familiar entity, Alexander. This time he would not catch her unaware, this time she'd show him just who she really was.

***

The wolf paused and cocked its shaggy head. A large, shimmery disturbance cut through the night like a blade. Lowering his muzzle, he sniffed around the portals outer edge. The blades of grass were choked with the stench of sulfur. He whined and fought the animal urge to run away from what he did not understand.

With a bravery far surpassing that of any natural wolf, he padded forward. The curtain before him shifted like sand, colors twirled in giant arcs of rainbow vibrancy.

When he stepped through, a large pressure built in his head, he howled into the night as the fires of the Underworld ripped through his skin. The werewolf was lifted into the air and bent double, his skin pulled taut against his body. It was as if a titan had taken hold and jerked, he was slowly being ripped apart. Daggers of light flared behind his eyes and exploded in his brain. Reddish-gold hues shot through his pores and the lights of a million stars sped past his mind's eye. The endless expanse of midnight blue sky tinged with rose pink nebulas opened before him.

Nikolas dropped heavily to the packed earth, his coat matted with dirt, his breath labored.

Painfully he stood and dragged his tongue, seeking moisture and coolness. The red haze of a mindless werewolf now replaced with the mind of a calculated and lethal killer. Trinity. His heart screamed with urgency to seek her out. Her scent lay heavy in the dew of the night; lowering his muzzle to the ground Nikolas sought his most beloved.

He walked the never-ending labyrinth of cobbled streets that was ancient Greece. The night was lit only by the lush moon. He stayed well within the shadows attracting no attention to himself. Several garbed maidens in diaphanous gowns scuttled past him, no doubt tending to their nightly duties. In the center of a square sat a large water fountain; the water reflected the soft blue glow of night.

He snapped back to his mission when the laden scent of death and carnage greeted his sensitive nostrils. Alexander. The odor was unmistakable and on the heels of that trail laid another, sweet and smelling of morning dew. Trinity. He increased his pace until finally he reached an underground tunnel system.

His hackles rose as he sniffed Trinity's fear. Her emotions overwhelmed him and a low growl emitted from his throat. The red haze of fury began to cloud his earlier calm and with a lethal, predatory gait, Nikolas entered the underground lair.

***

Trinity called her spirits to her. Instinctively, she knew the battle for her soul was about to commence. Wailing shrieks of bloodlust echoed in her head. The undead craved vengeance and swirled within her mind. Even though her eyes were closed, she was able to make out their sparks of color, reds, blues, green and gold, all coalescing into a tower of orange flames. She gritted her teeth as their sorrow racked her body with needles of lancing fire.

Their haunting moans hummed through her until she was one huge ball of electricity. She sizzled with raw power.

Alexander boomed with laughter, the resonate sound bounced off the stone walls surrounding them. His steady footsteps sounded in her direction.

Trinity's heart raced as adrenaline surged through her veins.

"It is time, my queen." His words crawled over her skin like a thousand tiny maggots. The hairs on her arm stood at the insidious sound.

She felt his gaze on her, burning her with its intensity. His moist breath fanned against her face, but she was prepared for it this time. She didn't stir when his hands traced the curve of her jaw and the firm skin of her breast over her shirt. She waited for the perfect moment to unleash the volcano inside her.

"Tell me you've missed my touch." At her lack of comment,

he continued, “You’ve been a bad girl, Trinity, but now you’re all mine and you’ll never leave my side again.”

She pushed back the revulsion of his touch. She could nearly taste his desire for her. With a forceful yank, he ripped her shirt off, exposing her nipples to the chill air. They pebbled in response.

“Look at the evidence of your desire for me, my queen.” He pinched he nipple between his thumb and forefinger in a rough, circular motion. She gasped at the searing pain that ripped through her chest.

“Do not think to rape me, Alexander, I will kill you first.”

She heard the whistle of displaced air, seconds before his hand contacted with her cheek. The sting exploded on the left side of her face, every nerve ending screaming from the heat of the pain, but she wouldn’t give him the satisfaction of knowing that.

“Ha!” She laughed, goading him on. She wanted him in a blind rage. “Is that all you have for me? Is that all you can do, slap me? I’m beginning to think, Alexander, your bark is worse than your bite. You fear me, don’t you? Fear my powers. You know I can kill you!”

Again, she heard the whoosh through the air, but this time it was his fist connecting with her jaw. Her head snapped back with a crack and thudded against the wall behind her. The metallic, salty taste of her blood welled in her mouth. She licked her bleeding lip, and then spit with as much force as she could muster.

She grinned when she heard it slap him on the face and hoped the slimy, red contents of her mouth was a sufficient insult to his over inflated ego. “You can kill me, Alexander, but I always come back and I’ll never forget you!”

“I’ll kill you, whore. I meant to show you mercy and honor by placing you by my side. Now you're dead!"

***

An explosion erupted behind them. Trinity turned her head toward the sound, old habits died hard; and sought frantically to study her surroundings with eyes that could no longer see. Alexander's intake of breath told her it was not good.

A lone howl rent the air, spilling its mournful song into the room. Her beast had come after all. The fuzzy feeling of victory spread through her breast.

***

Maidens scattered to the four winds, screams of fright echoing in their wake. Nikolas gazed at the black-clad figure kneeling before Trinity. His lip curled, exposing long canines; his body trembled with fury at the sight.

He walked cautiously, his focus solely on the figure now standing twenty yards from him.

Alexander smiled; his scarred face looked ready to sluice off with the effort. Rotted pieces of flesh hung as worms off his cheeks, where there should have been a nose was now nothing but a vacant hole.

"How wonderful." Alexander gave two powerful claps of his hands. The noise was startling in the near deathly silence of the room. "The were-beast has come to save his damsel in distress." He narrowed cold, lavender eyes and sneered. "Guards!"

A crash, like that of a giant ripping through a stone parapice erupted behind Nikolas. He swiveled and gaped at the endless supply of Semere filing into the room from every crevice of the palatial temple. They crawled as ants, marching in a row, their fangs gleaming and exposed and dripping with saliva.

"I've kept them purposely locked up and deprived of food for some time," Alexander exclaimed with a giddy quality to his voice. "They should find were-meat intoxicating. This one," he pointed to Trinity, "shall be all mine!"

Nikolas ran, heedless of anything but Alexander standing triumphantly before him. A sea of arms reached for him, yanking fur and whatever else they could get their hands on.

He growled and snapped at a busty vampire. She licked her lips as if she enjoyed the sport and dove for his throat. With his teeth, Nikolas tore into her face coming away with pieces of flesh. He spat them on the stone floor and grappled with another Semere who grabbed him by the tail. Desperately he fought and cast a quick glance in Trinity's direction, praying she was all right. She lay helpless in a corner, her white eyes staring at everything and nothing.

A Semere's claw ripped into his back, another into his haunch, and he howled in pain.

***

Trinity heard the battle raging around her. The hiss of wounded Semere, the cry of her lover, and the gleeful cackle of her captor. Now was the time to unleash her powers, while Alexander was distracted. She closed her eyes and concentrated on opening her senses.

Alexander yanked her hair and tugged upwards. She screamed and lashed out at him with a massive explosion of energy. In her mind, she saw the orange flames licking at his skin, gouging out his eyes and sizzling the blood in his veins.

He wailed and lifted her by her throat, then smashed her into the wall. The air knocked out of her lungs and she gasped like a dying fish.

"I want you to see what your disobedience has earned," he yelled and instantly her sight returned. A kaleidoscope of color poured over the gray world like a waterfall.

In the midst of a great battle, stood Nikolas panting and heaving. Large lacerations tore into his sides, red foam escaped his mouth, but still he fought. For each Semere he killed, two others took its place. She cried out for him, her heart broke and she frantically struggled against Alexander's powerful grip. She kicked, she clawed and she yelled, but still he was relentless and punishing with her.

"Watch your lover die!" Alexander's hand shot out and he yelled, "Grab his amulet."

"No!" Trinity watched in horror as the Semere turned as one and yanked the powerful vial of cold-fire off Nikolas's neck. Several hands pried apart his muzzle and poured the fluid down his throat.

Alexander's deranged laughter echoed in her head. Time slowed, she was powerless to help Nikolas. The room convulsed with insane hilarity and the Semere clapped their hands as Nikolas's form began to shake. His body stiffened and he dropped lifeless to the ground.

Trinity felt it then. His life force ebbing slowly away, the color in her world faded. Ice spread through her stomach, her misery like a steel band. The pain in her heart became a sick and fiery gnawing. A raw and primitive grief overwhelmed her. "I'll kill you all," she replied in a low, tormented voice.

Then she shrieked her despair and allowed the spirits to overwhelm her, to completely devour her. They exploded within her and she flung her hands upwards. Trinity transformed, into the burning phoenix. Her mighty flame lit wings cracked through the air as she flew upwards, then she dove with a cry of vengeance. Her eyes watched Nikolas's form grow larger and larger before her. In a blaze of red-gold flame, she entered his body and absorbed every trace of the poison. She breathed life back into him and massaged his heart to get it started again. Then she erupted and flew as a blur of light toward each Semere.

Zeus's poison spread as the plague. Bodies exploded into rain of ice and fire. Trinity beat her wings and devoured anything that stood in her path. Blue-green light flared as a beam of pure light. She screeched; the sound was an earthquake like vibration.

Chunks of stone fell around them. She hovered above Nikolas's body shielding him from further harm. The floor cracked into a jagged tear. Semere's screamed as they fell into the black pit.

A brilliant flash of white lightening arced through the edifice, cocooning Alexander in its midst. Trinity cried out and shot the poison directly toward his body.

Seconds before the deadly fluid met its mark, he disappeared. But for the stench of sulfur, it was as if he'd never been.

With Alexander gone, her fury was spent, and the poison took hold of her; she tumbled to her death. She crashed with a loud clap next to Nikolas's inert body. Her eyes gazed at her act of defiance. The steaming carcasses of dead Semere sizzled in the early morning light. As the suns rays touched them they exploded.

Weakly, she turned to Nikolas. His nude, bronzed body

glistened in the early dawn. Sadness welled inside her at the deep gouges in his beautiful flesh. Black hair partially concealed his features. She touched her hand to his cheek. "I'll always love you, Niky," she whispered, succumbing to her fate.

Chapter 30

A hard object pressed into Nikolas's side. He sat up and fought the waves of vertigo that battered him relentlessly. His stomach twisted in knots and his mouth tasted of cotton. Why hadn't he died? Zeus's weapon was deadly and he'd been forced to take a lethal amount. He shivered as chills wracked his body and sweat poured from his fevered brow. He would survive the cold-fire, but in the meantime, he felt like hell.

Opening one eye, he fought to focus on the object pressing against him. With his vision blurred, he relied on his other senses to figure out the mystery. The sweet scent of almonds and vanilla wafted on the air choked with the foul stench of blood and charred flesh. His heart gripped in his chest. He knew the scent. Her scent.

He crawled toward Trinity and lifted her head onto his lap. "Cat eyes, baby, can you hear me?" He rocked her back and forth, smoothing her long red tresses as he did so.

"Trin, wake up!"

Slowly his eyes focused and as they did so, he realized to his horror why she lay lifeless. Half her body was encased by ice, the other half had gray curls of smoke wafting from it. She had somehow ingested the cold-fire to save his life. The knowledge twisted and turned inside him.

Nikolas lowered a trembling hand and ran a finger along her brow line. The nauseating sinking of despair overwhelmed him. Her firm skin had turned an ashen shade of blue. Closing his eyes, Nikolas searched for a heartbeat; anything to tell him she still lived.

The stillness of the room reminded him of a crypt. Sweat dripped from his brow and he concentrated harder. He expanded his sensitive hearing. Outside, a field mouse scampered through the woods, a hawk cried and a brook gurgled lazily along. Then he heard it, the soft bump, bump of a failing heart, seconds away from death.

Nikolas breathed a sigh of relief. He pulled Trinity to his chest and laid a tender kiss upon her forehead. He refused to see her die again. His stomach flopped and uncertainty gripped his heart. He clenched his jaw; it was time.

Nikolas invoked the chant Athena taught him and reaching inside himself made contact with her soul. It fluttered against him, like butterfly wings, enveloping him with love. Heat radiated throughout him and he pulled Trinity's soul from his own. His body screamed out in protest at the absence of her warmth and he doubled over at the loss.

He had been able to go through life without her by his side, only because of the part of her he'd carried with him for so long. Sweat coated his body and an empty void consumed him. All that was good, all that he loved, lay in the tiny blue orb he now carried in his hand.

It glittered like a stream reflecting the warm rays of sunshine. He swallowed and gazed at Trinity's lifeless body. Her lips were slightly parted, her features smooth and a soft smile laced the corners of her face. As he lowered his hand, her heart stopped.

An ethereal blue mist covered her body as she was lifted into the air. Fire spiked through her and shot toward Nikolas. The heat pouring off her was like an inferno, consuming him. His skin pulled, tendons popped and bones stretched. He roared but stood his ground. The prick of a million scorpions would hurt less than the pain he now endured.

He dropped to the ground and transformed to his wolf form, hoping to find some form of relief.

The pain was slightly less severe, but still very intense. His fur pulled together, the lacerations closed and he was complete once more. Trinity's magic had accelerated his natural healing process.

A loud eruption cracked through the air and his hackles rose. Shards of jagged ice shot as an arrow through the air. He took cover behind an upturned table; all the while keeping an eye on Trinity's floating form.

A blinding white light surrounded her. He turned away, but still red spots showed up behind his eyes. Finally, sensing that the light had vanished he peered over the top of the wooden slab.

Trinity lowered to the ground, her arm hanging useless by her sides. A rosy flush suffused her cheeks and her hair cascaded as molten lava over her shoulders. A pleated aquamarine gown fluttered through the breeze. Nikolas held his breath expectantly. Hope nestled in his heart and he padded toward her.

He listened but there was no heartbeat. He waited but she did not stir. He whined and nuzzled her neck with his muzzle. She looked like the Greek goddess he'd fallen in love with. His sense of loss was beyond tears. Nikolas sat back and lifted his head. He howled, singing to the world of his grief.

***

A thick stain lay heavy over Trinity's mind. She opened her eyes to gaze at her surroundings.

She stood on a rocky precipice, behind her the banshee-like wail of the wind howled with fury. The land bore jagged tears in its soil; the silhouettes of large trees bowed and loomed overhead. The wind screamed and tore a chunk of rock off the cliff. She followed its noiseless descent down the rock face. It landed with a splash into a green, viscous sea.

The gelatinous waters erupted and thousands of blue, pulsing souls spewed forth. They cried and laughed, and surrounded her with their icy embrace. Her lashes fluttered shut as she accepted their touch. Her heart bare and devoid of warmth or life, she had no emotions, no feelings of despair or grief, happiness or anger. She was what she was. A spirit being accepted by her kind.

She lost all sense of time. All she could do was replay her last moments of life. Fighting off the screaming and clawing Semere to save her lover. Nikolas's torn and battered body. Had she saved him?

Cold fingers ran through her hair, across her face. "Come with us, Demi-goddess," they pleaded and chanted in unison. The thousands of wailing spirits clutched at her arms and legs, lifting her high into the air.

Maybe it was better that she hadn't lived. At least this way she wouldn't have to witness Nikolas's own death. She mourned the fact that she no longer felt a stirring of emotion within her shriveled heart. Trinity remembered love. The need to touch and affirm with words what he'd meant to her. She clung to those memories, because that's all she had left.

She was pulled beneath the churning waves and heat spread through her core. A blinding red light grew in intensity before her eyes and then darkness engulfed her once more.

She peered blindly through the gloom. "We leave you now, Demi-goddess." Several shades leaned in and laid a kiss upon her cheek. Shards of ice seeped into her at the contact.

"My daughter, come forth!"

She whipped her head around and beheld a shadowy blue figure sitting regally upon a throne of gold. There was a cruelness to his handsome features. His was a face that showed no remorse or leniency for the dead begging to be given life once more. He had an aristocratic nose, high cheekbones and lips that were set in a haughty sneer. But when his blue eyes lit on her, they softened just a tad and in them, she read genuine love and affection.

Should she feel fear? Probably. But she was incapable of any emotion, save curiosity.

"Who are you?"

"Hades." His voice was gruff as if he himself were unused to showing any type of emotion.

"My father?" Her brows knit and she wondered whether to bow or stay standing before him.

"Don't bow. I do not expect it of you. Come closer to me, my daughter."

No more had Trinity thought it, than she was standing before him. She inclined her head and waited for him to speak.

"Look at me, child."

Her eyes trailed a path from his throne, to his armored chest, to his face.

"I refuse to allow Hera this victory. I've seen you die over the centuries and have much enjoyed your companionship." He reached out a massive hand and rubbed along the top of her head. "You have always been my favorite, sharing my gifts as none of my other children have. I've hated this world I've been allotted and realize now, this is no place for you." Hades swept out his hand encompassing the barren landscape.

She glanced around and spotted a large three-headed dog standing alert and vigilant before a gated castle.

"So, Trinity, my beloved daughter, you shall receive a gift from me very few ever do." As he spoke, he unfurled a fisted hand. A tiny blue orb shimmered with streaks of white light. Her eyes were immediately drawn to it.

"What is that?" she whispered.

"It is your immortal soul. Nikolas tried to save you. His Goddess had given him possession of your soul long ago. But, before he could help you, you needed to believe in what you truly were. He'd kept it in his capable hands for so long. You were finally ready, Trinity. Finally ready to receive back your gift of immortality. But, you died. The soul came to me and now I give it back to you." He stood and took two steps toward her. Power and dominance radiated from him.

Hades blew upon his hand and the orb flitted through the air, landing square in her chest. Heat radiated through her. She threw her arms out and her head back as the electricity traveled through her body.

She took a deep breath and then it was all over. Fierce, blinding love raged inside her as she gazed at her father. A few memories of her past lives came flooding back. Hades walking with her along the gloomy banks of the river Styx. Showing her the ethereal beauty of the Underworld, and always keeping her sheltered from Hera's suspicious mind. Her shared lunches with Persephone, Hades wife and her stepmother.

Hot tears gathered in the corners of her eyes. The ice surrounding her heart melted and she threw herself into her father's arms.

He hugged her and laid a gentle kiss upon her forehead. "Welcome back, my daughter." His voice was thick with emotion and she could sense just how much it cost him to be vulnerable.

"All this time, I thought you'd wanted nothing to do with me. I never remembered the history we shared. So much I've forgotten because of Hera's curse." She stepped back and knuckled a tear from her eye. "So much I still can't remember."

"My daughter, I knew I'd be forgotten every time you re-birthed yourself. I couldn't show myself to you then because you had the fragile psyche of a mortal. You wouldn't have even understood, so I sat back, awaiting the time of your death when you'd rejoin me for another two-hundred years. And the other memories will come back slowly, give it time. Someday you'll remember everything."

"And Hera? How will she feel?"

Hades gave a negligent shrug of one shoulder. "I never knew where your soul was hidden or I would have returned it to you long ago. I could care less what that spiteful Goddess does now."

A longing to be with Nikolas overwhelmed her, her face

pulled down into a frown and the tears that had threatened earlier now fell in large cascades. "He will die eventually won't he?" She turned her face to the side; the lancing ache of losing him pierced her heart. Her body shook as she thought on him.

"Daughter." Hades laughed and the sound shook the stone foundation beneath her feet, the vibrations traveled up her legs.

"No mortal can come into Olympus; to do so is instant death." He gave her a knowing grin. "Nikolas is also an immortal, and perhaps even more than I, that were-beast has suffered through each of your deaths." Hades shook his head. "I hear that boy's keening wails every time you experience death. If you listen, you'll hear him howling his grief for you now." He lifted a brow and smiled.

Trinity closed her eyes. A haunting ballad rode the winds. One of lost love and desire, despair and heartache. Her heart grew to twice its size, threatening to erupt from her chest. She swallowed convulsively and a cry of relief broke from her lips.

"I can have him for the rest of eternity?" Her joy knew no bounds and she reveled in it.

Hades leaned forward and pressed a tender kiss to her cheek. "Come visit me often, my love. When Persephone is gone, I get dreadfully lonesome."

"I will, father." She hugged him.

Hades clapped his hand and the gated entranceway opened. Persephone walked toward them, her head bowed and her hands clasped before her. With each step she took, verdant grass and flowers sprang up. The smell of mint and pomegranates traveled in her wake. What was once barren and lifeless was now a beautiful and warm spring day.

"Yes, my lord." Persephone's tiny voice winged around her head.

Hades sighed. Trinity saw the look of disappointment cross his face before he had time to mask it. It was such a shame that Persephone had never come to love her father, but he could be brutish at times and he'd certainly been with her.

"Take my daughter to your sister. It is time this was all straightened out."

"Come, Trinity." Persephone held out her hand, Trinity clasped it within her own. A blinding white light surrounded them and a slight feeling of vertigo overcame her.

The gentle breeze of a summer wind kissed her temples. Trinity blinked her eyes to adjust them to the blinding sunlight.

"Hello, sister." Persephone nodded toward Athena.

"Pers," Athena said, a sly grin crossed her face. "Do you go to rejoin your master?"

Persephone stiffened and then disappeared in a flash of light.

Athena laughed. "I do so love teasing her, no sense of humor that one." She swept her chestnut curls over her shoulder and turned her attention to Trinity.

Trinity shifted from foot to foot, her nerves taut, her mouth dry. Athena just sat, beating her fingers upon her throne and stared. Her gray eyes were unfathomable and burning with zealous light.

Just as Trinity was about to scream to release the tension, Athena spoke. "You did not kill Alexander."

Trinity's mouth dropped open. Not kill him? How could she not have killed him? She'd seen him disappear.

Athena shook her head. "No, you did not kill him. Seems, my *friend*," she spat the word out, "Aphrodite, saved him just in time. And where he's gone is anyone's guess." She slammed her fist on the chair's arm and the sound was like lightning splitting the trunk of a tree.

Trinity's heart caught in her throat and she licked her parched lips.

Athena smoothed out her pleated white gown and composed herself. "The Fates decreed that you would be the one to abolish that monster."

"Then why is he not dead?" Her pulse pounded in her ears.

"Because the Fates are vague little gals. What they decree is always true. However, the time when you succeed may not be for years yet." She shrugged an ivory shoulder and sneered.

"What is the meaning of this?" A loud shriek split the air. A swirling mass of peach and gold lights coalesced into Hera's form.

Her bronzed skin flushed shades of burnished reds and her large black curls hung as a veil around her head.

Trinity's knees buckled and she flung out a hand, grasping a tree branch before she fell. Her stomach twisted in knots and a lump worked its way up her throat at the sight of her nemesis.

Hera advanced with a menacing step toward her.

"I cursed you once. I'll curse you again." Hera lifted a finger and pointed it straight at Trinity's heart.

A cry erupted from her lips.

"Stop at once!" A man's voice rumbled over the land.

"Ze…Zeus?" Hera stuttered and turned on her heel.

A massive man, as thick as the trunk of a tree came striding forward. Pure gold light surrounded him in a halo. Blond hair trailed behind him. Eyes the color of moss stared into Trinity's own and a dimpled smile flashed across his face. "Welcome back, daughter of my brother."

Trinity trembled and nodded once. She ached for Nikolas's touch, for his kiss, for him to tell her everything was all right with the world once again.

Zeus swung his head around and gazed at Hera, his eyes cold and calculating. "Athena told me what you did, *wife*," he stressed the name. "And, I see you sought to do so once again." He crossed his arms across his barreled chest and planted his feet wide apart.

Hera fell to her knees and bowed. "I only sought to punish her for her crime of seducing you, my love."

"Hera, what I do is my own business. From now on Trinity is under my protection, any who try to harm her will be dealt a swift and harsh punishment. That includes you!"

Hera shook and stood. "What?" She clutched at her chest. "But, I'm your wife. How could you…"

"Quiet, you insufferable woman." Zeus snaked out his arm and grabbed Hera by the waist, then flung her over his shoulder.

"Zeus, put me down at once. How dare you!" Hera kicked ineffectually into his gut.

Zeus's body shook with his laughter and he gazed once more at Trinity. "You have my word." He nodded his head and turned around.

Hera glared at Trinity, shooting spikes of poison through her eyes. Then, a flash of lightning engulfed them and they disappeared.

Trinity's breath came out ragged and she slipped down the trees face, until she knelt upon the grass. Sweat poured from her brows and she took huge gulps of air into her lungs.

Athena laughed. "My father always has to make those spectacular entrances." For the first time, Trinity heard genuine love in Athena's voice and she looked up.

Something clicked in her brain and Trinity spoke up. "Athena, what's happened to the others? Where are they?" It shamed her to realize she hadn't thought much of Nikolas's band since her fight with Alexander; she needed to know they were okay.

Athena inhaled and rubbed her chin between her fingers. "Agape's fine, but changed."

Trinity's brows dipped. "Changed? Changed how? What's wrong with her?" She'd come to trust and care for the white werewolf and the thought of anything happening to the blond beauty made her dizzy with fear.

"Your powers didn't harm her per se, but since then she's been in hiding. I think Alexander tainted her when he entered her body. She won't respond to my summons." Athena gave a negligent shrug. "I'll let her go. For now. As for Damien he's sticking close to Mercedes's side." She lifted a delicate brown brow and shook her head; a look of bewilderment crossed her features. "There's a story there between those two, but the bastard won't speak to me." She clenched her teeth and glanced over Trinity's head.

She waited, hoping to hear the goddess say something about Gabriel. The silence stretched between them, growing into an uncomfortable bubble. Trinity held her breath. Why wasn't Athena saying what had happened to Gabriel? Was he seriously injured? Her heart twisted in her chest, things weren't supposed to end this way. "And…and Gabriel?" She stuck her bottom lip between her teeth, afraid to hear Athena's answer.

The Goddess stared her straight on, her eyes narrowed but devoid of any emotion. "He's gone."

She let out a tiny cry and covered her mouth. This couldn't happen. The memory of her last words to the harpy seared through her mind. Trinity swallowed forcefully, refusing to cry. "So, he's dead?" she whispered around the lump in her throat.

"Not necessarily, no." Athena waved her hand through the air. "It just means I can't find him. He could be dead, only time will tell I suppose."

"Anyhow. I'm sure you're just dying to be reunited with your lover. He's been whining over you for a while now and it's driving me insane." Athena clapped her hands and Nikolas fell twenty yards away from her, still in wolf form.

"Oh my God!" Trinity launched to her feet and ran toward him. She was blissfully happy, fully alive. Her steps felt as light as air and she threw herself into him, burying her face in the scruff of his neck. The thick emotions of sorrow threatening to consume her evaporated in his presence.

Nikolas stiffened and transformed, glistening like a bronzed statue in the hot sun. His jaw clenched and he closed his eyes.

Trinity's heart dropped and she laid her hand upon his chest. "Nikolas." Her voice came out in an unsteady whisper. Did he not want her anymore? The thought caused her knees to sag and panic to riot within her mind.

"Now you see me for what I am. " His voice cracked with tortured self-loathing.

"Oh, my love, I've known for quite some time." She gave him a weak smile and took a hesitant step toward him. "I don't care. I love you, Nikolas Theophalus."

His arms shot out and he dragged her violently to his chest, raining kisses upon her brow, her cheeks, her neck and hair. "Trinity. I thought I would die if you rejected me. I love you so much. When I placed your soul inside you and you failed to return to me I thought my life was over." He rubbed her back and she purred in his loving embrace. She delighted in the rough texture of his hands upon the smoothness of her back and kissed his chest and neck.

"Then when your body disappeared, I searched for you everywhere," he choked and nuzzled her neck. "I love you, Trinity."

Warmth spread through her heart and joy bubbled in her laugh. Nikolas leaned in and touched his lips to hers. Feather soft at first, tasting and teasing. Trinity melted into him and surrendered her passion fully. His tongue sought entrance and she parted her lips. He tasted of sweet red wine. Their tongues mated and danced together. She lost all sense of time and reveled in being in his arms once more.

She shivered when his hands cupped her behind and kneaded the tender flesh beneath his palm. She moaned into his mouth and inhaled the spicy fragrance upon his skin.

A groan ripped them apart. Trinity hung onto him and panted; her heart heavy and full of love.

"I was amused at first, but I have no desire to see you two rut and moan like swine." Athena flared her nostrils. "Go and be happy."

She shooed them away.

Nikolas turned to Trinity and flashed a white grin. Her heart did a thump, thump and she squeezed his hand. Butterflies swirled and dived inside her belly.

"Thank you, Athena." Trinity beamed her joy.

"Oh, please," Athena scoffed. "You've lived around mortals far too long, Trinity, if you think I did this solely out of the kindness of my heart."

"Then why did you do it?" Trinity's brows dipped.

"Because it amused me to do so."

"And Aphrodite? What should we do about her?" Nikolas spoke up.

Athena smiled. "Leave her to me. Go now, before I change my mind."

Nikolas turned and pulled Trinity behind him, but not before, she saw a secretive smile grace Athena's smooth face and gray eyes glittering with happiness.

A soft smile touched Trinity's lips. So the Goddess wasn't as cold as she'd always made herself out to be. She shook her head and giggled.

Nikolas threw her a quizzical glance. "What?"

"Just that Athena is not as tough as she likes to seem."

Nikolas pulled her behind a tree and dragged her into his side. "So where were we?"

Trinity ran her hands down his flat abdomen and wiggled into him, enjoying the feel of his ramrod organ against her thigh. "What did you have in mind?" She batted her lashes and reached down to cup him.

He groaned and laid his palms against the sides of her face. "I'm glad to have you back for good, Cat eyes."

Trinity laid her head against his chest, savoring the steady beat of his heart against her cheek. "Take me to our home, Nikolas."

He deposited a kiss on her head and swept her into his arms, she snuggled into his warm embrace. "I love you, Trinity."

"And, I you. Oh no, I forgot." Her palm pressed against her lips.

"What?" He whipped around.

"Pierce. I forgot to tell him."

"Tell him what, Trin?" Nikolas's brows lowered.

"Who Storm is."

He shifted her in his arms. "Then tell him now."

She nodded. "Pierce, come to me."

Pierce materialized before her, his body drooped with fatigue and sadness. His green eyes held no warmth.

"Pierce, I've done you a grave injustice. Your Storm is none other than my friend Trish Montrose." She shrugged and gave him an apologetic grin. "I hope that somehow you can find your happiness."

Pierce transformed before her eyes. Light infused his body and she read the love written all over his face. "Trish," he tested the name then turned toward her, a wide grin on his face. "Thank you, Trinity, thank you." He dematerialized and Trinity felt a sense of completeness. She'd done the right thing.

"I'm proud of you." Nikolas stared at her.

As she gazed into his aquamarine eyes, overwhelming love nestled in her heart. "Take me home, baby, take me home."

About the Author

So let's see? The real Clara?

Well, she's married to the perfect husband; her "muse" she likes to call him. He's a tall dark-haired man with brilliant green eyes. Sound similar to one of her characters?

Yep, he was the inspiration for Nikolas, but that's where the similarities end. Her husband doesn't turn into a shaggy black beast when the moon goes full, though she's not sure she'd mind that. Two years ago they had a little boy, she like to call puppy, because he gets into everything.
Someday she hopes science will get to the point that we can learn to breath underwater and fly through the air. Until that day comes, feel free to join her in her dreams.

She loves to hear from her readers. Please visit her website at www.claraverone.com for news on contests and information on upcoming books. Or email her at songbird72180@aol.com

Printed in the United States
23949LVS00001B/45

9 781596 480049